LEARNING TO FEEL

N.R. WALKER

COPYRIGHT

Cover Artist: M.A Rivera
Edited: BM Edits
Learning to Feel © 2015 N.R. Walker
Third Edition

Learning to Feel

CHAPTER ONE

———————————

I SAT IN THE CAR, waiting for the real estate office to open and replayed the conversations I'd had with my family about my coming here.

My parents... well, my parents were both supportive and saddened. They supported my decision to quit the hospital in Boston and take up a doctor's position in a small town three and a half hours away. They knew I wasn't happy...

Which was what saddened them.

I'd never been happy, not really. Something in my life was... missing. I think my mom felt guilty that her son wasn't happy, though it was hardly her fault. I grew up loved and never needed for anything. I'd gone through high school happy enough, studied hard and was proud to follow in my father's footsteps by being accepted to medical school. I pushed myself to excel, rarely going out and having no social life to speak of. I *did* excel. I was an excellent doctor. I'd finished my residency two years ago and worked long hours to garner a reputation of my own.

No one thought I got where I was because I was

Thomas Tierney's son. I held my own, and they knew it. But still, something was, and had always been... well, missing.

I'd tried dating, for years I'd tried. My brother, Brendan, had tried relentlessly to fix me up, get me laid, or whatever. But I was just not interested. Sure, I found women beautiful enough and could become aroused by them if I needed it bad enough, but it was unfulfilling, lacking...

I remembered my last encounter with Laura... Lauren, whatever her name was, and it made me shudder. Surely that wasn't a normal response. I just presumed to lead a life that wasn't sexual.

I'd even done some research on it for fuck's sake, some people have low libidos. There were medications or therapies or some shit, but my job kept me busy enough, I just didn't miss it. I'd never *enjoyed* sex. It was simply a means of release. I usually fell into bed too tired to care, woke up a few hours later and went back to work.

That was my life.

Except for whatever it was that was missing. It had been eating away at me, this cloud of unhappiness that had settled over me, until it was something I couldn't ignore anymore. I'd tried to reassure my father it wasn't depression, being overworked, or the fact that I didn't sleep much.

"I trust your judgement," he'd said, though I knew he kept a close eye on me.

I loved my job, I had a great family, a fantastic apartment, and some close friends. I should have been happy. But I wasn't. Something was incomplete, and I had no idea what it was. I'd gotten used to the idea long ago of having a sexless life. But I knew I had to do *something*. I had to do something before I looked back in twenty years, wondering why the fuck I didn't do something sooner.

I just didn't know what that *something* was.

That was until there was a memo circulated at work for Belfast's County General Hospital looking for a locum, or permanent, whatever-the-hell doctor they could find. I'd sat in the staff lunch room, wondering what the fuck I was doing with my life, when I spotted the memo on the notice-board, and I wondered if the change of scenery would do me good. They were desperate, and I needed something different in my life, so I called them.

The job included a house as part of the contract to sweeten the deal, a furnished, two story, older style home with a patio on a couple of acres out of town. All I had to do was pack my things, and they'd take care of the rest.

I told them I'd take it.

When I told my family I was moving to Belfast, their reactions were the same.

"IRELAND?"

I'd laughed. "Uh, no. Belfast, Maine. It's a twelve month position."

So my family had a dinner for me on my last night, a quiet send off. My sister Alana, my brother Brendan, his wife Kat and my parents made for good company, and though they were happy for me, they were sad to see me go.

"It's only three hours away," I told Alana. "Give me a couple of weeks to get settled in, sort my schedule out, then come and stay."

She'd hugged me and whispered, "I hope you find what you're looking for."

My brother joined our hug. "And I hope she's hot."

My mom had cried when I said goodbye. "We just want you to be happy," she'd said, wiping her tears with a tissue.

Dad had pulled me aside and looked uncharacteristi-cally nervous. "Nathan, you're a good doctor. They're privileged to have you," he said. "But don't let being a doctor be the only thing you are. Take happiness wherever you find it, Son. Don't deny yourself anything."

It was an odd thing for him to say, and he was nervous and unsure, which told me that there was a double meaning to his words. I was about to ask him to just spit it out when Mom hugged me and started crying again.

"I'm only three and a bit hours away, Mom. It's not like I'm actually moving to Ireland or anything." I shook my head at her. But her overly maternal tears guilted me, so I hugged her and kissed her forehead. "I'll miss you, too."

Someone walking past the car window jolted me from my memories, and I realized sleepy little Belfast had woken. It was ten past nine, and when I looked back at the real estate office, I saw the open sign.

I was met by a small, round woman with a red bouffant hairdo that should have rightfully died in the sixties. "My name is Nathan Tierney," was all I got out before her eyes widened, she smiled hugely and started her spiel about how lucky Belfast was, and how the good people of this little town were abuzz that a new doctor was arriving. She was talking so incessantly, I started to wonder if this woman actually required oxygen.

She handed me a set of keys to my new house, I'd signed the paperwork and still hadn't said more than my name. She was still babbling on about how the house was old but there was a guy living in it while he fixed it up. He still had a few weeks work to do, but I'd hardly even know he was there, and it wouldn't be long until it was all mine for the rest of my time here.

"Pardon?" I interrupted her. "There's someone else living in the house?"

"Oh, yes," she sighed, like I hadn't been listening, which

I kind of hadn't been. "He's a nice young man, a Southerner I believe." Then she looked around conspiratorially, "A little strange. He's a painter, and a very good handyman. Can fix anything."

I was about to object, saying there was no mention of me having to house-share, but this woman just kept on talking. "You must have left Boston early to be here before nine, you must be keen to start here. Belfast's such a nice place," she told me again.

I didn't even bother explaining that I'd left Boston a little after five in the morning because I couldn't sleep. Her never ending voice, because she hadn't shut up yet, was fraying my nerves, I needed to leave. Quickly getting some directions, I left the office with a "thanks" and she was still talking at me when I got in my car.

I had no doubt all of Belfast knew I'd arrived by the time I found my house.

I almost missed the driveway turn off, but I eventually found my destination. The house was surprisingly beautiful, a grand old thing sitting in the middle of a clearing, not another house for miles, surrounded by trees, right on the Bay. If I wanted a change from Boston, this was it. It couldn't be more different.

I got out of my car and noticed the silence first, the lack of noise, except for the sounds of the forest and water. As I walked up the stairs, I could hear the faint sounds of a radio, or music, and I remembered I had a housemate, a *strange, handyman/painter* housemate.

Great.

I opened the door and called out, "Hello?" not knowing who or what would come out to meet me.

There were heavy footfalls upstairs and the odd sound of scratching on wooden floorboards. The odd scratching sound, I soon discovered was the sound of a dog's paws on a polished floor, since it was a golden retriever-looking dog which bounded down the stairs to meet me first.

He was friendly enough, with a happy face, wagging its tail. Apparently he was named Bentley.

"Bentley, stop!" a voice called, and I looked up to find my housemate.

A guy about my age, with blond hair, bright blue eyes and an even brighter smile. He casually walked down the stairs, wiped his hands on his shirt and said with a Southern accent, "Sorry 'bout my dog, he gets a bit excited."

I ruffled my hand on the dog's head. "He's fine."

"Are you the new doctor?" he asked.

I nodded. "I'm Nathan Tierney."

He extended his hand. "Trent Jamieson."

I shook his hand, and he grinned at me, his eyes intensely curious and for a moment I was caught in his stare. His eyebrow flinched, and his smile became a smirk. I felt a warmth spread over my skin and I pulled my hand away, embarrassed at my reaction. "I've gotta grab my bags," I blurted out, and quickly walked back outside to my car.

I popped the trunk and took some deep breaths, wondering why I noticed that he had dimples and nice lips, why I noticed that his hand was warm, why I noticed that he smelled of paint and coffee.

What. The fuck. Was that?

CHAPTER TWO

I GRABBED my suitcase and when I turned around, Trent was walking toward my car with Bentley at his heels. "I'll help you grab your stuff," he said.

I wanted to tell him it was okay, that I'd take care of it, but he was already beside me lifting boxes out, and again, I was stuck staring at him.

He looked at me, smiling but wary. "Wasn't expecting you so early," he said.

"I wasn't expecting a housemate," I replied and realized my tone was less than pleasant.

"Oh," he blinked back his surprise.

"Sorry," I said quickly. "I'm tired, please excuse my manners."

He gave me another grin as he walked back toward the house carrying boxes of my books. "So, they failed to mention me, huh?"

I carried two of my bags, and he waited for me at the porch steps. "Yeah," I said with a smile this time. "No one mentioned a housemate until the woman at the real estate office told me just now."

Trent walked inside and put the heavy boxes on the dining table. "So, you met Jenny Knight... the mobile telecommunications officer of Belfast," and he motioned his hands like squawking bird beaks, the universal hand symbol for talking.

I chuckled. "Uh, if you mean the woman who wouldn't shut up, then yes, I have."

He grinned. "Did she give you the run down on Belfast? All the gossip, who to talk to, where to shop."

"She might have," I admitted, "but I stopped listening before my ears bled."

He laughed, and it was an honest sound. "Don't believe everything you hear in this town. The people of Belfast think I'm strange... " he said cheerfully.

"Um, she might have mentioned that," I admitted.

He laughed again, and it made me smile.

"Well, I'll be out of your hair in a few weeks. This old house needed some TLC," he stopped and looked at me, "unless you want me to leave sooner."

I figured it was only a few weeks and not wanting to tread on any toes my first day in town, I told him, "No, it's fine. Really it's fine. I don't mind."

He grinned again and walked back out to my car, lifting more boxes and carrying them inside. When we had the car empty, he said, "Come on, I'll give you a quick tour."

He explained as we walked through the ground floor that this house belonged to the hospital, and that was how he ended up the official caretaker. "I've been here in Belfast for about six months now. Originally, I was just passing through," he said as we walked through a large open living room.

We walked into the kitchen, and he explained, "I was in the diner minding my own business when two guys started talking about how the hospital needed painting. They knew I was painter, because everyone knows everyone else's business, and they offered me the job. I told them there was a difference between painting hospitals and painting on canvas," he rolled his eyes. "But I figured why not."

He looked at me and shrugged. "Anyway, it took a month or so to do the outside of the hospital, and they told me 'bout this place. It needed painting, and I needed somewhere to stay... "

"So, you're a traveling painter?" I asked.

He laughed at that. "I am actually a painter, sort of. Well, I want to be. But the traveling painter gig pays better." He stopped at the bottom of the stairs and corrected himself. "Actually, it pays... period. I've yet to make it in the painting world."

He turned and climbed the stairs, and I followed him. I didn't look deliberately, but he was right in front of me, and I found myself looking at his legs and the shape of his shoulders. It wasn't until I got to the top of the stairs I realized I'd just checked him out.

Him.

A guy.

"Hey, are you okay?" he asked me. "You looked a little pale."

I exhaled in a huff. Fuck. "Yeah, I'm fine." But my heart was pounding erratically.

He didn't look convinced. So I smiled and looked down the hall, hoping he'd stop looking at me, which thankfully he did. He showed me the bathroom and which room would be mine. He said it was the biggest and brightest. "I painted it first," he told me, "knowing you'd be needing it soon."

Trent pointed to the other doors. "That's the spare room, and the other room is the one I'm staying in."

I noticed a door at the end of the hall. "Where does that door lead to?"

"Oh, the attic," he said. "If you don't mind, I do some painting up there. The canvas type," he said with a grin. "If you need the space, I can clear out."

"No, it's fine," I reassured him. "I can't imagine I'll need to use the attic."

"It's just that the lighting is perfect up there," he explained.

I pointed to the door. "Can I see it?"

He hesitated. "Um, I don't usually show my work to anyone... "

"Oh," I shrugged. "That's okay."

"No, it's all right," he said, walking toward the end of the hall. He hesitated again but opened the door and walked up the narrow flight of stairs, as I followed him.

It was a huge, loft-style space, and there was incredible light streaming through the dormer windows. He moved quickly, nervously, and his hair looked a lighter blond in the sun. Jesus, now I'd noticed his hair...

I looked elsewhere, anywhere else, and I saw some canvases, square, rectangular and different colors leaning against the far wall. I didn't look too closely, he was obviously uncomfortable at my being in his space, but I recognized what I saw.

There were colors which mimicked outside, blues, greens and greys. Only colors, minimal shapes, mostly lines and textures.

"You do abstract?" I asked him.

He looked a mixture of shocked and shy. "Contemporary abstract," he corrected me gently. "You know art?"

I smiled. "Not really. My mother does. I've not had much time for anything but work... " my words trailed away as I looked out the window. I saw the forest, mountains and the bay. "Holy shit! The view is amazing!"

He chuckled. "I know. Come on, I'll show you the outside."

We left the attic and headed back downstairs, and Trent talked as we went. "I've painted the living rooms and the kitchen, fixing things as I found them. I still have to do the other bedrooms and the hall, but I was finishing up the bathroom today," he said.

"I thought you smelled like paint before," I said without thinking. I cringed at admitting I noticed what he smelled like.

He smirked and did that eyebrow flinching thing again. "Is that so?"

Feeling my face flush, I said, "I might just wash up," nodding to the bathroom door, ignoring his question completely.

I wasn't sure if he stepped closer or if the walls were closing in on me, but I could have sworn he wasn't that close a second ago. He pulled his bottom lip in between his teeth, and his eyes seemed to spark with something unfamiliar. "I'll just be downstairs."

I closed the bathroom door and leaned over the basin, I hung my head while I concentrated on breathing. Fuck. I had no idea what was going on with me or what it was about this guy.

A guy.

A *man* for fuck's sake!

I looked in the mirror and saw myself staring back. Messy brown hair, pallid complexion and dark circles under hazel eyes. Though it wasn't me. Not really. The man that looked back at me was the unrecognizable guy who just noticed another man's eyes, his dimples, his hair, his shoulders, his smell... oh, fuck.

I washed my face with cold water and told myself to pull my shit together. I was just tired and hungry.

Yeah, that was it. I was hungry. My blood sugar must have been a little low. I wasn't even sure if there was any food in the house, but I headed back down the stairs toward the kitchen, convinced that eating would clear my head.

Trent. He was there, of course, in the kitchen, right where I didn't need him to be. I smiled awkwardly, found the coffee and filled the coffee machine then started looking through the cabinets for a cup.

Without a word, he stepped up next to me and pulled a mug out of a cabinet I hadn't got to yet. He smiled at me, amused it would seem.

"Coffee?" I asked.

"Sure," he said and grabbed a second cup.

We walked outside, along with the dog, and our coffees. We stood on the patio overlooking the huge sloping yard, and Trent told me which direction was best for walking or running. As he told me about the bay and the town, I noticed he had such a melodic voice.

I deliberately didn't look at him and took in the lack of other noise. I heard the sounds of the forest, the birds and even the wind through the trees and the gentle lull of the water.

"It's so peaceful here," I told him.

He looked at me for a fraction too long, then he smiled. "It sure is," he said, his eyes still on me.

His stare unnerved me. It didn't make me uncomfortable in a weird kind of way, it made me uncomfortable in a why-the-fuck-do-I-like-that kind of way. Before I lost my shit completely, I finished my coffee quickly and went back inside.

I couldn't even begin to rationalize what I was thinking until I had more caffeine. Lots more caffeine.

Trent followed me inside and sat at the island bench in the kitchen. "So, Nathan," he said nonchalantly, "is anyone else moving here with you? Is there a Mrs. Nathan?"

I looked up at him. "No."

"Is there a Mr. Nathan?"

I wasn't sure what he meant by that, and the confusion must have been clear on my face because he clarified, "A boyfriend?"

My breathing stuttered, my eyes never left his and all I could do was shake my head no.

And he smiled.

Fuck.

CHAPTER THREE

"I'LL JUST FINISH PAINTING the bathroom upstairs. I'll take your bags up to your room," Trent said with a smile and before I could respond, he walked out of the kitchen.

I made another coffee, black and strong. I looked through the cabinets and the fridge, making a mental note of supplies I'd need. I popped some bread in the toaster, and by the time it was toasted, I had a friend.

"Want some?" I asked, and Bentley sat and wagged his tail.

Just as I was hand-feeding him my crust, Trent walked in and smiled. "I wondered where my offsider went. Shoulda known food was involved."

I offered an apologetic smile. "Sorry, I should have asked if it was okay."

Trent chuckled, and it was a warm sound. "It's fine," he said. "His manners get away from him sometimes, but now that you've fed him, he'll expect you to share all the time."

I patted Bentley and told him, "That's okay, buddy."

When I looked up, Trent was smiling again. I was quick to explain, "I used to have a dog when I was a kid." I wasn't entirely sure why I'd just said that. "I used to share my food with him all the time."

I quickly washed my plate and cup then told Trent I'd head back into town, get some groceries and a few other things, and have a look around.

"I could come with you," he said quickly. "I need to grab some supplies from the hardware store, if that's okay?"

"Oh," I said hesitantly. "Okay... "

"I could show you the sights of Belfast," he said, still smiling. He was always smiling...

We walked outside, Trent told Bentley to "stay" on the porch, and we got in my car. "I think he's a little disappointed," I said, nodding pointedly at the dejected dog.

"He can come if you want him in your car," Trent said with a raised eyebrow, and I looked into the pristine back-seat of my car. Trent laughed, "Didn't think so."

My nerves around him seemed to have settled down, and I wondered if I was imagining things, imagining my attraction to him. I'd never been attracted to men before. I'd never been attracted to *anyone* before, not really. But a *guy*? The thought had never crossed my mind.

Even in college, not that I ever went out or socialized much at all, but surely if I had tendencies for guys instead of girls, I'd have realized this then? Or even back in high school?

But I'd never really had tendencies for girls either.

I snuck a look at him as I was driving. God, why was the line of his jaw so intriguing? And when he looked out the window and his neck stretched just so, why did I want to touch it? I wanted to lick it.

Fuck. My cock throbbed at the thought. Jesus fucking Christ, what was happening to me? I'd never had this kind of reaction to *anyone* before. I was libido-less, for crying out loud.

Now? My libido sparks *now?* For a guy?

Fuck.

"So, you're the new doctor?" Trent asked, making small talk, oblivious to my internal catastrophe.

"Um yeah, it would seem so," I said, and tried to smile.

"Why'd you leave Boston?" He asked personal questions so easily.

My hand left the steering wheel and ran through my hair. I was so unfocused, so conflicted, so not me. This guy, who I'd known for all of an hour and a half, had completely derailed me. "I needed a change," I told him, opting for honesty.

"Think you'll find it here?" he asked, a smile playing at the corner of his lips.

His lips...

My dick twitched. Fuck.

Before I could answer, he pointed and said, "Turn up here."

So I turned where he directed me to and soon found myself looking at the hospital. "Just thought you might like to see your new place of employment," he said.

I pulled over and looked at the small, single story building. It wasn't anything like Boston General.,That was for goddamn sure.

"When do you start?" Trent asked.

"Day after tomorrow," I answered him. "But I thought I might go in and do the meet-and-greet thing in the morning."

"The whole town's been talking about the new doctor," he said and flickered his eyebrows. "The nurses will love you."

I looked at him, shocked at his blasé comment.

He laughed. "I think they are expecting some old retiree. Dr. Hine was about two hundred years old when he left. I don't think they'd be expecting a single, obviously attractive young man."

I blinked at him. "Obviously attractive?"

"Seen yourself lately?" He said with a chuckle and pulled down my sun visor so the mirror was staring back at me. "Surely I'm not the first person to call you that."

My head shook, and I was left speechless. He was so open, so free about personal subjects and said the most unguarded things—the polar opposite of me.

I folded the sun visor back up to its rightful position. "Um, you might be," I said quietly. "The first person to call me that." I cleared my throat and pulled the car back out onto the street.

He stared at me. I swear I could feel it. And it was both awkward and exhilarating, and the fact that I half liked it was disturbing to me.

"Where's the market?" I asked him, trying to take his attention off me.

He pointed up ahead. "Turn left up here and follow it to the main street," he said, still looking at me.

I found a local Thriftway and pulled up out front, just as Trent spoke again. "Surely there was a line a mile-long of broken hearts when you left town?"

I looked at him, and a bubble of uncomfortable laughter escaped me. "Uh... no," I muttered, and quickly grabbed my keys and darted out of the car.

I grabbed a basket the front of the store, and Trent was soon behind me. "No?" he asked incredulously.

"Please, just drop it," I urged him. Surely he could see the pleading in my eyes.

"Okay," he said softly as he nodded. Then his tone changed, as did the topic of conversation. "So, what's on the grocery list?"

We grabbed a few things from each aisle, and it was easy. We liked a lot of the same things, ate similar foods. He told me he enjoyed cooking and shook his head at me when I confessed that being a doctor in the ER usually meant I lived on coffee and sandwiches from a vending machine.

I paid, at my insistence, and we made a quick stop at the hardware store. Back in the car, he showed me the police station, the library, the high school, the diner and the park.

"Aaaaaand now you've seen Belfast," he said with a smile. He offered to show me the National Park and Searsport, a smaller town about twenty minutes away, tomorrow after I checked in at work. "It's a little tourist town, markets and stalls and hippie stuff."

He smiled when I agreed.

That afternoon, he finished doing whatever he was doing upstairs while I finished unpacking. I was sorting my books when Trent came back downstairs. "Beer?" he asked, but didn't wait for my response, he just walked back into the room and handed me one.

"I'm not much of a drinker," I told him.

He looked at me, baffled. "So, you don't eat real food, you don't drink, you don't sleep, you don't have a girlfriend... " he took a mouthful of his beer and swallowed. "You don't have a boyfriend... "

His words trailed away suggestively, and I was again unable to answer.

"What *do* you do?" he asked with a tilt of his head.

"I work."

He stepped closer to me, like he might have touched me, but instead put his beer on the shelf beside me. I exhaled shakily, and my body responded to the close proximity of him. My chest tightened and my cock twitched, and I blurted out, "I'm not gay."

He looked at me, both surprised and amused. I wasn't sure if I was trying to convince him or me.

"Really?" he asked with that goddamn smirk. "I thought I had a pretty good radar for things like that." He stepped up close to me again, so close I felt his body heat, and he reached out for his beer as he watched me.

I was so thrown by my reaction, my body's reaction, my mind's reaction, I was a doctor for fucks sake. He rendered me speechless with his blue eyes, full lips, strong jaw and those dimples turned my mind to mush.

He could tell I was stuck, but thankfully he didn't push me. He stepped back and said, "I'll start dinner," and he left me standing in front of the book case trying to control my breathing.

I was deciding whether to stay where I was, to join him in the kitchen or to hide in my room when my phone rang. Pulling my cell from my pocket, I checked the caller ID before I answered. "Mom."

She asked me fifty questions, and I reassured her everything was fine. I talked to her for a while, told her of my plans to meet the hospital staff tomorrow and about the house and how the *house* came with a *housemate*. That of course ensured another fifty questions, to which I answered as vaguely as possible, knowing Trent probably heard me.

"Well, he sounds nice," Mom said. "I'm glad you're not there alone."

When I said goodbye, I found myself on the sofa, exhausted. I smelled whatever it was Trent had started cooking, and it smelled good. But I was tired, thoroughly fucking confused, and my stomach turned.

Trent came into the large living room and said dinner wouldn't be too far away.

I stood, and for some reason I couldn't look at him, like if I did, I'd change my mind. "I'm not hungry," I told him. "I'm sorry, but I think I'm gonna head upstairs."

He didn't speak for a second, while my feet felt planted to the floor. He walked right up to me, but he wasn't smirking or smiling. He looked concerned. "I'm sorry if I came on a bit strong, Nathan. I thought... " he stopped talking, smiled and started again, "You look tired. Get some sleep."

But he stood too close again, and my brain had stopped working. So I nodded and tried to swallow. I somehow made it up the stairs and into the bathroom. I closed the door behind me and quickly undid the button of my jeans and palmed my aching dick.

I was so hard. I'd never been so aroused. Sure, I'd been with women, but this was different. I was aroused at the mere proximity of this guy. A guy, for fucks sake! I ran the water as hot as I could stand and let the heat of the shower run over my shoulders and down my back, but my cock was throbbing, swollen and leaking.

I was a fucking intelligent man, a doctor, who was resigned to living a life without true physical gratification. Yet there I stood, more turned on than I'd ever been, fisting my cock in the shower, because of a man. A man, who, if I closed my eyes, I could picture on his knees before me.

And it wasn't the hot water and my hand around my dick, it was his hot mouth and his tongue that lapped at and sucked me. The image of this, the idea of Trent; blond hair, blue eyes and succulent lips taking my cock in his mouth, sucking and swallowing... God, I came so fucking hard.

My cock pulsed and lurched, erupting thickly onto the

tiles. My whole body convulsed as the mental images of Trent swallowing my come sent spasms through me. I stood in the shower, leaning my spinning head onto my arm against the tiles and waited until I had regained some semblance of control before shutting the water off and getting out.

I crawled into bed, confused but sated, and fell asleep with the words my father said to me echoing in my brain.

"Take happiness wherever you find it, Son. Don't deny yourself anything."

CHAPTER FOUR

———

I WOKE from a rare solid ten hours of sleep. It took me a while to realize I wasn't at my apartment or in a hospital cot after a thirty-two hour shift. I was in a strange bed, in a strange house — my bed, my house for the next twelve months, in Belfast, where I was currently sharing a house with another man.

Trent.

I recalled last night, how I jerked off to images of him, how being near him made my chest tighten, how his smile transfixed me.

And I was surprisingly okay with it.

I'd always thought something was missing. I'd never had real sexual urges with women, and I'd never been particularly attracted to anyone. It was new for me, and while it fucked with my head, I convinced myself to just go with it.

For once in my life, I *felt* something. Really, really *felt* something. Even if it was fleeting, even if it was with a guy —fact which I tried not to dwell on – I just wanted to let myself have this. Just once.

Throwing back the covers, I took a deep breath and went downstairs. Bentley was in his bed by the rear glass doors and looked at me as I walked into the kitchen. "Hey, Boy," I whispered, and he padded over to say hello. I told him I might go for a walk and he could have some breakfast when I got back, then it occurred to me that he might like to come with me.

It was still dark, barely five a.m. So I got changed quickly and quietly, not wanting to make too much noise, and Bentley and I headed out into the back yard. The property was quite large, and the water met the edge of the yard, maybe one hundred yards from the house.

By the time I'd walked a few trails, explored a bit and breathed in enough forest air for one morning, we headed back. I threw some rocks into the water and laughed at Bentley, who was utterly confused by rocks that sank in the water, and I was still smiling as I walked through the back doors.

A sleepy looking Trent was sitting at the kitchen island with a coffee in his hand, and I was certain he had been watching us down by the water. "I thought you'd run off with my dog," he said, sipping his coffee. "But then I saw you," he added, jutting his chin toward the yard.

Oh shit. I didn't even think of letting him know. "I'm sorry. I should have left a note."

Trent laughed. "It's fine, Nathan," he said, and his eyes were a dazzling blue. "You seem happier today. I trust you slept well?"

"I did, thank you, which is rare for me," I said. I set about making my coffee and told him, "It really is beautiful here. The trails would make for some great hiking."

Trent nodded and told me about the National Parks that surrounded Belfast, which trails were good for hiking or sightseeing. He asked, "Did you still want me to show you around this afternoon?"

"Sure," I told him, and my heart thumped in my chest, making me smile.

He smiled too and told me what work he'd get done upstairs while I went to the hospital to meet the staff. We talked so easily, and I thought I was getting a handle on my nerves around him, until he leaned across me to put his cup in the sink.

My heartbeat spiked, my skin warmed and when my breath hitched, he looked at me and smiled. "You okay, Nathan?" he asked with a smirk, as though he knew damn well what he did to me.

I took a deep breath and nodded. "Yeah... I promised Bentley some breakfast."

He stepped away from me and grinned. "You're gonna spoil my dog."

"He doesn't mind," I replied, and Trent chuckled as he walked out of the room. I was left holding onto the kitchen counter like it was holding me up.

Breathe in, breathe out, and feel.

I repeated my mantra a few times until my heart rate was back to normal, and Bentley had had two pieces of toast.

I walked into the Emergency Department of Belfast County General Hospital and approached the triage counter. The woman, a nurse, looked up from the desk, then looked me up and down, twice. I was used to this reaction from nurses – or women in general – and I looked away and rolled my eyes.

"What can *I* do for *you?*" she asked breathily, in a poor attempt at being seductive.

"You can get me the Chief of Staff or your Unit Manager. I'm Doctor Tierney."

Her eyes popped, and she backed away, not taking her eyes off me until she'd backed around a corner. I turned to face the waiting room, which a few people were sitting in, and they were all watching me too. I smiled at them, resisting the urge to bang my head on the counter.

I had a fleeting moment of *what the hell have I done?* But then I was met by an older man wearing a doctor's coat. "Doctor Varner," he introduced himself, and I shook his hand. He was professional and businesslike, though like most doctors I knew, he looked tired.

We immediately talked work, and I was introduced to staff and shown around the hospital. By the time I left an hour later, I had a pile of paperwork to fill out and rosters to go over, but I felt much better about my decision to come here.

I called into the bakery and grabbed some fresh bread rolls before heading home. Bentley met me at the door, and I presumed Trent was still busy upstairs. I unloaded my paperwork onto the dining table and decided to let Trent know I'd bought him some lunch.

I climbed the stairs and found him in the hallway with his back to me. I saw he had earphones in, and I heard the quiet buzz of music coming from the iPod shoved in his pocket. I watched him; he was wearing paint-splashed faded jeans and a white paint-splashed shirt. His hand held the brush like a surgical instrument as he ran the bristles along the door frame at the end of the hall with both precision and finesse. His forearm flexed, and his shoulders moved with each stroke of his hand. My eyes fell to his waist where his shirt bunched at his jeans, and I wondered what he looked like underneath the material.

Fuck. Now I was checking him out again.

I was. I was attracted to him. I couldn't deny it.

Fuck.

Breathe in, breathe out and feel. Let yourself feel...

I called out his name, but he didn't hear me, so I walked up behind him and touched his shoulder. He jumped, startled, and I blushed. "I brought you back some lunch," I told him quickly and all but raced back downstairs so he couldn't see the semi in my pants.

"Be down in a sec," he yelled out, and I was grateful for the few minutes to garner some self-control.

It was a heady feeling, it was heightening and for the first time *ever*, I think I saw what all the fuss over lust was about.

It was intoxicating.

As I bit into my salad sandwich, my mind wandered into the whole 'but it's a guy' territory, and while half of me was okay with it, half of me wanted to fight it. What did it mean? Why now? Why hadn't I been attracted to guys before? Why hadn't I been attracted to *anyone* before? Was it some early mid-life crisis? Was that why I up and left my life in Boston? Because I was having some kind of stress-induced freak out?

Oblivious to my mental tirade, Trent sat down beside me and said, "Thanks for lunch." He smiled with dimples and his eyes danced, and the part of me that simply didn't give a fuck, won.

Just like that.

He asked about the hospital, how the meeting went and what I thought and we talked long after our lunches were finished. He said it was rare for the good weather and suggested we head down to Searsport first. There was a beach and markets where the locals sold their wares.

So that was what we did. We took his old Chevy truck, chained Bentley into the back so he could come with us, and headed south to Searsport. My nerves seemed to take a back seat as we chatted effortlessly, and he told me stories of his travels that made me laugh.

We spent a good hour or so in the small town, at the markets, watching Bentley pounce and play in the bay before we climbed back in the truck and eventually found some nature trails perfect for hiking. We didn't go in too far because we weren't prepared or equipped for hiking, but it was different to see Trent outdoors, and just *hanging out* with him. By the time we got back to the house, it was getting dark.

Being back at the house changed the energy between us. It was like my body knew we were finally alone, just the two of us, and I was both praying that Trent would make a move and that he wouldn't. I wanted to *feel*, I wanted to feel desire, to *be* desired. It thrilled me and terrified me at the same time.

Trent seemed to pick up on the shift in my emotions. We were in the kitchen, and I was leaning against the counter. He stood barely two feet from me, handed me a beer and clinked his bottle with mine. "Have a good day?"

I took a mouthful of beer and answered him honestly. "It was been one of the best days I've had in years. Thank you."

His eyebrows shot up. "Really?"

I chuckled, embarrassed, and drank some more of my beer. "I haven't done much else aside from work and study."

"You've done the good people of Boston an injustice," he said with a smile. "All those girls and boys who've missed out on you."

I felt my face heat and redden at the mention of boys,

and I explained, "I've only been with girls before... well, women."

He tilted his head like he was trying to figure something out. "But you're attracted to men, right?"

My heart rate took off, and my breathing accelerated. "I've never..." I started to explain and stopped, but I knew this was it. It was now or never. So I told him, "I've never been attracted to anyone."

He blinked.

I didn't want him to think I was a freak, so I tried to explain. "I've never been attracted to anyone, not girls and not guys, I never even thought of guys that way, until... until... "

And I stopped talking because I needed to breathe.

Trent put his hand on my chest, over my heart. "Calm down, Nathan," he said soothingly, like he was the doctor, not me. "Breathe for me."

So I did. I took some deep breaths, even though his hand was still on my chest and he was standing too close.

When he was sure I was breathing more steadily, he kept his hand over my heart. "You've never thought of guys that way until... until what, Nathan?"

His voice was musical, soft and smooth, and I answered him without thinking. "Until you."

He smiled. It was a shy smile, a knowing smile. "But you're warring with yourself, aren't you, because I'm a guy?"

All I could do was nod.

He took the bottle from my hand and sat it on the counter. "Close your eyes, Nathan."

He saw my eyes widen, so he added, "Do you trust me?"

And I couldn't explain why, but I did. I did trust him. I nodded.

"'Then close your eyes," he repeated. His voice was just a

whisper, and he was so fucking close. I felt the heat from his body against mine, and my eyes slowly closed.

"Breathe, Nathan," he said, and I did, like I'd somehow forgotten to before.

His hand that was pressed to my chest moved slowly up to my neck, and his fingers grazed my skin. "Does that feel wrong?" he whispered.

My whole body felt alive, and I shivered. I shook my head no.

Then his fingers moved to my jaw. He traced my cheek with his thumb, and he whispered again, "Does that feel wrong?"

My skin burned, and my cock throbbed. I couldn't speak, so I shook my head again.

"How does it feel, Nathan?"

My voice was a whimper and a groan. "Good. Very good."

"Is it wrong that I make you feel good?" he whispered in my ear.

"No."

"Has a woman ever made you feel this good?" he whispered against my skin.

My chest tightened, and my voice croaked. "No."

"Breathe," he whispered again, and I felt the heat of his breath on my skin.

Then both his hands cupped my face, and I felt the warmth of his skin on mine.

"Look at me," his voice was just a breath.

I opened my eyes, and he was so close, barely an inch away. His eyes were dark and determined and his pink lips were parted right in front of me.

"Can I kiss you?" he asked.

I nodded, and he sighed softly. His eyes fluttered closed

before he pressed his lips to mine. My heart hammered, and my insides combusted as he moved his lips just a fraction, keeping them against mine, and he kissed me.

I thought my knees might buckle, but they didn't, and I kissed him back. My lips opened, and I tasted him, and I needed... I needed to taste more of him. His hands still held my face, but I pushed my mouth onto his. I was urgent, and my sudden desire shocked him. I felt it in the way his lips froze.

I groaned in frustration, in want and need. This sparked something in him because he quickly matched my desire. His hands left my face and curled around my back, and he pulled me against him at the same time his tongue touched mine, making my entire body convulse.

Fuck, my cock ached and throbbed. I was about to explode in my jeans. I'd never known such pleasure, such ecstasy. I was torn between wanting more and embarrassing myself by coming in my pants.

He was devouring my mouth with his tongue, his hands were digging into my skin and it felt so fucking good. I knew one more hard push against him, and I would surely come. I pulled away from him. "Stop."

His lips were swollen, and his eyes were pained. "Why?" he asked, out of breath.

I closed my eyes, and with ragged breath, I admitted, "You're gonna make me come."

He groaned. "Please. I want to watch," he murmured, and his hand palmed my bursting cock through my jeans, making me cry out.

He pushed and squeezed as best he could through the thick denim, and I was gone. He somehow pushed himself against me, between my legs, squeezing and pumping me with his hand until I pulsed and shot my load into the fabric between us.

My senses were obliterated. My body felt boneless. Trent thrust himself against me. I felt his denim clad length against my hip as he sought friction, so I grabbed his hips and pulled him against me. I opened my eyes in time to see his jaw clench. His eyes rolled back and his whole frame jerked against me, as he groaned through his orgasm. I wrapped my arms around him as he slumped against me, still trembling. He made the sweetest whimpering sound.

I leaned against the kitchen counter, and Trent was still in my arms, leaning heavily against me. The room was spinning, and I wasn't sure I believed what I'd just done. *Don't freak out, don't freak out...*

Breathe in, breathe out and feel. Let yourself feel...

Then Trent chuckled into my neck and looked at me with a post-orgasm haze in his eyes. "Fuck," he said, smiling. "You're so fucking hot when you come."

I couldn't help but laugh, and he rubbed his nose along my jaw before kissing me again.

"I uh... I um... I think I need a shower," I said quietly, needing to put some distance between us, but not really wanting to let him go.

His eyes lit up. "Need some help?"

"No," I laughed. "I think I've got this."

He pouted playfully as I left him alone in the kitchen and went upstairs.

CHAPTER FIVE

WALKING BACK DOWN THE STAIRS, I heard noise coming from somewhere in the kitchen ... Trent. I'd just showered to clean myself up because we'd just made out and dry humped each other to orgasm. A little unsure of how to approach him, I hesitated in the foyer. But I had made the decision yesterday to allow myself to feel, so taking a deep breath, I walked into the kitchen.

To find it empty.

"Can you bring out the oil?" he yelled from the patio. When I looked out the window, I could see he was busy at the grill. He smiled at me, and I saw my beer on the table next to his. I grabbed the oil and walked out to join him, leaned against the table and watched him do his thing.

He was oiling the grill, explaining it was so the meat wouldn't stick. He'd changed his clothes and was wearing a blue shirt that matched his eyes. Something I doubt I'd have realized two days ago.

He stopped for a pull of his beer and quickly turned to peck my lips before he turned his attention back to the grill.

I felt myself blush, which gave me away every time. "Is that okay?" he asked. "If I kiss you like that?"

I smiled, but couldn't form the words to say it out loud, so I nodded.

He could tell I was nervous. He put down the bottle of beer and stood in front of me, between my legs. "Nathan, talk to me."

I said nothing, so he took my hand in his and said, "It only gets weird if we let it."

I found myself squeezing his fingers. I could feel him looking at me, his eyes were burning into mine. "What we did, in the kitchen earlier, was that weird?" he asked. "Or did it feel good?"

I bit my lip, but I answered truthfully. "It felt good."

"Not weird?" he asked, smiling as he bent down to look into my eyes.

I grinned. "No, not weird."

"It was very fucking good, Nathan," he said with a chuckle, then leaned in and whispered in my ear, "You made me jizz my pants."

I laughed, and he chuckled again before taking my chin in his fingers to lift my face and kiss me sweetly. Then he tapped my forehead, "Let go of what's in here," he said, then his hand slid down to my chest, "and just feel."

And he just said the magic word: Feel.

During dinner Trent talked about everything and nothing in particular. I found myself smiling as I listened to him. He looked at me every so often, smiled and just kept talking. It was so easy to be with him.

His words, *it only gets weird if we let it*, played in my mind, and I knew he was right. So I relaxed and just let myself enjoy his company. I had no idea what this thing was between us or what I wanted it to be. But by the time we finished dinner, I was fairly certain I didn't care. I'd just let it be whatever it was.

I couldn't deny the attraction I felt for him, but if our earlier make out session was all I got from him, I'd take it. If he did want more from me, I had no idea just how much of myself I was willing to give. But I was willing to give something...

Well, I thought I was...

"So, work tomorrow?" he asked as I finished drying the dishes.

"Yeah," I said with a nod. "I'm looking forward to it." I insisted on dish duty because he cooked. When I put the last dish away, I turned to find him ogling my ass.

He knew I'd caught him and grinned without shame. He walked over to me, and I thought he might kiss me, but he grabbed my hand instead. "Come on," he said and pulled me into the living room.

He sat on the sofa and patted the seat next to him as he flicked on the TV. Taking a deep breath, I sat beside him. He was so comfortable and relaxed, like it was the most natural thing in the world, and although it was so very new to me, he put me at ease.

His hand casually sat on my thigh, and I felt it burn my skin causing the nerves in my dick to pulse with excitement. He was only touching me on the leg for fuck's sake, and I felt my cock harden.

"Is it okay if I put my hand there?" he asked. And I liked the fact he asked. He knew this was new to me, and he didn't want to push me.

I smiled and puffed my cheeks out as I exhaled loudly. "It's fine."

He chuckled. "You're so nervous," he observed. "Relax,

Nathan. I'm not about to throw you down on the sofa and have my wicked way with you."

His words clenched in my stomach, and my breath caught.

His eyes widened a little. "Do you like how that sounds?" He leaned forward, and his voice was husky when he asked, "Do you want to find out how it feels?"

I swallowed loudly, and my dick was now fully hard and rather uncomfortable in my jeans. I needed to relieve the pressure because it was bordering on painful. But I didn't want to dry hump him again, and I wasn't sure if I was ready to be naked with him just yet. "I um, have an early start in the morning. I better go upstairs."

I stood, and his eyes trailed from my face to the prominent erection I was now sporting. I could see his eyes darken. "You have sweet dreams now," he said, and his gaze fixed on mine.

I picked up the paperwork I'd left on the table earlier that afternoon and ran up the stairs. I heard him say, "Goodnight, Nathan," then he chuckled.

I threw my papers on the desk in my room and headed straight for the shower. I almost groaned in relief when I stripped off my jeans and my cock sprung free. By the time the water was hot enough, the head of my dick was purple. The intensity of my attraction to him, how he made me feel, baffled me.

A few words, a look of lust in his eyes and I was so fucking hard. Using shower gel as a lubricant, I stroked and pumped myself, relishing the feeling that hummed through me. I'd never been a sexual being. I'd never... fuck, I'd never been so turned on.

This time instead of picturing Trent on his knees in front

of me, I imagined him pushing me down onto the sofa, his body on top of mine. How he'd kiss me, how his hands would touch me, big hands, rough hands, would skim over my chest and hold my waist as his cock would slide against mine.

That image, *that image*, of his naked body, his hard cock, was all it took. My whole body lurched, come erupting forcefully from me in long, thick spurts. I squeezed my dick, and God only knew what sounds escaped me. But I came back to earth from my orgasm and found my breathing laboured and my forehead against the tiles.

I dried off, crawled into bed and read through my paperwork until well after midnight. I fell asleep to pictures of a blond haired, blue-eyed man with a beautiful smile flickering through my mind.

The next morning I was up early again. I took Bentley for a run, and we shared toast for breakfast, then I got dressed for my first day at work.

I came back into the kitchen and found Trent making two cups of coffee. He looked up at me and hummed approvingly. "Looking good, Doctor Tierney," he smirked. I was dressed in my usual work clothes; dress pants, a button down shirt and tie.

"Ready for your first day?"

I nodded. "Yeah, I think so."

"You'll do just fine."

I let out a shaky breath. "I'm sure I will." Then I asked, "What's on your agenda?"

"More painting," he said with a smirk. "Bit of this, bit of that."

I found myself smiling back at him, just as Bentley trotted up to Trent and looked up at him expectantly. "He's had breakfast already," I told Trent, "don't let him tell you otherwise."

Trent laughed, and I smiled all the way to the hospital.

I barely had time to settle in at work before we were bombarded with patients. I soon realized the majority of Belfast had come to see me, curious and nosey, but not ill or injured.

"Gossip fodder," a deep voice said with a chuckle.

I looked up to find a uniformed officer smiling under a greying moustache. "Chief Peters," he announced with a firm handshake. I immediately liked him.

"Don't mind the locals," he told me. "They'll lose interest in you when someone new comes along."

He talked of his town like it was in his blood and told me *he*, meaning the entire town of Belfast, was pleased to have me. He asked me how I was finding it, and I told him how I did a bit of sightseeing yesterday and how my housemate showed me around.

"Ah, the painter... Trent Jamieson," he recalled. "How's the house coming along? Is he nearly done?"

I remembered the real estate lady telling me my housemate would only be staying in Belfast for as long as he was painting the house. "Still a bit of work to do," I said. "It's a big old house."

Chief Peters launched into the history of the house and who'd lived in it for the last however many years. I didn't pay much attention because my mind was stuck on Trent leaving town.

And I wasn't sure I liked that idea.

"He seems like a nice kid," Chief Peters said, "a bit of a wanderer." Then he grinned. "The women of Belfast won't know what to do with *two* new youngbloods in town. Tongues are wagging, hearts are aflutter already," he laughed at his own not-funny-at-all joke, and I smiled obligingly, though I wasn't about to tell him the women of Belfast were wasting their time.

He told me his daughter worked at the hospital pharmacy, and I thought I knew who he meant. My suspicions were confirmed when the mousy-brown haired girl I'd seen a few times today walked out and called him "Dad". Chief Peters put his arm around her, and they walked out, her head was down as she mumbled something to him. I thought it was sweet.

The day wrapped up, nothing too strenuous, more administration than anything else, and I headed home. It was late and I didn't expect to find Trent awake, but he was. He was watching TV with Bentley's head in his lap.

His eyes glistened, and he smiled his one-dimple-smile when I walked through the door. "So, how was your first day?" he asked.

He rolled his eyes when I told him how the entire female population of Belfast stopped by to see what the fuss was about, but apart from that, nothing too exciting to report.

"Oh, I met Chief Peters," I said, taking a seat next to him. "It's nice that his daughter works at the hospital."

He looked a little baffled by my comment, so I explained, "It was great to see placement positions for people with learning difficulties in small communities."

He huffed out a laugh, but still looked confused. "What?" he asked.

"The Chief's daughter, Danielle, Dani? Is that her name?" I asked, and Trent nodded. "She has cognitive impairment... doesn't she?"

Trent burst out laughing, scaring the dog. "No Nathan, she doesn't."

I thought back to every time I saw her that day. "Oh, but she... every time I saw her, she... " and then I got it.

Trent leaned toward me, but he was laughing. "Every time she saw you," he said through his laughter, "did she have a glazed-over look in her eyes with her jaw hanging open?" And he imitated the exact look, a thoroughly stunned look, the very look the Peters girl had when she saw me.

I nodded, and he laughed louder. "Oh my God," he croaked. "That's priceless! She's totally hot for you. Please tell me you said something to the Chief about his daughter having diminished learning capabilities. What did you call it? Cognitive impairment?"

I pushed his shoulder, but started laughing myself. "No, thank fucking God I didn't."

He was chuckling at my expense and smiled brilliantly. "I don't think he'd have shot the new doctor."

I got up and walked into the kitchen, leaving him still laughing on the sofa. He soon followed, still grinning. "So, did all the other women that came to ogle the new doctor have cognitive impairment?"

"It's not that funny," I told him.

"Then why are you smiling?"

"Because you're cute," I answered, but I froze when I realized what I'd just said.

He grinned spectacularly, but still looked surprised. "Am I?"

I huffed out a breath and ignored his question, I opened the fridge and scouted for something to eat.

"Nathan," he said softly. When I finally looked back at him, he was still smiling. "Do you think I'm cute?" he asked in a teasing manner, but I couldn't handle it.

"Look, Trent," I said exasperated. "This is a lot for me to take in, okay? This is all new to me, that you're a man, that I'm finally feeling *something* for the first time in my life. I've had barely forty-eight hours to deal with the fact I'm attracted to a guy, okay? I'm trying to get my head around what it means that I'm attracted to *anyone*, so give me a fucking break."

My words were louder and harsher than I intended, and I saw the sting of them in his eyes. I closed my eyes tightly and pulled at my hair with both hands.

When I opened my eyes to tell him I was sorry, he wasn't there.

CHAPTER SIX

WHEN I GOT up the next morning, last night's outburst at Trent was heavy in my chest. I took Bentley for his morning run, fed him his toast—and mine—then got dressed for work. There was still no sign of Trent by the time I left, and I couldn't say I blamed him.

I got to work and started with some paperwork, but the day soon turned busy enough with the usual admissions. I saw the Peters girl scurrying through the halls. When she was talking to other people, she was smart and witty, but she still got that glazed look every time she saw me. It made me smile.

When I got home that night, the house was dark and quiet. Bentley greeted me cheerfully, but I was disappointed Trent still didn't want to face me. I knew it was late, but it wasn't *that* late. I knew him avoiding me was my own doing. He probably thought he was doing me a favor by giving me space.

But I didn't want him to.

I sat and stared at the TV for a while, but I couldn't tell

you what I watched. Finally I crawled into bed, hoping tomorrow would be a new day in more ways than one.

But it didn't start out that way. I got up to find Bentley was not in his bed or in the house, and Trent's truck was gone. He must have gotten up and left early to avoid me. I did my best to ignore thoughts of him and the hollow aching lump in my stomach, and went to work.

I was kept busy until mid-afternoon by two kids from a nearby town, who thought motorcycle riding without protective gear would be fun. Nothing critical, just scrapes, cuts and bruises, and one had a torn cruciate ligament in his knee. But they would both live to boast about it.

The Chief was there, of course, and his daughter was not far behind him. She was lecturing the two boys about the dangers and the stupidity. "Jeez Scott, what the hell were you thinking?" she scolded him. "Adam will tan your hide."

Then the other kid laughed. "Toby, it's not funny," Dani chided, "you could have been seriously hurt."

They rolled their eyes, and I couldn't help but chuckle. It was then she looked at me and got that glazed over, stupid look on her face. I found myself smiling, and she blushed before scurrying away. I couldn't wait to tell Trent because he'd think it was funny. Then I remembered that Trent wasn't exactly talking to me, and my smile drained away.

Goddamn it.

The rest of the afternoon blurred by, and all too soon I was walking up the front steps of the house wondering what I'd find. The house was dark except for the kitchen light, and the silence was deafening.

I threw my bag on the table, and with a defeated sigh, I walked into the kitchen. And he was there. He was standing with his back to me, wearing grey sweat pants and a black tee shirt. He knew I was there, but he still wouldn't look at me.

I quickly crossed the space between us and stood behind him. His chest rose and fell with his rapid breathing, but his head was down, and he was gripping the counter.

I leaned in toward him but didn't touch him. His skin prickled where my breath touched him, and I whispered, "I'm sorry." His breath stuttered, but still he said nothing. I ran my nose against the curls at the nape of his neck, and he shivered. "I didn't mean what I said."

His voice was raspy. "Yes, you did."

I leaned my forehead against the back of his head, and my hands ghosted over his back. He knew he was right. So I amended, "I didn't mean to hurt you."

He exhaled loudly, leaned back against me, just a little. For a long moment, we didn't speak.

But my heart was pounding, and my stomach twisted with nerves. I felt his body heat, and it was heightening. The exhilaration, the thrill of just being near him... "What is this," I asked, "... between us? Is it always like this?"

He shook his head. "No, it's never been like this."

My hands touched him with more certainty. He felt so good, so fucking good. My hands stopped at his waist, my fingers digging in to hold him tighter. His head fell back against mine. I pressed my lips to the exposed skin of his neck and whispered, "I don't want to fight it anymore."

He turned in my arms and pulled me against him. All of him. His entire front was flush with mine. I felt his hardening length pressing against mine, and he kissed me. He wasn't being careful or hesitant. He was demanding and urgent. His mouth devoured me, and I was lost. I gave myself to him in this kiss, as our mouths opened and our tongues collided, our bodies meshed together.

And I surrendered.

I didn't want to fight this, whatever *this was*, again. I didn't want to question my desire. I just wanted to allow myself to feel.

My whole body was on fire, burning deliciously, and my head started to spin. He pulled his mouth from mine and kissed along my jaw, up to my ear and back down my neck so I could finally breathe. He continued licking and sucking on my neck, and I realized I was groaning.

My arms were tight around him, and I loved the feel of his strong muscular frame, his broad shoulders. My hands pushed against his back, pulling him against me and it still wasn't close enough. I pulled his shirt up and started pulling it over his head. He pulled his lips away from my neck as I discarded it. His eyes were wide, his lips were swollen and beautiful, and his bare chest was heaving in ragged breaths. "Nathan, what are you doing?"

I smiled at him. "I have no fucking idea," I told him honestly as I pulled at my tie, loosening it just enough to pull it over my head. Then I started on the buttons of my shirt.

I got most of them undone before he batted my hands away and undid the rest himself. I busied my hands on his chest, feeling the hard planes of his pecs under my hands, the feel of another man under my touch. It felt so good, and so fucking right. My hands continued down to his abs, not too defined but taut, and perfect, my hands kept going.

I needed to feel him, to touch him, so I did. I slid my hands over the fabric of his sweat pants and wrapped my hand around his long, hard dick. I wasn't entirely sure what I was doing, and the sensation of pumping another man's cock was unusual, even through his pants. But I handled him like I'd handle myself; firm, sure, squeezes.

His whole body convulsed at my touch, and when he groaned the sexiest sound I'd ever heard, I knew I was doing it right. He kissed me, hard and urgent, while I pumped him the best I could through the fabric.

My shirt was hanging open, and his hands were at the button of my pants. The next thing I knew, my fly was open, and his hand was down the front of my pants, skin on skin. His hand wrapped around my aching cock, and my kiss faltered as my mouth stammered in sensation.

It felt so fucking good, so real and so fucking right. I let go of his dick and slipped my hand under the waistband of his pants. He hissed beautifully when I wrapped my fingers around him.

His cock was like silk on steel as he thrust into my fist, and he groaned low in his chest. His tongue was in my mouth, and I sucked on it, making his hand pump harder on my cock. It was all I needed. My length swelled and twitched as I thrust into his hand, against his body. My mouth broke from his so I could tell him, "Fuck Trent, gonna come."

His lips were at my ear, his breath shivering down my spine, tightening my balls. "Come on me," he whispered and like his words were the key, my cock exploded in his hand.

Thick, hot come spurt violently onto his stomach as my orgasm sent white lights through my senses. My hand that still held his shaft reflexively squeezed and pulled as he rammed himself into my tightened hold. I felt his cock pulse and thicken as he shot his load onto us both.

He squeezed me as his orgasm sent his body into spasms, and he milked my dick of come. I continued to stroke him as he softened in my hand and slumped against me. We were sweaty and sticky, and I didn't care. His eyelids were heavy, and his lips were curled in a post-orgasm smirk. I couldn't help but kiss him.

"Fuck, baby," he murmured against my lips.

"Baby?" I asked.

"Shut up," he chuckled, "Baby."

I laughed and kissed his lips again. "Mmmm, shower," I said, and without waiting for a response, I took his hand and led him up the stairs.

CHAPTER SEVEN

I TURNED THE WATER ON, and I knew he was behind me. I felt his eyes on me. I could sense him. My pants were undone, so I pushed them off my hips and collected them off the floor, folded them in half and hung them neatly over the rail. I shrugged out of my shirt and folded it too, while Trent peeled off his sweat pants, leaving them crumpled on the floor. He smiled and shrugged as I grinned at him.

I stepped under the shower spray first, quickly scrubbing at the mess that was drying on my stomach. I leaned my head back into the water, and when I opened my eyes, Trent was standing before me. His eyes were dark, and he hummed as he took me in.

I lathered up some body gel and pulled him under the spray, trading places with him. He leaned back in the water, and I took my time while I washed him down so I could admire his form. He was lean, muscular, his uncircumcised dick hung heavy and limp, and he had a star tattooed on his hip. I washed his abdomen, his chest and up to his neck. He was watching me watch him, and I wasn't shy about it. He was beautiful.

As a doctor, I'd seen thousands of naked bodies. Granted, I'd never been naked in the shower with them, but the naked human body was simply anatomy to me. It always had been.

Until now.

I was naked, in the shower, with a man. A man who I'd just given a hand-job to. A man who pumped me into orgasm. A man. I thought I wasn't anywhere near ready to be so intimate, skin on skin, with a guy. Guess I was wrong.

Because this felt right.

I leaned into the spray of water and kissed him. He pulled my bottom lip in between his and bit it softly, playfully, before releasing me. He turned the water off, and I handed him a towel. I couldn't help but watch him as he dried himself.

I wrapped the towel around my waist. I needed to say what was on my mind before we left the bathroom. I wanted to get it out there, knowing if I put if off now, it would go unsaid. "Trent, I need to tell you... I really am sorry for what I said."

"But Nathan," he countered, "you *do* need time. I don't want to rush you into anything you're not ready for."

"I won't do anything I don't want to do," I told him.

He looked at me thoughtfully. "Nathan, are you scared of what *this* means?" He indicated to the space between us. Then he quickly added, "Being with a guy?"

"No, not anymore," I answered. "I was, I mean, at first. The whole guy thing was weird at first. I've never thought of myself as being one thing or another, straight, not straight. I was neither..." then I admitted, "I've never been very sexual."

He shook his head, like he couldn't believe it. "You seem pretty sexual to me."

"Um, about that... " I trailed off. I needed to ask him this. "Look, I'm a doctor, so forgive the clinical approach. I don't want all the details, but I need to know you've practiced safe sex." He blinked, and I explained, "As a doctor, I have regular blood tests, and I know I'm clean."

He grinned. "My last test was just before I left New York, and I haven't been with anyone since."

I chuckled, relieved, and I felt my cheeks heat. Trent leaned against the bathroom counter and smiled.

"Nathan, I'm gay, as in *not* straight," he said outright. "And we've been...well, we've been pretty sexual. I need to know if you're okay with that."

"Yes, I am," I said immediately. I stepped closer to him. "What we've done together, what you've done to me, I'm very okay with," I told him and cupped my hand to his jaw. I looked in his eyes and told him very seriously, "And I'm pretty fucking happy you're gay."

He laughed, and for the moment, the seriousness was over.

"Look, Trent," I told him, "I have no idea what I'm doing, and that scares me. And I have no idea how long you'll even be here, but I'm in this, whatever the fuck it is."

He smiled; his whole face smiled. He pushed himself off the bathroom counter and kissed me. It was a sweet, happy kiss. Then he repeated my words. "I'm in this too, whatever the fuck it is."

"Yeah? Really?"

"Yeah, really," he said with a laugh. "Don't sound so surprised. You can practice being sexual with me anytime."

I was smiling like an idiot.

"One thing though," he said playfully. "Maybe next time you make me come, we could try somewhere other than the kitchen."

I laughed and nodded. "Sure, next time." And the mere thought of that made me smile harder.

Trent grinned at me like I amused him. He pulled the towel from around his waist, exposing himself fully to me, and dried his hair. My eyes were drawn to his dick, his thick, heavy, limp dick, and when I forced my eyes to look at his face, he was smirking.

I swallowed hard and exhaled loudly, and he chuckled. "You have an early start, Doctor." He laughed as he walked out of the bathroom, rubbing the towel into his hair. He was naked, so of course I watched him. His back was as beautiful as his front. His ass was... well, it was fucking perfect.

It took me a second to even think of moving, and when I made it to my room, I fell into bed expecting my mind to be racing about conversations, decisions, sexual orientation...

But it didn't.

I fell asleep smiling.

I got to work the next day, and I still couldn't help but smile as I recalled saying goodbye to Trent. I'd already taken Bentley for a run and shared breakfast with him. When I came back downstairs showered and dressed for work, Trent was in the kitchen.

He was standing at the counter stirring his coffee mechanically, still half asleep. I walked up behind him, put my hands on his hips, and ran my nose along his shoulder. He sighed, and I smiled, pushing his groin against the counter and squeezing his hips so he groaned. I kissed the back of his neck and said cheerfully, "Gotta go to work."

I took a step back from him. He turned around, his eyes dark. I picked up my car keys and grinned at him as I walked out. He yelled at my back, "You don't play fair!"

I smiled all the way to work.

I was still grinning, and when the hospital staff saw me,

they noticed. There were numerous comments about fresh country air, compared to the stress and perils of city living, smog and being overworked in city hospitals. I smiled and agreed with them to be polite, not bothering to correct them.

It wasn't the fresh air. Not at all.

Work filled my day, and I found the familiar routine comforting. The hospital was small, and there wasn't the influx of varied cases, but I enjoyed the more personal interaction with the patients.

The female staff tended to hang around me a little too much, lingering, watching, and flirting.

I ignored it, of course. I always had. The Peters girl stammered and blinked her way through another awkward conversation, though I couldn't help but smile. Not because what she was saying was funny or witty, but because I knew Trent would be laughing hysterically if he witnessed it.

When I got home the TV and lights were on. Trent walked down the stairs wiping his hands on his shirt.

"Were you painting at this hour?" I asked, putting my satchel on the table.

"Not house painting," he said with a grin, but he didn't elaborate. He walked into the kitchen and retrieved a plate from the fridge. "I made enough dinner for you. Figured you wouldn't have eaten."

His thoughtfulness warmed me, and I gave him a genuine smile. "Thank you."

When I turned to put the plate of pasta in the microwave, Trent was quick to stand behind me. He put his hands on my hips and pushed me into the counter, pressing my groin against the cabinet, just as I had done to him that morning. He ran his nose through the hair at the nape of my neck and breathed a sigh across my skin, causing me to moan and shiver. Then he was gone.

"Gotta go take a shower," he said with a laugh, and I knew he was getting me back for doing the same to him earlier. I groaned in frustration, and he chuckled all the way up the stairs.

Ignoring my hardening dick, I ate the pasta Trent cooked for me. It was good, hearty comfort food, and I ate all of it. I washed up my plate and was drying it when Trent came back downstairs. He called out from the living room, "Wanna watch some TV?"

I walked into where he was. "Sure," I told him, and he pulled me down onto the sofa with him. He was wearing sleep pants and a tee shirt and stretched his feet out onto the coffee table.

I pulled my tie off, and Trent quickly asked, "Do you want to get changed?"

I leaned over and shook my head *no* before I pressed my lips to his. His lips formed a smile before he kissed me back, opened mouthed and sliding tongues. My eyes closed as I melted into this kiss.

His hands were on my face, and he slowed the kiss before pulling away. I pouted, and he smiled. "I've thought about kissing you all day," I told him.

"Is that all? Just kissing?" he asked in a teasing tone.

"Well, maybe more..."

"Like what?" he prompted me.

"Like this," I told him, pulling him by his shirt so he was leaning over me. I laid back on the sofa and took him with me. His eyes went wide, but he smiled. I let go of his shirt and held his waist instead, lifting my head up to kiss him.

He held his weight off me, but I didn't want him to. I wanted to feel him. I lifted my foot up, resting it on the sofa so I was lying down more, and he was between my legs. I pulled his hips into mine, feeling, savoring the feel of him, hard, angular, muscular. Male.

He groaned, and the sound set my blood on fire. He was kissing me hard, deep and perfect. My hips were rising to meet him, setting a slow, but desperate pace. I felt his stubble against my chin, my lips and tongue as I was licking and sucking his mouth and jaw.

I peeled his shirt off, and he made quick work of the buttons on mine, exposing my chest to his. His fingers roamed over my skin and then he tweaked my nipples. "Fuck!" I cried out, my back arching off the sofa.

My reaction to his touch spurred him on, and he thrust his hips, rubbing his cock against mine. I dug my hands into the skin of his back, pressing hard enough to bruise him. I dipped my fingers under the waistband of his pants and slid my hands over his ass at the same time pushing his sleep pants down to his thighs.

Trent leaned up on one knee and pulled his pants down the rest of the way, freeing his engorged dick. I pulled my own pants open and pulled my cock out of my briefs, moaning at the relief.

But then Trent got up, half pulling his sleep pants back up over his hips. "Don't you fucking move," he said huskily and bolted up the stairs. I blinked, unsure of what the fuck just happened, but then Trent ran back into the room out of breath.

"Pants off," he huffed and pulled my dress pants off by the hems at my feet. He threw them somewhere and quickly pulled his own pants off. It was then I noticed he had a bottle in his hand. He kneeled between my legs, and I suddenly felt vulnerable. Exposed, open and so very vulnerable.

"It's lube," he told me. "It'll make it feel better when I pump your cock with mine."

His words made any fears of what he might have needed lube for fade away. When he took my length in his now-slick hands, I groaned so fucking loud it didn't even sound like me. But then he rested on his knees between my legs, still pumping me slowly. I watched as he added more lube, then he leaned toward me and took both our cocks in one hand. Fuck. The feel of his cock against mine, sliding, squeezing and pumping was so fucking hot, I almost bucked off the sofa.

When he leaned over me on his other hand and kissed me while he stroked us both, I thought I would die. I was moaning and thrusting, kissing and grinding, completely overwhelmed with the sensation.

"Fuck, Trent," my voice was a groan, "you feel so fucking good."

He answered me with just a shudder and a whimper. When his shoulders started to shake, I wrapped my hand around his and started to stroke our cocks with him.

"You feel so good under me," he said, his voice was so husky. "You're gonna make me come."

So I squeezed harder, pumped him faster and thrust my cock into our hands until he was moaning incoherently. With my other hand, I ran my fingers over his chest and rolled his nipple with my thumb and finger. His reaction was immediate, he bucked, his cock thrusting, and he grunted and growled as he poured his come onto me. It was such a turn-on to watch as his entire body orgasm. He was all lithe and beautiful, his cock was lurching, surging, as it emptied.

My hand kept pumping us both. I could see and feel his

come on my stomach, my hand, my cock, and it was enough to tip me over the edge.

My back and hips left the sofa, and I bucked against him. The feel of him against me, his hand wrapped around me, the feel of his come on me made my cock erupt.

"Yeah, baby," his sexy voice prolonged my pleasure. "Come for me."

My entire body flexed, and a strangled cry ripped from me as both our hands pumped me. My cock twitched with every stroke, pumping every last drop from me, and we were both moaning. I felt warm all over. Boneless. It made me chuckle. Finally, Trent slumped against me. We were both spent, hot, sweaty, sticky messes and neither of us cared. Our breathing simmered, and I felt his heartbeat return to normal against my chest. "Shower with me," I said, not really asking.

He hummed and nodded, while sitting up, I took his hand and led us up the stairs. This time when we showered, we stood under the spray together and kissed, our mouths never parting until the water ran cold.

CHAPTER EIGHT

I GOT home from work a little earlier than normal and took the opportunity to call my sister. Listening to her chatter away about coming to visit, I changed the ear I was holding my phone to. "Change of plans, Alana," I told her. "I thought I might use my first few days off to go back to my apartment. There are a few things I need to grab."

I pacified her by suggesting everyone could come for a few days next time I was off. "It's only three weeks away, plus I'll see you all next weekend."

It was kind of a spur of the moment decision, and I hadn't actually asked Trent if he wanted to come to Boston with me, but I figured he'd jump at the chance.

"I get four days off every after two weeks, Lani," I reminded her, calling her by her nickname. "We'll catch up next weekend for dinner when I'm in Boston, then you can come here next time, okay?"

She whined and sulked but in the end, had little choice. I told her I missed her, that I loved her and that I'd see her soon. When I disconnected the call and looked up, Trent was watching me.

"My sister," I said by way of explanation. "Hey, are you busy next weekend?"

He looked at me, curious, and shrugged.

"I was going to go home to Boston. Did you want to come with me?"

"Why, Doctor Tierney, are you propositioning me?" he asked, teasingly.

"Only if you say yes."

"Then yes." His grin was huge.

I laughed, and his yes made me happier than it probably should have. But then his face fell. "Oh, I can't...I can't leave Bentley."

"Bring him," I suggested. "My apartment has a courtyard with some grass. It's nothing like here, but at least he'll have a bathroom."

Trent smiled his eye-crinkling smile. "We'll have to take your car. My trucks reliable, but it's not too comfortable."

"It's fine," I said, making a mental note to put blankets down on the backseat first.

"So, Boston, huh?" Trent mused. "I've never been. I spent a while in New York and was headed to Boston but decided on a detour up the coast and came to Belfast."

I asked him about his time in New York while I made dinner. He answered, though it was obvious there were parts he wasn't willing to divulge, but we laughed and talked all the same. It was so easy. There was an occasional gentle touch of a hand, my hand on his hip when I leaned past him, and our conversation never waned.

During dinner we talked music, books and current affairs. He knew so much about the art world, a subject I knew very little about, I could have listened to him talk about it for hours. He was so passionate, so enthralled about what he did. It was refreshing.

He said the same went for me. That like him, I too loved what I did, but I had basically stopped living my life for my work.

"I didn't stop living my life," I told him. "I just didn't know any different. I spent so much time working because there wasn't anything else, any*one* else..." my words trailed away.

"But there were women...?" he asked, and while his tone was joking, I knew he wanted an honest answer.

"There were," I told him the truth. There was no point in lying. "But it was never... it was... *deficient*..." I wasn't sure how to explain it. "It never felt right."

He nodded knowingly and then started to clear the table. "I kissed a girl once," he admitted, and I looked at him shocked. He grinned at my expression. "It was horrible. I was sixteen and tried to be into girls like everyone else. Her name was Suzie. It was like kissing my Grandma." He shuddered at the memory.

I laughed at this, and Trent chuckled. But I wanted to ask him something. "So you always knew you were gay?"

He nodded. "Pretty much, yeah. When I was about fourteen and the guys were watching porn, they'd make comments on tits, and I'd be thinking, *mmmm, look at his back, his hips.*" He shook his head and chuckled. "I never even looked at the girls in those movies. I was always watching the men."

Trent watched me for a second before he asked, "Did you never notice the men in porn and think there might have been something there?"

I cleared my throat. "I've never watched any..."

Trent blinked. Twice. "Never?"

I shook my head and busied myself with cleaning up in the kitchen. "I told you, I was never into sex."

"You've never watched porn?" he asked incredulously. "Never?"

I felt my cheeks heat and deliberately wouldn't look at him, but I shook my head again. "No."

He mumbled, "Oh, my God."

I finally faced him, and he was staring at me, a smile slowly spreading across his face. "You've got a laptop and internet connection?"

I nodded, and I knew what he was suggesting. I wasn't opposed to it, not at all. In fact, I was rather interested.

"If you wanna grab it, we could get comfy on the sofa..." he trailed away suggestively.

Avoiding his stare, I looked at the floor when I said, "Or we could watch it in my room?"

He grabbed my hand and pulled me out of the kitchen. "What about the dishes?" I asked.

"Fuck the dishes," he said flatly and led me upstairs.

I set up my laptop, a little nervously, and he patted the bed beside him, inviting me to join him. So, climbing up to rest against the headboard like him, he took my computer and typed in some website address.

Before long there was a screen filled with images where you could select which scene you'd like to watch. "Are those all videos?" I asked, naively.

He nodded and smiled. "The net's full of free porn. There are short videos or long ones that go for thirty-odd minutes. But I think we'll start with some shorter ones. They can be a little crude," he warned.

But he pressed play and soon enough, there were two guys making out on a bed. They started with kissing, and I could feel myself getting aroused just by watching them. Then they were naked and pumping each other. I watched their cocks. I was transfixed.

"You like that?" he asked softly, and I nodded in response.

Then the scene cut, one of the guys was bent over the side of the mattress, and the other guy slid his dick into the other guys waiting ass. It was hot, and it made me hard, but to imagine doing that was scary as hell.

"I don't think I'm ready for that," I said in a whisper.

Trent's hand squeezed my thigh. "I know you're not ready for that, baby."

I looked at Trent then, and he was looking straight at me. "But you've done that?" I asked.

He laughed quietly and nodded. "Sure have."

I looked back at the screen and something confounded me. "The guy..." I didn't know what to call it, "getting fucked," I cringed at having said that. "He seems to like it."

Trent grinned. "The guy *getting* fucked is called a 'bottom', and the guy *doing* the fucking is called a 'top'," he explained. "And he does seem to like it, doesn't he?" he added sardonically.

I wasn't sure if it was rude to ask, but I needed to know. "So, which one are you?"

He took his time to answer, and I was about to apologize for asking when he told me, "I switch."

The guy on the screen was thrusting harder, and they were both groaning and it was really quite distracting. "What does that mean? Switch?" I asked.

"Both. I like to do both," he said with a chuckle.

I could hardly take my eyes off the guys fucking on-screen. My cock was aching, so I palmed it, tried to relieve some pressure. It was then I remembered I wasn't exactly alone, and my eyes quickly darted to Trent. He was watching me.

His eyes were dark, and his lips were parted. He looked... hungry.

The sound of the two guys on-screen coming demanded my attention. I looked to see the guy, the bottom, coming hard while still being fucked.

"Does being a bottom hurt?" I asked, though my voice was strained.

Trent's voice was husky. "Not if you have a patient lover."

I looked at him, into his eyes. His face was barely inches from mine, one of his hands was on my thigh, his other hand was slowly stroking himself. I hadn't even noticed. Swallowing hard, I asked him, "Are you a patient lover?"

Trent blinked slowly, and he groaned. "Oh, baby." Then he kissed me, softly, sweetly. His lips and tongue were caressing my mouth. Slowly, deeply and almost tenderly, Trent devoured my mouth, my jaw, my neck.

He pushed the laptop to the edge of the bed and settled himself between my legs. My cock was so hard it hurt, and he quickly undid the fly and exposed me to him. I expected him to palm me or wrap his fingers around me, but he didn't.

Without saying a word, he pulled my shirt above my head and leaned down, taking my nipple into his mouth. My body reacted at once, my hips rose, trying to push against him, but he denied me. He trailed opened-mouthed kisses across my chest and down my abdomen.

Then he took my cock into his hand, only to lean down and kiss the head.

I gasped in absolute pleasure. My entire body was shaking in desire, in anticipation.

He smiled as he licked the length of me, from base to

tip, his eyes never leaving mine. He rubbed his hands over my hips and along my stomach as he licked me again.

The laptop screen was now showing a different couple, one kneeling taking the entire length of cock down his throat.

I shuddered, and then Trent took my cock into his mouth. "Holy fuck!" I cried out, and he hummed.

I fisted the blankets at my sides, and Trent started to slide his lips up and down my dick. His mouth was warm and wet, his tongue was swirling and lapping, and I knew I wouldn't last long.

It didn't help that the laptop screen was still running a close up of a guy fucking some other guy's face. He was thrusting his cock while the other guy opened wider to take him. They were moaning, and I was so fucking close to coming.

I ran one hand through his hair and felt how his head moved up and down my shaft. Between watching Trent work me over, feeling what he was doing to me, and watching the two men on-screen, I was on the edge. "Fuck Trent, I'm close," I warned him, and he groaned around my cock.

Then the guy on screen started yelling, "Take my cock, suck it! That's it boy. Take my cock, all of it!" and my back arched off the bed as my orgasm ripped down my spine, and I exploded in Trent's mouth.

He sucked and swallowed, and my seams completely unravelled. His mouth, his hands, his moaning, sent warm shivers through my body as my orgasm wracked my whole frame. I was still twitching, and the room was still spinning and even when Trent bit playfully my hip, all I could manage was a giggle.

He crawled up my body and pressed his erection

against me. Even in my orgasm-addled brain, I could feel his desire pressed against my thigh. He wasn't expecting it, and when I flipped us over and pressed him into my bed, his eyes went wide and he grinned.

I laughed, and the room tilted a little, the blood had still not returned to my brain properly. "Whoa," I chuckled, "give me a second," and he laughed with me. "It's not my fault," I defended myself, "you're the one who jellified my insides."

He laughed again, but the sound died abruptly when I pulled his sweat pants down, and his engorged cock sprang free. "Nathan," he gasped, "what are you doing?"

I looked at his throbbing dick, I'd never been so close to an erect penis. I'd most certainly never attempted to have one in my mouth, and then I looked at his face. "I don't know... but I want to try."

"Baby, you don't have to."

"I want to," I told him. "I really want to." And I did. I really fucking wanted this.

"But...?"

"But I don't know what I'm doing," I admitted. Leaning back on my knees, I took him in my hand and stroked him.

He bit back a groan. "Shit babe, mmm..."

But then I licked him, pressing my tongue to his frenulum. "Ah, fuck!" he cried.

And I did it again, and this time he hissed. I smiled, and next, I licked the head and he moaned. When I did it again, I was rewarded with precome. The taste assaulted my senses, it shocked me at first. I'd never tasted another man before, but I wanted to taste more.

So I closed my eyes, parted my lips and took him into my mouth. Trent's breath stuttered, and he moaned like I'd never heard. It spurred me on, and I started to move up and down a little, and flattened my tongue against his shaft.

I didn't take him too far into my mouth, but I sucked hard and flicked the head of his cock with my tongue. Opening my eyes, I looked up at him. His eyes were wide, and he was staring at me. "Ohhhmygod..." he murmured.

I used one hand to wrap around the base of his shaft and pumped him while I continued sucking hard. Trent's hands flinched around my head like he wanted to grab hold of my hair, but he quickly fisted the blankets instead.

Giving him so much pleasure, seeing him writhing under me, was empowering. I sucked and licked him with a new confidence, and when my fingers grazed his balls, his voice rasped, "Fuck baby, coming, coming..."

I pulled my mouth from him but continued stroking him, squeezing him and massaging his balls, watching his reaction to my touch. He thrust his hips up, ramming his cock into my fist. His hands were clawing into the blankets at his sides, and his jaw was clenched as his orgasm erupted in hot thick spurts onto my hand and his stomach.

I was still panting when he came back to earth, and I wiped him down with his disregarded shirt. I closed the laptop, he pulled his sweat pants up and pulled me into his still-trembling arms. He mumbled something about me *trying to fucking kill him,* and settled himself against me. When his breathing evened out not long after, I knew he was asleep.

I brushed the hair from his forehead with my fingers, kissed his temple and fell asleep, for the first time in my life, in the arms of a man.

CHAPTER NINE

IT WAS an odd whining noise that woke me from the best
sleep I'd had in years. Peeling back my eyelids, I found my
bedroom bathed in sunlight and the source of the whining.

Two big brown eyes and a wet, black nose were mere
inches from my face, and very curious. He whined again
and huffed, making Trent stir. Trent lifted his head, looked
at me then at his dog and smiled sleepily, but he dropped
his head back down and sighed.

"What do you want, Bentley?" I asked the dog.

Trent answered with a chuckle, "You're late getting his
breakfast."

It made me laugh.

But I glanced at the alarm clock and realized I was late.
"Shit!" I flew out of bed, grabbed the quickest shower ever
and didn't bother shaving.

I went back into my room to get dressed, to find my bed
was empty. I was a little disappointed I didn't find a sleep
rumpled Trent smiling at me, but the fact he was even in my
bed at all made me grin.

I raced down the stairs and into the kitchen to grab my

tie and satchel. Trent had toast ready and he had one piece cut up. Handing a portion to Bentley, he told the dog, "Dr Slacko here's running too late to serve you today."

Trent looked at me and grinned. He was so fucking cute, all messed hair and blue eyes. He handed the other piece of toast to me. I took it with a smile and turned and walked to the door, and he said, "Is that all the thanks I get? Just a sexy smile?"

So I turned on my heel and taking two long strides, I grabbed his face with my free hand and kissed him so hard his wide eyes rolled back in his head. His back was bent, and I leaned over him, kissing him, thoroughly and fucking deliciously hard. I tilted my head, so I could force my tongue into his mouth, demanding to taste him.

His hand slid along my face, and he moaned when he felt the unshaven stubble along my jaw. I pulled my mouth from his abruptly, and he whimpered. It took a second for his eyes to open and focus. "Thank you," I said with a smile in my voice.

I think I'd rendered him speechless because his mouth opened and closed, but he said nothing. I prompted him with, "You're welcome," and he nodded.

I bit into my toast and chuckled all the way to work.

THE NEXT FEW days were some of the best I could recall. Trent and I spent every night together, exploring each other's bodies. He slept in my bed, and it was pretty fucking perfect. I was getting more confident in my skills of pleasuring him, and I was learning what I liked as well. Sometimes we didn't do anything overtly sexual, just cuddled up and watched TV, and that was pretty great too.

I worked late one day, and when I got home, I knew Trent had been painting, I could smell it. I asked him if I was allowed to see what he was working on, but he denied me. "Maybe when it's finished," he said, but I could see how me asking made him uncomfortable, and I realized whatever he was painting must be very personal to him.

I dropped the subject, for which he was undoubtedly grateful. I tried not to let it bother me. After all, what we'd been doing for the last two weeks was very fucking personal, but I pushed the matter to the back of my mind.

Work was busier. With a few days of sunshine, there were more broken bones, sprains, scrapes, cuts and falls, from visitors and hikers alike, out making the most of the good weather.

My last day before I left for the weekend in Boston, was a busy but good day. When the evening settled down and I grabbed a bite to eat, the Peters girl found me. I smiled politely, and she asked if she could sit with me. "Sure," I told her.

She blushed and she stammered. In the end, I think she avoided looking at me so she could maintain a decent conversation without getting that dazzled, far-off looked on her face. It still made me smile. I silently thanked God that Trent wasn't there to witness it.

"So, you're off tomorrow?" she asked cautiously.

"Yes. I can't believe I've been here two weeks already," I told her as I finished my sandwich.

"It's supposed to be another nice day tomorrow," she said, and I realized she was nervous. "I usually head down to Northport when the weather's good. I was thinking... I um, maybe..." she finished in a rush, "Ithoughtmaybeyoumightliketogo?"

Oh shit.

"Um, I can't." I told her. "I'm heading back to Boston to pick up a few things I left behind. I'm leaving in the morning."

"Oh," she said quietly, and her disappointment was palpable.

"Maybe another time?" I said and immediately regretted the offer, but my intention was to let her down gently. She must have mistaken my awkwardness for regret, because she brightened a little.

"Okay," she said and smiled at the prospect of our future date. I stood and collected my lunch tray. Not game enough to make eye contact, I looked at the empty tray as I told her I was due back at work. Dani gave a little wave of her hand, "Bye, Nathan."

I busied myself with paperwork in the hope she wouldn't find me again, knowing that in a few short hours, I'd be off for four days and I was spending them all with Trent.

I'd never done anything like it. I'd never actually used time off for anything other than catching up on sleep. Now, I was hoping like hell we didn't sleep much at all.

When I got home, I tried to hide how excited I really was. I knew Trent was enjoying whatever the hell it was between us, but I wondered what it meant to him. I knew the house painting was almost done and I wondered what that meant for us. I certainly didn't want to ruin what time we had left together by talking about feelings and emotions, and risk scaring him away.

So I did the only logical thing, I said nothing.

I climbed the stairs to get myself changed, and Trent was cleaning up in the bathroom. "You know," I told him from the doorway, "if someone were to blindfold me and put turpentine and acrylic paints in front of me, I'd think it was you."

He grinned and dried his hands on the hand towel. "Mmm, I'm sorry, what were you saying? You said the word 'blindfold', and I had all sorts of wonderful images in my head. I didn't hear the rest of what you said."

I laughed and shook my head at him. I'd just taken my tie off, and it was still in my hands, so I decided to tease him a little. I lifted the tie to my eyes and asked him, "You mean, like this?"

"Don't tempt me, Nathan," he said. His voice was husky. "Not sure if you're ready for that."

I raised my eyebrow at him. "I think you might be surprised what I'm ready for."

He looked at me for the longest time before he stepped close enough I felt the heat from his body. His eyes became darker, more intense, and his nostrils flared. He took the tie from my hands and covered my eyes with it, tying it off at the back of my head.

I was suddenly nervous, but excited, and I jumped when he took my hand, leading me out of the bathroom. "I'm walking you to your bedroom," he told me, and I followed him, willingly, keenly.

He stopped me, and I presumed we were in my room. His fingers left my hand, trailed up my arm and across my chest. He undid the buttons and slid my shirt off my shoulders, letting it fall to the floor. He pushed me backwards, and I felt the bed against the backs of my legs. "Sit," he commanded, and I did. He pulled my shoes and socks off and then said, "Stand up." His hands were undoing my pants, and he pushed my briefs down. As I stepped out of them, I could hear his breathing was as loud as mine.

"Now sit back down and scoot up the bed."

I couldn't believe how intoxicating this was. How, at this point, I was pretty sure I'd do anything he told me to. I was so turned on, I could feel how hard and aching I was when I lay back on the bed, and I gave my dick a squeeze.

"No touching," Trent's voice startled me, and I could hear the rustle of his clothes coming off.

When he joined me on the bed, he hovered over me, starting at my feet, I knew he was naked. I just knew. He kissed his way up my thighs and nibbled my hips, ignoring my throbbing cock. He licked my navel, kissed and scraped his teeth along the lines of my body.

The sensation, without sight, was overwhelming. I felt everything. I heard everything. I reached out blindly for his face and fisted his hair, making him groan.

"Oh fuck, Trent," I whispered to him, "please, touch me."

He moaned and chuckled. "I am touching you," he murmured against my ribs.

And he was. His hands were rubbing over my chest, pinching my nipples, digging into my skin, but I needed him to touch me where I ached the most.

I didn't care if I had to beg. "Touch me, touch my dick, please. Please..."

His knees were between my thighs and his hands were gone from my body. I heard the familiar click of the lube bottle, and he pushed my thighs further apart with his knees. I was suddenly very aware of our position, my vulnerability and my need.

I heard the slick sound of Trent rubbing the lubrication on his fingers and hands. I wondered if this was it, I wondered if we'd have sex, if he was about to fuck me. It scared me and excited me. But I knew I wanted it. I wanted it, and I needed it...

"Trent? Baby?"

Then his hands were on my cock. "Is this where you want me to touch you?"

"Yes," I rasped out.

"Fuck, have you got any idea how fucking hot you are right now?" Trent's voice was barely audible. "So fucking beautiful."

He gripped me harder, and I wished I could feel him. Blindly, I reached my hands out, but could only feel air.

"Whatcha lookin' for, baby?" he asked.

"I need to touch you," I told him. He leaned forward, resting on one arm, while his other hand pumped me.

I still couldn't see anything, and it was so heightening. My hands found his face, I leaned up and kissed him, but after a few passes of my tongue he pulled away with a groan.

I lifted my thighs higher across his and raised my hips off the bed, thrusting my ass blindly toward his cock, and he moaned loudly.

"Oh Trent, please," I pleaded with him.

He squeezed my cock with his hand. His voice was so gravelly with desire. "Is this what you want?"

It felt so fucking good, but it wasn't quite what I wanted. "I need to feel you..."

"Feel my hand on your cock, baby," he urged, "how good you feel in my fist."

I shook my head, because he didn't seem to understand what I meant. "I need to feel you inside me."

And his ministrations on my cock stopped. His breathing hitched and I wished I could see his face. I tried to pull the blindfold off my eyes, but his hand stopped me. "Leave it on," he said quietly.

"I want to see you," I told him.

But then both his hands were at the sides of my face, his

fingers over my tie-covered eyes and his legs between mine. He was lying with his weight on me, all of him on all of me and it felt amazing. I felt his engorged length pressing against me and mine against him. Instinctively, I thrust into him, our lube covered cocks slid between our bodies.

"Oh, Trent," was all I could say before his mouth was on mine, and he was fucking my mouth with his tongue.

My hands ran along his back and pushed his ass into my hips as I pushed back up against him. My whole body shuddered. I was so fucking turned on. He was still kissing me like I'd never been kissed, and then he started thrusting his cock into mine, making us both groan.

His hands curled under my shoulders, and my arms were wrapped tightly around him. We rocked and thrust, and devoured each other. My whole body was on fire, every nerve set alight with need. My stomach warmed, and I knew I was about to come. "Trent," I warned him, "Oh, fuck..."

I flexed against him one last time, locking my legs around his and pushing myself against him so hard that when my cock throbbed and twitched, spilling between us, it made him groan. He bucked against me forcefully, drawing out my orgasm and beckoning his own.

He growled and groaned as he came, and I felt his hot come spurting on my stomach in time with his grunts. Finally he collapsed onto me, smearing our mess with our bodies. He sighed and chuckled into my neck. His breath was warm on my skin as he kissed my neck and shoulder. I pulled the tie from my eyes, my eyes taking a little while to adjust to the light.

Trent leaned up on his elbow and looked at me with a lazy smile and dreamy eyes. He was fucking beautiful, but his post-coital face was by far my favorite. "Come on, gorgeous," I said with a kiss to his swollen lips. "Shower with me."

He chuckled again but climbed off me and led the way. We walked to the bathroom, both of us naked, and Trent started the shower. He had his back to me while he tested the water, and I couldn't resist running my hands from his lower back up to his shoulders and neck and into his hair.

I liked touching him, feeling his hard body against my skin. It wasn't soft and supple like a woman's, it was hard, defined and masculine. And I liked it.

Trent stepped into the shower, waiting for me to join him. "Is that your thinking face?" he asked with a grin.

I smiled and nodded, joining him under the water, cleaning the cooled mess off my stomach and chest. "Just marveling at the male physique," I told him.

Trent laughed, putting his head under the spray of hot water, but he didn't say anything.

"Trent, can I ask you something?"

He looked at me curiously, still smiling.

I grabbed the body wash and started scrubbing at my arms, so my next question seemed nonchalant, though I felt anything but. "I thought, well," I paused. "Well, I was kinda hoping we'd have sex."

His smile faded, and his eyes widened, though he tried to hide it. His reaction didn't sit well with me. "Nathan..."

"I just thought, earlier, on my bed when you were between my legs... I couldn't see anything, but I heard the lube and thought for a second that maybe you were about to... I thought maybe... I was hoping..."

He was quiet, and wouldn't look at me. "Nathan, I don't think you're ready for that."

Oh.

I was so new to this. I didn't know what I was supposed

to do, what was expected of me. I pulled his chin up, making him look at me. "When will I be ready?" My eyes flickered between each of his eyes, searching. "Trent? You'll tell me, won't you? When I should be ready? Because I feel like I'm ready."

Something flashed in his eyes, or maybe it was the steam and the water, I couldn't be sure, but he nodded.

Then something occurred to me. "Do you need something else? Someone else... who's more experienced...?" I asked, even though the thought of him with someone else twisted my stomach.

His eyes darted to mine. His mouth fell open, and he shook his head. "Why? Why would you say that?"

I was quick to explain, "I just thought you might need *that*, and if I wasn't ready..."

He smiled, kind of, and told me, "It's fine, Nathan. What we're doing is pretty fucking great. Don't rush anything. This is about you learning what you want."

Stepping back so I could see him more clearly, I told him, "It's not just about me."

He chuckled, but it wasn't exactly a humorous laugh. "I'm not exactly hard done by, Nathan. You've made me come every day since you got here."

But his words stung, and I knew it showed on my face. He looked... wrong. Sorry, remorseful and hurt, not the smiling Trent he normally was. But I couldn't face him, so I stepped back under the water and put my head in the spray, closing my eyes.

He got out of the shower and asked, "Are we still on for Boston tomorrow?"

I cleared my throat and took a breath. "Yeah."

"Better go pack then. See ya bright and early," he said a

little too cheerfully and left the bathroom. And I knew tonight I was sleeping alone.

Fuck.

By the time I got out of the shower, I was determined to be in this, *whatever the fuck it was*, for the fun of it, just like him. It was only physical for him. He practically just said so. I felt kind of stupid for thinking it was ever something different...

When I first decided to allow myself into this *"sexual learning,"* as Trent just called it, I'd told myself to just *feel*.

I just wasn't expecting the *feeling* part to be a heavy ache in my chest.

CHAPTER TEN

I LAY in bed but sleep wouldn't come. My mind was replaying everything that had happened since I got here. When I met him, my reaction to him— my first real reaction to anyone, and to a man, no less. My decision to allow myself to feel, whatever the hell he made me feel, and his decision to join me.

I recalled how he'd repeated my words, *"I'm in this too, whatever the hell it is."*

But at no point, not once, did he ever say his heart was in it.

To be honest and fair, neither had I.

But there I was at one in the morning, staring at the wall. My heart felt kind of strangled. I'd never felt the sting of rejection before. He hadn't even really rejected me... just said that whatever the hell this was, was just meaningless sex.

And it fucking stung.

I could have kicked myself for being so stupid. Trent had never said he felt anything for me, so maybe I'd misread the times when he'd held my hand, or the way he'd looked at me sometimes. He was only ever in this for sexual gratification.

He hadn't lied about it, he didn't mislead me. I knew what I was doing when I went into this. And now I was about to spend the weekend with him in Boston.

But it didn't mean anything to him.

So, I told myself it didn't mean anything to me. I could convince myself it was just physical. And that was exactly what I'd do. Just sex, just physical, nothing more. He was so much more experienced than me, in this— whatever the hell it was— and he told me I wasn't ready to take the next step. Oral sex, hand jobs, yes, but sexual intercourse, no. I felt like I was ready. I wanted that with him. I wanted to feel that with him, to give myself to him— even if it meant nothing to him— and I wondered what it would take for me to be ready.

Then I heard footsteps down the hall, the wooden floorboards squeaking softly told me he was having trouble sleeping too. I waited and listened for him to walk past my room, but he didn't. I looked up and found him standing at my door.

"Can't sleep?" I asked.

"Mm mm," he murmured softly with a shake of his head.

I took a deep breath, and before I realized what I'd done, I'd thrown the covers back, inviting him into my bed.

I could see his face in the moonlight, and his lips twitched into a smile before he crossed the room to climb into my bed. He snuggled down with his back to me and pulled the covers back up over us both. My arm slid around his waist, and I was spooning him, just how we'd slept all week, and he sighed at the contact of my skin on his.

His breathing evened out almost immediately, and I knew he was sleeping already. I rubbed my nose into the back of his head, smiling at how his hair tickled my nose, and how relaxed and sleepy I was with him in my arms.

My last thought before sleep claimed me, was how this – whatever the fuck it was – apparently didn't mean a thing.

I WOKE up to the feeling of my fingers being licked. It was kind of startling but not too unpleasant... until I realized my hand was hanging over the side of the bed. Peeling back my eyelids, I found the four-legged culprit with happy brown eyes, a toothy grin and a long, slobbery pink-tongue.

Bentley.

Groaning, I got up and changed into some sweats and sneakers. Reluctantly, I left the sleeping man in my bed and went downstairs. Bentley bounded happily out before me, and we set off for our morning run. I went further on the trail this morning, figuring Bentley could use the exertion before a three and a half hour car trip, and I used the run to clear my head.

I loved running through the woods that hugged the Bay. It sure beat pounding on concrete or running fruitless miles on a treadmill. The air was crisp, the ground was damp and the sounds of the living forest spurred me on. We had easily covered several miles, and when we finally got back to the house, we were both panting.

Bentley's long coat was wet and kind of dirty, but he looked rather pleased. My shirt was soaked through with sweat, and my hair wet with the damp, forest air. When we walked through the back glass doors, Trent was fixing himself a coffee. He looked at the both of us and asked, "Did you run or swim?"

I leaned over, resting my hands on my knees and caught

my breath. "Cardiovascular workout," I told him, "you should come with us next time."

Trent laughed loudly at me. "It gets my heart going enough just watching you," he said.

And it was comments like that that confused me. But it meant nothing to him, the sexual innuendos, the flirting, and the nonchalance about it all. I knew that was just him, always joking about sex and feelings and never being serious.

Maybe that was how I should be with him.

So I took off my shirt, and he watched me, his eyes raking over my naked torso. He smirked at me, so I twisted the shirt in my hands and flicked it at his ass. It connected with a resounding thwack, and he spilled his coffee. "Ow."

I laughed. "I'm the Master Towel Flicker," I told him. "Growing up with Brendan, I have years of practice."

He pouted and rubbed his ass. I chuckled at him, "Would you like a doctor to have a look at that for you?"

He grabbed the dish towel from me, twisted it, aimed it at me and told me to piss off, but I just laughed at him and raced upstairs to the bathroom.

When I was showered, shaved and packed, I went back downstairs. I dropped my bag in the foyer and headed toward the kitchen to find Bentley, looking very excited at something behind the open laundry door.

I walked past him, and when he barked, I turned to find Trent behind me, armed with a twisted tea towel. "Oh Bentley," Trent scowled, "you gave me away."

I laughed incredulously. "Because he's my breakfast buddy," I said as I patted and rubbed the dog. "He sticks up for me.

"He's a traitor," Trent said with a pout, but his lips twisted, trying not to smile.

"It's a shame," I told him. "I'd have let you rub my ass, too."

He groaned and threw the towel at me. I smiled at him and asked, "You ready to go? I have a surprise for you this afternoon," I told him, and his eyes widened. "Can't be late."

He was a little more than shocked. My suggestion of a surprise had thrown him. "I'm packed," he said quietly. "I'll just grab my bag."

I found an old blanket and laid it on backseat of my car. Trent came out with his bag and some strap looking thing, which he called a harness, for Bentley. Ten minutes later, we were on the road.

We stopped in Portland for coffee, and so Bentley could pee in the park. Conversation was easy. The changing scenery prompted changes of topics, and there was rarely silence. Bentley laid down and napped while we talked, and my fears of having to clean the car of dog urine smell went unfounded.

We passed a bus that was advertising for men's cologne, and our conversation went from male models, to sports stars, to body image, to piercings and tattoos.

I asked him about the tattoo, a solitary star, that I'd seen on his hip.

"Is it a Texas thing?" I asked, and he chuckled.

"No, it's a gay thing," he said with a smile.

I was surprised by this. "Oh."

"It's a symbol of sexual preference, as a way to make it known to other gay guys," he explained.

"But it's on your hip. How do guys see it?"

Oh. I realized they'd see it when he was naked with them...

He smiled and explained, "I don't advertise my sexual-ity, Nathan, but I also don't hide it. I'm not embarrassed and have nothing to be ashamed of," he said simply. "This symbol is more of a badge I wear to remind myself to always be true to who I am."

"I like that," I told him honestly. "It takes courage to wear your heart on your sleeve, so to speak. It's commendable."

It was quiet after that but not uncomfortable, and we were soon in Boston. I wove through traffic as Trent took in the sights. I pointed out things of interest, which he was probably not too interested in, but I explained that while I was born in Chicago, I grew up in Boston. I told him how much I loved this city.

"Then why'd you leave?" he asked, a fair question.

I sighed. I didn't know how I felt about divulging the truth to him. "I'd just worked a thirty-six hour shift without a day off in about two months. I was running myself into the ground. I think my boss was ready to sideline me, and I saw that Belfast County General was in need of a doctor..."

Trent nodded contemplatively. "Pretty big change of scenery," he noted.

"What?" I said with a smile, "You mean Belfast County General isn't like Boston General Emergency?"

Trent rolled his eyes at me then looked out the window. "Why'd we stop?"

I pointed to his left. "That's my place."

"You live here?" he asked with his eyebrows raised.

"No," I grinned at him. "I live in Belfast."

I got out of the car, and he joined me. I grabbed the bags, and he took care of Bentley. My apartment, technically a townhouse, was one of a row of joined cobblestones that someone with foresight had the brains and finances to develop in the nineties. I'd loved this place from the moment I first saw it two years ago, made an offer that same day, signed the paperwork three days later, and I'd secured my own private slice of Boston real estate.

I opened and held the door, allowing Trent and Bentley to walk in first. I followed them down the short hall and into the open kitchen/living area, where I put the bags down and flicked on some lights.

I could tell Trent was taking in the dark-hardwood floors, white rugs and the expensive furniture, but what hit me, like a ton of bricks, was how...*bare* it looked.

Everything was just as I left it. There wasn't a thing out of place. Yes, it looked bare, but there was something else. I just couldn't define what the difference was.

"Something wrong?" Trent asked me.

"No," I answered quickly. "No, no, it's all good. Come on, I'll show Bentley his ensuite."

I opened the back doors, and my once ample court-yard looked tiny. There was a patio that covered half of it, and the rest was grass. The outdoor furniture was pulled to one side and was covered, but it looked so small compared to the yard at Belfast. God, had it only been two weeks?

Bentley quickly bounded outside, sniffing and explor-ing, then peeing on the large pot that sat in the corner. Trent looked at his urinating dog, then at me, and shrugged. "Bentley owns that one now. It's got his name on it."

I laughed, and we left the back door open and went upstairs. "There are two bedrooms upstairs and the bath-room," I said as we got to the door of my room. I walked in and dumped both of our bags on my bed.

"A little presumptuous, aren't you?" he asked, looking at his bag on my bed.

"You can have the spare bed if you like," I told him, as nonchalantly as I could, and opened the curtains.

"Oh, shut up," he said, rolling his eyes. "You know I'm gonna end up in here anyway."

I grinned, and he chuckled at me then changed the topic completely, "Now, you said you had a surprise for me this afternoon?"

"Yes," I told him. "Lunch first though, I'm starving." I walked back down the stairs, grabbing my keys and Bentley's leash.

We walked two blocks to one of my favorite places in all of Boston. "Ah Nathan, we miss you," the short, smiling Japanese woman greeted me.

"Hello, Mrs. Lin," I greeted her in return. "I told you I was moving away."

"You not staying?" She asked, and I laughed and told her no. "But my sales are down," she scolded me. "My best customer move away, and I go broke."

"Can you deliver three hours away?" I asked her.

She scowled at me, then smiled. "What could I get for you, Nathan? Your usual?"

"Two, please," I said.

"Oh," she said suspiciously. "Lunch for two?"

I looked quickly back at Trent, who was standing outside with Bentley. "Um...yeah."

"Mmm," Mrs. Lin hummed. "He's a cute boy."

I coughed and felt my cheeks flush. She handed me my lunch order, I paid and she was still smiling when I walked out the door.

We ate our sushi, California rolls, and drank our green tea in the park. "God, I've missed this," I told him, indicating to our lunch.

"Do you ever eat anything that isn't healthy?" he asked.

"I'm a doctor," I reminded him. "Do you want to know what eating fast-food will do to your body?"

He stuck his fingers in his ears. "No, I like not knowing. Please don't ruin it for me. I love burgers."

I laughed at him and spared him the lecture on trans lipid fats and refined sugars. He grinned at me, and we finished our lunch and took Bentley home.

"Should I change into anything in particular?" he asked, still not knowing where we were going.

"Jeans are fine," I told him, and when he came back down stairs, he was wearing dark denim jeans and a blue button down shirt that matched the color of his eyes. His blond curls were somehow brushed back off his face, and he lifted one corner of his mouth into that smirk he had.

"Pick your jaw up, Nathan," he told me.

"You look... um..."

"I look what? C'mon say it," he taunted me.

"You look fucking hot."

He laughed then and said, "You're not too difficult to look at either."

I walked straight up to him and stood before him. My shoes were touching his, and I had to kiss him. I needed to kiss him and touch him, feel him. My hand touched his face, my thumb skimmed his jaw and I pressed my lips to his.

I told myself to kiss him without feeling, but then his lips moved against mine as he kissed me back. I held his face and pushed my mouth onto his, opening my lips and caressing his tongue with mine. His hands held my hips, and I couldn't help but moan when he pulled me against him.

I felt this kiss building in desire, and as much as I wanted it, I wanted to show him his surprise more.

I broke the kiss, and leaning my forehead against his, I took a second to breathe. I licked my lips, but couldn't help kissing him again, chastely. He smiled against my lips, and I told him, "If we don't leave now, we won't be going anywhere."

He chuckled and took some deep breaths. We fixed Bentley some dinner and water, a blanket on the floor, one more bathroom break, and we finally left.

It wasn't far to the city from my place, so we jumped in a cab. I gave the directions to, "Huntingford Avenue," and Trent looked at me in wonder. I grinned at him. "We're going to see MoFA," I told him.

"MoFA? Who's that?"

I laughed. "Not a who, but a what."

"Oh enough with the cryptic shit," he moaned. "I'll just wait to see for myself."

"Don't like surprises much, eh?" I teased him, and he pouted. He was so fucking cute when he tried to pout, and before long his pout became a smirk.

We arrived at our destination and had to walk just a few yards. Trent still had no idea where I was taking him, but when we rounded the corner and he saw the Museum of Fine Arts, he stopped walking, apparently so he could smile.

"You brought me here?" he asked, still grinning, with his eyes wide.

I nodded. "There's a new exhibit on contemporary abstract, and I thought you might like to see it. I haven't been here in a few years, but considering you're an artist and all..."

"Oh my God," he whispered and looked at me for the longest time. Then he looked at the building before us, and his look of awe made me smile.

I told him, "You can stay out here and look at the build-ing, or if you'd prefer, we could look at the art inside..." and without thinking, I took his hand and led him toward the doors.

It wasn't until I went to pay our admission and I had to let go of his hand that I even realized I'd just held another man's hand in public.

I wasn't sure what surprised me more, that I *did* just hold his hand in public, or that I didn't care. Trent could tell I just realized what I'd done, and he was watching me, waiting no doubt, for me to freak out. But instead, I just smiled at him.

I led the way, taking him through the grand foyer first. He took in everything, admiring and staring, but it was when we found the new exhibit of abstract art that his reaction floored me.

He was moved by what he saw. He stared at each painting for ages, as though he was deciphering a hidden language, from one abstract artist to another. He tilted his head every so often and the fingers on his right hand moved, as though the textures meant something, even though he was some meters away.

I didn't pay particular attention to the paintings. I was watching him. The hours felt like minutes, time flew so quickly, I wished I'd brought him here earlier. We eventually did look at other rooms, but he wanted to go back to the abstract exhibit.

He was drawn to the painting that was a dozen shades of white, the one of lines and boxes and what appears to be a horizon.

I stood behind him and whispered in his ear, "Tell me what you see."

He gasped as my voice surprised him, though his eyes never left the painting in front of us. "This is someone who won't be defined, won't conform, he won't bend. He has strong beliefs and he wants to be heard."

Wow. His perception amazed me. "Then why isn't it bold, with loud colors? Why is there no color?"

"The artist wants you to see the meaning, to hear what he has to say. Colors tell a story, but here in this painting, the artist isn't saying *look* at me, he's saying *listen* to me."

My heart flipped in my chest at his words, his Southern accent spoken low and thoughtful, made me shiver. He was so insightful, and I envied how he saw the world. I saw black and white, rational and cogent streams of thought my medical training had ingrained in me. Yet he saw between the lines, he saw hidden meanings, how color interpreted emotions and how lines defined agenda.

I realized I wasn't as good as him at being in this *what-ever-the-hell-it-is* without any emotions attached.

I leaned my forehead on his shoulder and whispered, "Incredible."

"Yes, it is," he answered softly.

I wasn't talking about the painting, but I didn't correct him. I kissed the side of his neck instead.

CHAPTER ELEVEN

I DIDN'T REALIZE how late it had gotten by the time we left the Museum. "Come on," I told him, "there's a restaurant here. I'm starving."

We were given a table, and while we were waiting for our food, Trent could barely contain his excitement. He talked about the paintings, the textures, the language, like I hadn't just seen them with him. And in a way, I guess I hadn't, I didn't see any of what he saw.

He was describing them in ways I couldn't have imagined before now. I only saw large canvases of colors, defused a dozen different ways. He saw life, emotions and energy. Even when we left the restaurant and walked out into the cool, Boston night, he was still smiling.

He pulled out his phone, looked something up online, and his face lit up. "Now it's my turn to show you something."

Two blocks later there were neon lights and security men at the door. It was a bar. Not just any bar, but a gay bar. Trent walked right up, confident and knowing, but I wasn't. "Trent..." I said hesitantly.

He stopped and looked back, he walked back to me. "Nathan, you need to experience this, just once."

I shook my head. "But I don't drink, or dance," I told him.

He grinned like I'd just dared him, and I exhaled loudly. He knew he'd just won. "Come on, Baby," he whispered seductively in my ear, and I didn't stand a chance. "You won't be disappointed."

So, reluctantly I followed him, and Trent offered a cheerful and very Southern, "Evenin', boys," to the two burly men at the door.

They smiled and asked for our ID's before letting us enter. When they checked Trent's license, one of the men said, "You're a long way from home, Cowboy."

Trent grinned and winked at him. "Just a heel click of my ruby slippers away, baby."

Both men laughed, while I stood there a little shocked at seeing this side of him. They opened the doors, and Trent pulled me inside.

The room, lit by neon and strobe lights, was otherwise dark. There was a bar in the back, dance floor to the right. It was full. Of men. Dancing. The music was loud and thumping, and I couldn't take my eyes off the men who swayed and grinded.

Trent still had my hand, and he pulled me to the bar. I couldn't hear what he ordered, but the barman returned with two very large, very green cocktails. Trent handed one to me and I sipped it cautiously. It was sweet and surprisingly, not too bad. I had to lean right up against Trent and yell in his ear so he could hear me. "What was the thing with the ruby slippers at the door?"

He laughed and leaned into me, and I felt his lips at my ear. "Just playing with them," he said. "It was fun."

When he looked at me, his eyes were bright and smiling. He was so close, and I was pressed against him. One hand held my drink, the other hand held his hip. But I needed to be that close so I could hear him. It didn't mean anything...

Taking a small step back, I sipped my drink, taking my time to look over the crowded room. There were men talking, with hands on thighs, men kissing, fondling and groping, and men like me who were watching everyone else.

I leaned into him again, pressing my lips to his ear. "They're staring at me."

"Because you're fucking beautiful," he answered. I looked at him, shocked. But he wasn't ashamed, he just smiled. "Finish your drink so I can take you out on that dance floor and show them who you're here with."

He saw me choke at his words, and he smiled. He was different here, he was in his element. He was comfortable and had an air of authority, and I liked it. I finished my drink in one mouthful and shuddered as I swallowed it. Trent chuckled, took my hand and led me into the sea of swaying bodies.

He pulled me against him, my hips fit perfectly with his. The alcohol buzzed my brain, and my blood was warm, furling desire in my veins. Trent ran his hands over my hips, around my back and down my ass. He ground against me, and the music thumped in my chest.

My eyes closed. I felt him against me, his chest against mine. His nose skimmed along my jaw, and when he pressed his lips to my neck, I moaned. I felt him smile against my skin, and I was helpless to what he was doing to me.

And he knew it.

Then he spun me so my back was against his chest and

when he ground his hardening cock against my ass, my body betrayed me and I shuddered. I felt exposed like this, there were other men so close, almost up against me, but Trent kept his hands on my hips and his mouth at my neck.

There was no doubt who I was here with.

I lifted my hands above my head until my fingers found his hair, and I pulled his face closer. His lips teased my neck, and he moved us to the music. We danced, on full display for the world to see and yet it was so sensual, and I felt so alive.

And a little bit drunk.

Trent whispered in my ear, "I think we need another drink," I felt his breath on my skin.

This time at the bar, there were more people. Trent ordered two more green drinks and dragged me to one side, away from the bar where it was a little darker, and I took a long drink.

"Thought you said you didn't drink or dance," he said, clearly amused. "Do you like it?"

Whether he was asking if I liked the drink or the dancing, I wasn't sure. I nodded, "Yes."

I finished my second drink, and Trent offered another. "Water," I told him. He laughed and went to the bar. My head was spinning, or the room was, and I was moving to the thumping beat, even though I was standing by myself.

Then a hand tapped my shoulder. "Dr. Tierney?"

Oh, fuck.

I turned to find a face I recognized, though my green-drink skewed brain took a second to place his face. He was on the staff at Boston General. "John Reitner," he reminded me.

Yes. That was him.

"What are you doing here?" he asked. Then he

amended, "Well, I know *what* you're doing here. But I haven't seen you here before."

"I'm here with Trent," I told him, and I suddenly felt very drunk. "He's at the bar. He's gay."

"Oh," he nodded and smiled, "right."

Then Trent was at my side, very close, and he handed me a bottle of water. I introduced them and explained that John worked at Boston General. Trent nodded and looked at me, alarmed. I imagine I looked the same.

"It's alright, Dr. Tierney," John told me, "I won't tell anyone I saw you."

And with that, he turned and danced himself into the middle of the dance floor.

Trent asked, "Are you okay?"

I shrugged and nodded. "Too late now," I told him. "And I'm too drunk to care."

He laughed, "Then we should dance."

We finished our waters and went back to the dance floor. This time he kept me facing him, flush against him, and surely he felt how aroused I was. We danced, or rather Trent danced with me. He kissed me right where everyone could see us, and I couldn't bring myself to care.

I was lost in the moment of being with him like this, on the dance floor, in his arms. It felt right. And so fucking good.

Eventually, we both needed to pee. When we came out from the bathroom, Trent suggested another drink, and I was drunk enough to think that was a fantastic idea.

This time when I was standing by myself, another man approached me. He looked me up and down like I was something to eat, and I didn't like it. "Well hello, gorgeous," he murmured and almost cornered me. "You look a little lost. You want to come home with me? Don't deny it, gorgeous."

I literally felt my skin crawl. "I'm not interested," I told him. I wasn't usually backward about being forward, but I was out of my element here. I looked for Trent, and then he was suddenly there.

He slid between us, so he was in front of me as he faced this guy. "I believe he told you he's not interested," his southern accent was strong. He stared the man down and took a step toward him. "He's mine."

It took me a moment to realize what Trent said. That I was his, that I belonged to him and while it shocked me, I couldn't deny I liked it. Because I *did* like it.

The guy disappeared, and Trent turned to face me. "I'm sorry," he said.

So I kissed him, I kissed him hard. I didn't care who saw. When I broke away from his lips, I told him, "Don't apologize. I liked it."

His eyes widened, but he grinned and took my hand, leading me to the bar. "You're coming with me this time," he said, "it seems I can't leave you alone."

Trent stood at the bar, and I slipped my hands in the back pockets of his jeans. I was quite content to play with his ass. He kept looking over his shoulder at me and it made me chuckle. "Care to remove your hands?" he asked me with a raised brow.

"Only if you remove your jeans first," I said, although it mustn't have been as quiet as I'd intended, because the barman laughed as he placed two more green drinks on the bar.

Trent picked up the two glasses, and I was forced to take one of my hands out of his ass pocket to take the drink.

"So," Trent joked, "never had you pegged for a handsy drunk."

I smiled at him as I took a long draw off my drink. The third one tasted much better than the first two, and I drank it probably far too quickly and told him we needed to dance. He shook his head at me, but he obliged.

The dance floor was pumping, and half the men were now shirtless. I wrapped my hand around his neck and kissed him. I was past giving a fuck. It felt good, and it felt right. I was in a gay club, dancing with and kissing a man, and I didn't give a fuck.

I didn't care that I was drunk. I felt good. I'd not felt this good, this alive, in my entire life. I had no idea how long we danced, but I was sweaty and so fucking turned on. Trent was grinding against me, rubbing his denim-clad cock against mine, and I could feel how hard he was, how hard I was.

I ran my hands over his back and ass, and up into his hair. I kissed him like there was no tomorrow - and he reciprocated. He was into this, there on the dance floor, I knew he was. He held me, his hands touched as much of me as he could reach, he moaned into my mouth, and his body shuddered.

"We need to leave," he breathed in my ear.

I'd kind of forgotten we were in a crowded bar. I looked around, and everyone seemed oblivious to us... not that I cared.

Next thing I knew, I was telling a cab driver my address, and we were falling into my apartment. Bentley was excited to see us, and I gave him a cuddle. I told him I missed him too, and Trent laughed at us and then dragged me up the stairs.

"For someone who doesn't dance or drink, you did quite well," Trent chuckled.

Three cocktails were obviously enough to make me say things I normally wouldn't, because I told him, "I can think of better things to do with your mouth than make smartass comments."

Trent grabbed the waist of my jeans, popping the button. "Is that so?"

I palmed his cock through his jeans and nodded. He pushed me down on the bed, took my jeans off for me, undressed himself and climbed onto the bed. "I'm drunk," I told him, though I'm pretty sure he already knew that. "And I want to taste your come."

"Jesus," he mumbled. "You can't say things like that to me."

Which of course made me say more things exactly like that. "I want you in my mouth. I need to taste you."

He didn't need much encouragement. He moved really fast and, I wasn't sure how it happened, but the next think I knew, his beautiful face was gone and I had his dick in my face. And then I realized my dick was warm and wet. He was sucking on me, and I was staring at his very erect and very swollen cock.

I'd never needed to taste something so bad in my life.

So I took him in my mouth, as much as I could, and I hummed my contentment. Trent moaned around my cock, sending shivers through me, and I bucked in response.

Then his cock was no longer in my mouth, and he was gone. "Hey, where'd you go?" I asked, licking my lips, and he chuckled.

Then he was back again. I grabbed his hips this time, so he couldn't escape, and devoured his erection. He groaned long and loud, "Oh, fuck," as I worked him over. "I had to get the lube," he told me. Then I heard the lid click on the bottle, and his hands were massaging my balls and the base of my cock while he licked at the head.

His fingers, slick with lube, were massaging everywhere, and when he pressed against my anus, I welcomed it. Maybe it was the alcohol. Maybe it was because I'd wanted it, and he wouldn't give it to me...but I moaned in encouragement.

And he did it. Slowly, just a little, he slid his finger into my ass.

I tightened my hold on his hips and took more of his length into my mouth, more than I'd ever taken. I wanted him to know I liked what he was doing, so I sucked him harder. I licked along his shaft, and I tasted him on the back of my tongue.

He pulled his mouth off my cock. "Oh fuck, Nathan! Baby," he cried out, "just like that." And he was fucking me with his finger harder and deeper, as he nuzzled his nose into my pubic bone. "Jesus..." he moaned. Knowing I was pleasuring him turned me on, and I worked his cock harder.

"You're gonna make me come," he told me, his voice barely a groan. He was still fingering my ass and pumping my cock with his hand, while his mouth licked and lapped at me. It was sensation overload.

"You want me to come in your mouth?" he grunted, and I groaned and nodded and sucked him harder.

His rock-hard length swelled in my mouth, and his balls tightened in my hand. I wanted him to come. I wanted to taste him, drink him. He thrust once, and his cock lurched as he exploded down my throat.

He roared, and his whole body flexed as his come spurted, hot and thick. And I savored him—he was sweet, salty and musky. His cock was at the back of my throat, I had no choice but to swallow. And I liked it. I lapped at him, sucking him clean, and he growled.

I couldn't help it, and it was probably not the reaction he was after, but I chuckled.

"Something funny?" his voice croaked.

"I swallowed," I told him proudly.

He barked a short laugh. "You blew my fucking mind."

I realized his finger was gone from my ass, and he shuffled out of my arms, only to push me onto my back and kneel between my legs. He poured more lube on his fingers, and then drizzled it directly onto my shaft.

He wrapped one hand around my dick and massaged my balls with his other. He sucked on the head, licking me, distracting me from the finger pressing into my ass.

My back arched off the bed, and he pressed deeper inside me. He pumped and sucked my cock while he finger fucked my ass.

"You like my finger in your ass?" he asked, and I moaned.

"You're so tight," he told me, and I whimpered.

"I want to be inside your ass when you come," he ground out, and I lost it. My pleasure built in waves, and I imagined it was his cock that was fucking me. I could picture his hips against mine, thrusting into me, his dick pulsing, my ass clenching.

"Fuck me, Trent," I groaned through gritted teeth. "Fuck me."

He pushed in a second finger and sucked my cock so hard, the pleasure consumed me. My orgasm came from the depths of my belly and spilled into his mouth, and he kept fucking my ass with his fingers while he sucked me.

When he pulled his fingers out of me, I was completely spent. The room spun as Trent fell against me. He chuckled and hummed against my chest as my arms wrapped around him.

Even as a sated, alcohol-induced sleep claimed me, I knew three things. One, I wanted this moment to last forever. Two, this wasn't just physical for me—I wasn't sure it ever was.

And three, I was drunk. And I was going to be fucking hungover tomorrow.

CHAPTER TWELVE

MY EXPECTATIONS DIDN'T DISAPPOINT me. My head fucking hurt.

I recalled the nightclub from last night, dancing, running into someone who knew me, and the green drinks Trent gave me. I rolled over to hit him or curse at him, but he wasn't there.

Throwing my feet over the side of my bed and sitting up seemed like a good idea...until I did it. The room tilted, my head pounded and nausea ran down my spine and twisted my stomach.

Fuck. Who the hell's idea was it to drink?

I never drink.

And being hungover rudely reminded me why.

I stumbled to my dresser and founding some boxer briefs, put them on and went downstairs. Trent was there, being all bright and bubbly with Bentley. I sneered at them both, and Trent chuckled.

I considered sneering again but decided trying not to dry heave in the kitchen sink was a much better idea.

"Jeez, you only had three drinks," Trent said with a laugh.

My stomach rolled at the mention of it. "Don't talk about it."

"You missed Bentley's breakfast," he teased. "He wasn't impressed."

"Could I care tomorrow?" I asked and leaned my head down on the kitchen counter.

Trent walked into the kitchen and stood beside me. "You need a greasy burger and a Coke," he told me.

I shook my head and mumbled into the marble counter-top, "I need water, vitamin B and electrolytes."

"God, it must suck being a doctor," he griped. "You need a shower, half a pound of saturated fat and sodium, and a hit of caffeine and sugar." I groaned, and he laughed. "Trust me," he added.

I looked at him, all showered and dressed and sunshiney.

"Go!" he ordered. "Upstairs. Shower."

I pouted like a petulant child, but did what I was told. The shower was a reprieve, and I felt better after brushing my teeth. I didn't bother shaving. I just got dressed and went back downstairs. Trent and Bentley were waiting, and we headed straight outside.

The sun was half obscured by clouds but was still fucking offensive. Trent dragged me past Mrs. Lin's, and he walked into a diner. I sat in the park with Bentley and cursed at the sun while Trent ordered our breakfast.

A double bacon burger and a Coke. Ugh. He swore it would fix me, so I humored him by eating it.

It was disgusting and really, really good.

I ate about half and fed the rest to a grateful Bentley. Trent shook his head at me. I opened the soda and took a mouthful and pretended to offer the can to the dog. Trent pushed my shoulder, "I draw the line at giving him Coca-Cola."

I laughed and leaned my head back and closed my eyes to the sunshine.

"Feel better?" Trent asked.

"I can feel my arteries hardening," I told him. "And I'm pretty sure after that drink I'm now pre-diabetic."

"Gee, overreact much?" he asked with a laugh. "But you do feel better, I can tell," he said with a smug smile.

I told him to shut up, and he smiled. We sat and watched Bentley roam around the small park, sniffing and exploring. Trent and I didn't talk, but every so often, I'd steal a glance in his direction. He'd be looking at me, and he'd smile.

We'd been back at my apartment for about twenty minutes when my urge to kiss him got the better of me. We were in the living room, Bentley was napping on the floor, and I just decided to do it. Trent was on the sofa and had asked me what was on the agenda this afternoon. I walked over and straddled him, and his eyes widened as he looked up to me.

"You, are on my agenda this afternoon," I told him before I kissed him.

He chuckled, then sighed into my kiss and his hands rested on my hips. It was an unusual position for me to be in, for a guy to be in, being the one who straddles, but before I could think too much about it, there was a knock at my door.

"If we ignore them, they might go away," I mumbled against his lips, and he smiled.

But then there was a jangle of keys, and I heard a familiar, "Nathan?"

"It's my mom," I said, climbing off him. I started toward the front door as my mother let herself in, just as Bentley decided to greet our visitor.

I grabbed his collar just as my mom walked down the hall. She stopped when she saw me, not expecting to find me wrestling with a dog. "Hi, Mom," I said. "Just give me a sec."

Trent quickly grabbed Bentley, and I laughed as my mom watched on bemused. Though she seemed oblivious to Trent, she was watching me.

I was smiling back at her, and she put the bags in her hands down on the kitchen counter so she could hug me.

It was then I noticed Trent. He was holding onto his dog, but he looked a little uncomfortable, or even nervous.

"I yelled out..." Mom said as an explanation for letting herself in.

"I was upstairs," I lied, and it was then that she looked to Trent.

I quickly made introductions, sparing the specifics. "Mom, this is Trent. Trent this is my mom, Julia, and this is Bentley."

"Nice to meet you," he said. "Sorry 'bout my dog. He gets a little excited."

"That's perfectly fine, dear," she told him, giving him the standard issue Julia Tierney motherly smile. "I was in the neighborhood and thought I'd drop by and see if you wanted to join me for lunch?"

"We already ate," I told her.

"Oh," she said, still looking at me strangely. "But you're still coming for dinner?"

"Yes," I reassured her. "That's the plan."

"And you, Trent?" she asked him, "You're coming, too?"

"Um," he said hesitantly, and he looked a little lost, not sure what to say.

"Don't be silly," Mom said quickly. "You're more than welcome." She then turned her attention to Bentley, "Brendan would love to meet you," she said as she petted his head.

"Mom..." I said, trying to downplay her insistence that Trent joins us.

When she looked at me curiously, I knew she was about to say something embarrassing. "You look good, Nathan."

I rolled my eyes.

"You do!" she exclaimed. "You look like you've actually slept. The country life agrees with you, I can tell."

"Thanks Mom, that's not humiliating at all."

My mother was oblivious to my sarcasm, and Trent chuckled.

"Well, I best get going," Mom said. "I'll see *both* you boys at about four." She eyed Trent, daring him to argue, smiled and breezed out as quickly as she'd come.

Trent was still staring at the door, and he blinked. I was quick to apologize. "Excuse my mom, she's a little... insistent. You don't have to go...

I don't expect you to want to spend the evening with my family."

"Will she have me court-martialed if I'm not there?" he asked, and I laughed. "And why would Brendan love to meet Bentley?"

"My brother's a vet."

"Huh," he nodded. "A doctor and a vet? What does your sister do?"

"Alana? She's in design school," I explained. "She's more like Mom. Brendan and I are like dad. What about your family?"

He was quiet for a moment before he answered. "My parents died in a car accident when I was sixteen."

"Oh, shit," I replied, shocked. "I'm sorry."

"It's okay, Nathan. It was eleven years ago," he told me. "I lived with my Uncle Peter and Aunt Carolyn until I finished high school. I used my inheritance money to pay for art school and hit the road after graduation." He looked at me and gave me a small smile. "And that is the Trent Jamieson story."

I wanted to ask him personal questions, but I didn't think that was what someone who's not supposed to care would do. So I didn't. "And you've been getting inspiration from the American countryside ever since?"

"Inspiration?"

"Yeah, for your paintings," I explained. "Like in Belfast."

He shrugged and nodded, but said, "The art museum last night was so good. You have no idea..."

"I think I do," I told him, and I stood in front of him. "Your face was priceless."

He looked into my eyes, really, *really* looked into my eyes. His voice was quiet, "No one has ever done anything like that for me before."

My hand cupped his jaw. "Well someone should have," I told him, and I kissed his lips sweetly. He looked away, I think I made him uncomfortable... and I was reminded that this, *whatever-the-hell-it-is,* was just physical. So taking the seriousness down a notch, I looked at my watch. "Well, we have three hours before my mother has us both court-martialed...and I want a nap."

"A nap?" he laughed. "What are you, three? Or eighty-three?"

"Shut up," I told him, glad that he was now smiling.

"Your hangover remedy is starting to wear off, and I'm tired because you made me drink and dance last night."

His eyebrows shot up to his hairline. "Me? Well the drinking, yes. But as for the dancing, I seem to recall you managing quite well on your own."

I smiled at him. "Hey, it's not my fault you're sexy when you dance. You know I wouldn't stand a chance."

He laughed again. "*You* are sexy when you dance. Didn't you see how all those men looked at you? They couldn't take their eyes off you."

"Yeah, right," I scoffed. "Now I know you're bullshitting. I'm going upstairs to have my *grandpa* nap, if you want to join me...?"

His smile became a smirk, and he looked at me with playful eyes.

"To sleep," I reminded him. "I'm going to go to sleep." He pouted, so I told him, "But I sleep better when you're with me, so..." my words trailed off, and he grinned and rushed past me, taking the stairs two at a time. I followed him, not quite as fast, but grinning like an idiot.

I set the alarm on my phone, peeled my clothes off, leaving only my boxers on and climbed into bed. Trent was already undressed and lying down, so I shuffled across the bed and rested my head on his chest. His arms wrapped around me and very quietly, he said, "I sleep better when you're with me, too."

I smiled, and the next thing I knew the alarm on my phone told me it was time to wake up.

We arrived at my parent's house, and I could tell Trent was nervous. Before we got out of the car, I asked, "What's wrong?"

"Um," he said with a nervous laughed, "just never been to meet someone's parents before."

Oh, fuck.

I didn't even think of *that*. I was so fucking out of the loop on this shit. "That isn't what this is," I told him to put him at ease. I didn't want him to think I'd set this up... "It isn't like we're *dating*, for fuck's sake. We're just going to have dinner. So my mother doesn't scalp us, remember?"

His brow furrowed for just a second, but then he smiled, he looked relieved, and I tried to not let that bother me. We got Bentley from the backseat and walked up the steps to the house.

I opened the front door and yelled out, "Hello?"

"We're out the back," came my mother's reply. As we walked out into the open entertaining area, five pairs of wide eyes were watching me. Kat, my sister-in-law, even had to close her mouth.

I made introductions as quickly and painlessly as possible. Hands were shaken, cheeks were kissed and the smiles were genuine. After Brendan had gotten over his shock of seeing me with a dog, he took Bentley and patted his head and tummy, finally settling to scratch him under his ears.

"See?" my mom announced to the room, "I told you he looked great."

I groaned and fell into a chair beside my dad. Trent took the only remaining spare seat beside me and my dad chuckled. "Your mother's been on and on about how the country air has been good for you," he said, still grinning. "You do look... refreshed."

"Sleep," I said by way of explanation. "It's amazing what it will do for you." So, with that the subject was dropped and I asked Trent if he wanted a drink.

"Just a soda or water," he said quietly.

Brendan declared, "There's beer."

"Ugh," I winced. "No alcohol."

And Trent laughed, causing more inquisitive eyebrows raised from around the table. "Um, Nathan is a little hung over today," he told them. My head lolled back, and I groaned.

"What?" Brendan cried. "*You?* Got *drunk?*" he asked me, and everyone stared, waiting for my answer.

"I had three drinks, and it nearly killed me."

"Where'd you go?" Alana asked, bright-eyed.

"Some bar in the city. I can't exactly remember," I lied.

"You can't remember?" Brendan asked. "What the hell were you drinking?"

"I don't know. They were green," I told them. They laughed, incredulous that I, the brother who never drinks, got hammered.

I grabbed us some sodas, and the attention turned to Trent. He explained that yes, the accent was Texan, and that he'd been traveling, seeing the country, for nearly four years. He'd spent a while in New York, and then he told them the story of how he came to be staying in the house at Belfast.

"So how long do you plan on staying in Belfast?" Kat asked him.

Trent's eyes darted to mine, then back to Kat. "Not sure. Haven't thought about that yet." Which I could tell was a straight up lie, but I didn't want to know the truth.

So I steered the conversation away from what I didn't want to know. "I took Trent to see the Contemporary Abstract exhibition at the Arts Museum," I said, knowing it would spark a long conversation about art—and not about Trent leaving town.

We talked through dinner about the exhibit, about art, and the Boston summer weather blessed us for an outdoor evening. Trent's excitement and passion for what he did really showed in the way he used his hands and how his eyes shone when he talked. I couldn't help but smile at him. Bentley sat by my chair, and I sneaked him some sausage. When I looked up, Trent was smirking at me with his eyebrow raised. "You're gonna spoil my dog."

"He doesn't mind," I answered, trying not to smile.

Brendan started to lecture me on animal behavioural habits and dining tables. I scrunched up my napkin, threw it at him and told him to shut up.

"Boys," Mom chided us. Brendan ignored her and threw the scrunched up napkin back at me. Just like always.

After dinner, I found myself sitting with my feet up on a lounge chair with Bentley's head in my lap as I was talking with my dad. Everyone else was still there, but dad was talking hospitals. He asked a hundred questions about Belfast County, and I told him, "When you visit, I'll give you the grand tour."

Trent was stuck talking to Brendan and Alana, and when I caught his eye, I smiled apologetically. I noticed Kat looking at me. She smiled, more to herself than to anyone else, like she was confirming something in her mind. I looked at her with my eyebrow raised in question, but Trent's loud laughter interrupted our silent conversation.

"It's true!" Brendan exclaimed. "It was huge!"

I chuckled and asked Trent, "Is he telling you why he became a vet?"

We'd been on a family camping trip when we were kids and encountered a bear. He'd been fascinated by animals ever since and told everyone he encounters the same story.

"It was just a cub," I told Trent, and he laughed. "That bear gets bigger every time he tells that story." Brendan snarled and threw his beer cap at me. I caught it and threw it back at him.

"Boys!" Mom chided us. Then she looked at Trent and said, "You'd think with their IQ's they'd act like adults... but no, they still act like they're twelve."

Trent grinned at me, the type of smile that made my heart thump, and I knew it was time to leave. I made a point of looking at my watch, "Better get going." Bentley had fallen asleep on me so I patted him to wake him, "Come on, little buddy. Time to go."

He shook himself awake, and Trent thanked everyone for their hospitality before he took his dog to harness him into the back seat. I invited everyone again to visit in two week's time. When we got in the car, Trent asked me, "What's the rush, doctor?"

I started the car and enthusiastically pulled out into traffic. "Somewhere else I'd rather be."

He grinned and put his hand on my thigh. "Such as?"

I tried to concentrate on driving, but his hand was burning through the denim to my skin, and my dick was getting hard. "Um, anywhere I can be alone with you."

"Anywhere?" he asked. With his eyebrows raised and that sexy smirk, his fingers edged closer to my hardening cock.

"Fuck, Trent," I moaned and shifted in my seat, trying to relieve some of the uncomfortable pressure in my jeans. "Yes, anywhere. In the car, on the floor, on the sofa, in the shower... I don't fucking care."

He laughed. "I think I've unleashed a monster!"

I grinned back at him. "You have. I feel like I'm seventeen years old! It's all I can think about."

Trent chuckled. "Mmm, so the car or the floor, huh?" He rubbed the denim, then deliberately squeezed my cock, making me groan. "I think we can arrange that."

I pulled up at the front of my place, and before he could

pull his hand away, I grabbed it. I pushed his hand down on my cock and pushed my hips into his hand. "You're fucking killing me."

Trent's head fell back, and he groaned, making Bentley bark from the backseat, and it scared the shit out both of us. "Now your dog's trying to kill me," I said, clutching at my heart.

Trent laughed loudly. "Come on, get that pretty ass of yours inside."

CHAPTER THIRTEEN

WE WALKED INTO MY APARTMENT, and my dick was throbbing. I was keen to head straight upstairs, but Trent suggested another pit stop for Bentley. He opened the back door for him but caught his finger on the handle. "Ow! Shit!" he said, rubbing his hand.

I took his hand and looked over his fingers. "Would you like me to look at that," I asked, then grinned at him. "Trust me, I'm a doctor."

He laughed at me. "Is that the infamous Nathan Tierney's pick up line? How you lure all the pretty blond girls back to your place?"

I shook my head at him. "I've never had anyone else here."

"No one?" he asked in disbelief. Then he laughed, "Don't you like blonds?"

I pulled a curl of his hair and twisted it around my finger. "Blond yes, I like very much."

He was uncomfortable again, like any words of emotion make him embarrassed, and he turned to watch his dog pee.

So I walked into the kitchen and grabbed a bottle of

water. I took a mouthful and told him, "I told you I was never sexual. I've been with four women – each time it was at their place, so I could just leave." He was staring wide-eyed at me, so I admitted, "I'm not very proud of just leaving like that, but it was never anything more than sex."

He was still staring at me. "Four?"

I exhaled a laugh, and I nodded, embarrassed. "How many guys have you been with?"

"Um, more than four... let's just leave it at that."

I smiled at him. "Well, you make five for me," I said. I laughed to hide my embarrassment, but my blush gave me away.

Trent walked over to me. "You're so fucking hot when you blush," he mumbled, which of course, made my cheeks heat even more. Trent groaned, and he ran his nose along my jaw and whispered, "I can feel how your skin warms when you blush."

And my already hardening dick twitched. He pressed his lips against my neck and up my jaw, then whispered against my skin, "You should not shave more often." Then his hands were on my face, his thumbs feeling my stubble, and he sighed. My dick throbbed at the sound.

"Take me upstairs," I murmured, and he crashed his lips to mine. His tongue was in my mouth, licking and tasting. His hands were holding my face and in my hair, and I melted into him.

Then his tongue was gone from my mouth, but his opened lips stayed pressed on mine. He breathed in my mouth, "Upstairs... now."

My feet propelled me forward, and he followed me closely. I was two steps in front of him on the stairs, and when he slid his fingers between my ass cheeks, I almost stumbled

Instead of pulling his hand away, he started rubbing my jeans, pressed against my ass and the back of my balls. I gripped the handrail and groaned. I stood there, not moving, not able to. His fingers probed forward, rubbing the denim over my ass, my cock was aching. "Oh fuck, Trent... please."

"God," he groaned, "all I have to do is touch you."

"Yes, touch me," I begged him.

Then his hand slapped my ass, and I yelped. His voice was gruff when he ordered me, "Get on the bed, boy."

Fuck. Me.

I staggered up the remaining stairs and had my jeans and boxers off in under a second. I knelt on the end of the bed, pulling my shirt over my head, when Trent gasped behind me. "Like that... don't move."

His voice made me freeze. His eyes were on me, hungry, wanting. He laid a towel down lengthways, from the pillow to the foot of the bed.

"Kneel on that and grip the headboard," he ordered. His voice was low and soft, I shivered.

I did as I was told, I was naked, straddling a towel, on my knees and holding onto the wooden headboard. I felt exposed and very fucking turned on, and then he was naked behind me. "Do you have any idea how fucking hot you are right now?" his voice was gravelly.

"Your legs spread for me," he said and ran his hand up my inner thigh. It made me groan.

"The flesh of your ass," he murmured, and his fingertips traced circles over my ass, spreading gooseflesh in their wake.

My cock was throbbing and leaking, precome seeped from the slit. "Oh please Trent, touch me."

He whispered, "I am touching you... here," his hands slid over my lower back, and he gripped me above my hips. His thumbs rubbed the divots above my ass, and he told me, "I'm touching the sexy dimples here."

My head rolled back, I was so desperate for him to keep touching me.

"Your spine," he said, and his fingers ran up the center of my back. "I'm touching your shoulders... God, your shoulders..." he moaned, sliding his palms across my shoulders. He gripped the top of my shoulders so my back arched. He whispered, "The way you stretch your back, Nathan... it fucking turns me on."

All I could do was whimper.

Then he brought his knees behind mine, slowly pressing the front of his thighs to the backs of mine, and I groaned, low in my throat.

He chuckled. "Mmmm, you like it when I touch the back of your thighs..."

"Yes," I cried. "Fuck, yes."

Then he pressed his cock against the top of my ass, and my whole body jerked. I could feel the weight of his length, heavy and hot. "Oh, fuck!" I pleaded, trying to press harder against him.

"So eager," he groaned.

"I want it," I told him, my voice raspy, like my breath. "Please."

I heard the click of the lube bottle, and I thought this was it. He was going to do it, he was going to fuck me. And I wanted it. I *needed* it. My knees widened farther, and I stretched my back, feeling his cock press harder against the flesh of my ass.

"Oh, Nathan," he mumbled my name as he poured the cool liquid over his dick and down the crack of my ass. I was moaning in need, and when I pushed against him once more, he hissed. "Fuck, baby," he groaned through clenched teeth.

But then I felt his fingers. Lower, lower, rubbing and spreading and slowly, he pressed one finger inside me. My head fell back, and I groaned. He kissed my shoulder as he finger fucked me.

I was moaning, it felt so fucking good, and I was pushing my ass toward him, offering more of myself to him. "Oh yeah, Trent. More, give me more."

His grip on my left hip tightened, and he grunted. I felt his breath on my shoulder. His lips kissed, and his tongue tasted my skin. He pulled his finger out, only to sink two more back in, as he bit my shoulder. He was slow and careful, sliding into me, stretching me, the most delicious burn setting my blood on fire.

His kisses became hurried, he used his teeth to nip at my skin, then he started to push his fingers inside me harder. I gripped the headboard and arched back into him, for him, and his fingers twisted inside me. He touched something, something that detonated deep within me.

"Fuck!" I cried.

And he did it again.

"Oh, fuck!" My body convulsed at his touch. "Trent, oh my God..."

"Yeah, baby," he groaned as his fingers still fucked me, pressing right where it sparked pure pleasure. "Right there?" he asked.

"Fuck, yes," I yelled.

"Pump your cock," he rasped out.

I was quick to obey, my fingers wrapped blindly around my length. I looked down at my dick and saw it was purple and swollen. When Trent brushed my prostate again, my cock lurched in my hand.

He did it again and again, and I pumped my fist hard, feeling pleasure in every cell of my body. My back stretched completely, arching, pushing my dick toward the bed. His fingers still fucked me, and my orgasm erupted from deep within, as come poured from my cock onto the towel beneath me.

Painless fire ripped across my body as my pleasure consumed me. Shaking and shuddering, I fell forward onto my arms. Then his fingers were gone from my ass, but I could feel his rock hard cock sliding between my ass cheeks. He was sliding his cock through the lube-slicked flesh of my ass. Both of his hands gripped my hips, and he grunted in time with his thrust, "Fuck, fuck, fuck."

The room was still spinning, I was completely spent, but I felt his fingers dig into me, and he flexed against me as he came. I felt his come splash hot onto my back, and he was almost growling as his orgasm rocketed through him.

Finally, he collapsed on top of me and pressed the weight of his spent body against me. He was mumbling words I couldn't hear, and he was kissing the sweat off my skin between his ragged breaths.

He rolled me onto my side and pulled the towel out from under me. He cleaned me up, my front and then my back, my ass. Then he wiped himself with the towel, threw it to the floor and collapsed back onto the bed.

He spooned me this time, wrapping his arms around me. I tried to stay awake. I wanted to talk to him... I *needed* to talk to him, about whatever-the-fuck-this-was, what he was starting to mean to me, but sleep took me.

I dreamed of him instead.

IT WAS DAYLIGHT. I was still in bed, and I was so fucking comfortable. Trent was wrapped around me, and he was hot and heavy. I didn't want to move, ever. I stayed like that, wondering how on Earth I could broach the subject of defining what this means to him without scaring him off. I knew our time together was limited, and I didn't want to shorten any time I had with him by making him want to leave.

So I resigned myself to say nothing and just make the most of what time I did have with him.

Bentley came into the room and looked at me, curiously. He made a whining noise, and I realized he must need to pee. Grumbling, I unfolded Trent from me and threw back the covers, pulled on some pants and went downstairs to let him outside.

I turned the coffee machine on and decided against going for a run today. I had a better idea.

I ran back upstairs and slid back into bed with Trent. He grinned, and I knew he was awake. "Want some breakfast?"

"Mmmm," he hummed his agreement.

So I slapped his ass. "Then get up. We're going out."

He groaned. "Coffee first."

"Machine's on. I'm taking a shower," I told him, and he quirked an eyebrow. Getting off the bed, I chuckled and told him he could make me a coffee while I jerked off in the shower, and he threw a pillow at me.

He was behind me before I even turned the taps on.

After soapy hand jobs in the shower, body washing and languid kisses, we dried off and got dressed.

It was like a new life for me, like I'd been walking around, living in this body, this skin, but I wasn't really living at all.

It wasn't just a sexual awakening... it was *living*.

"So, breakfast?" Trent's voice startled me.

"Oh, sorry. I was a million miles away. So, breakfast... we can hit the markets, if you like? We can take Bentley, too."

I told him we should pack, since we were heading back to Belfast after lunch, it made sense not to come back here. He agreed, and we packed our bags, closed up the apartment, loaded our stuff into my car and headed into the city.

We strolled through the market, drank coffee and ate a breakfast of bagels and fruit. I bought some gourmet pooch treats, and Trent rolled his eyes. "You're spoiling my dog," he told me for the fiftieth time.

I grinned. "He doesn't mind," I told him. Trent laughed and shook his head at me.

We strolled the stalls, stopping and looking as we pleased. Trent bought a few mementos while I waited with Bentley, and when he walked back to us, the first thing I noticed was that his jaw was tight, and he looked pissed.

"What's wrong?" I asked him.

His tone was curt. "Nothing, let's just go."

I looked around, back toward the store he'd just left and found a group of young guys, laughing and looking in our direction. "Did they say something to you?" I asked him.

"Nothing I haven't been called before," he replied. "Come on, let's go."

I was stunned, quite frankly, and followed him robotically. We walked back the way we came, and it wasn't until we were in the car and driving away that Trent seemed to relax.

"Just some small-minded little fuckwits," he said. Then he sighed. "It just sucks. We've had the best weekend, and then some little fuckers ruin it..."

"I'm sorry," I told him. I didn't know what else to say.

"Don't you *ever* apologize," he spat out, and I could see he was still livid. "You've got *nothing* to be sorry for."

"I'm sorry they upset you."

"And it doesn't upset you?" he cried. "Jesus, Nathan! How can it *not* piss you off when some fucking 15 year old punk calls you a faggot and a butt puncher?" He took a deep breath to calm himself. "They've got no fucking right to judge us."

"Trent, I've been a doctor in Emergency for two years," I told him. "I've seen every demographic of society and been accused of prejudice by everyone. The families of people whose lives I'd just saved either abuse me for racism, discrimination, favoritism and everything in between, or they thank me for it."

He stared at me and remained quiet, waiting for me to continue. "What I'm saying is, yes it bothers me. No, they have no right to judge. But I cannot control their behavior. I can only control my reaction."

"Just like that?" he asked sarcastically.

I smiled. "Yes, just like that."

"Well, Dr. Phil, that's great in theory and all," he huffed, "but wait until you're called derogatory names just because you're gay."

He stared out the window, and I was left with a deafening silence...

...*because you're gay*...

...because I'm gay...

Am I gay? Is that what I am? Well, I'm attracted to a man. He turns me on, so it would be a safe assumption that I'm not straight, but I'd been with women...so am I bi? Fuck if I knew. My mind raced, trying to make sense of it. I'd never thought of myself as *anything*... Trent's gay... and he just said *"because you're gay"*, so he obviously thinks I am. Those punk kids at the market obviously thought I was....

"I'm sorry." His voice distracted me from my thoughts. "I didn't... I didn't mean to..." he sighed loudly. "Fuck, I'm sorry."

I nodded and concentrated on the traffic for a while. I could see Trent was still upset, though now it was with himself.

"I'm sorry," he said again. "I know you're trying to sort shit out, trying to figure out what this means to you... I know how hard that is." Now his voice was quiet, resigned, "I shouldn't have said that."

"It's fine," I told him, though I hardly sounded convincing.

We didn't speak until I stopped an hour later to let Bentley out so he didn't pee in my car. We took a few minutes in the fresh air, and I decided a change of topic was needed. "Oh, I forgot to tell you, Dani Peters asked me out."

He spun around to look at me. "She what?"

"True story. She asked me to go to the beach with her."

His eyes were tight, and his jaw was clenched. "What did you tell her?"

"What do you mean?" I asked with a laughed. "I told her no. I was going to Boston with you."

"Oh," he nodded his head. "If I had known, I could have arranged the special bus for you."

He pretended to make the dazed, diminished learning capabilities face, and I pushed his shoulder and told him to shut the fuck up. He laughed, and it made me laugh, and when we got back in the car, everything was okay again.

CHAPTER FOURTEEN

THE REST of the trip back to Belfast was uneventful. Since we'd laughed in the park, the mood between us was back to normal, playful and easy. The tension from Trent's encounter with the kids at the markets seemed to have dissipated, and we were all smiles as we pulled up to the house.

Bentley was happy to be home, jumping out of the car and quickly sniffing out what he might have missed in the last three days. We unpacked our bags and spent a peaceful, lazy afternoon, doing our separate things.

Trent went up to his attic. I presumed him to be painting. He could lose hours up there. I longed to see what he painted, see his inner thoughts on canvas. He was always quick to laugh off any hint at emotion, joking and using sexual innuendos to downplay the real him. And I wondered what his paintings might say about him.

I knew I could always sneak into the attic when he wasn't home to see for myself, but I wouldn't break his trust like that. I quickly dismissed the idea, likening it to reading someone's journal.

I took Bentley for an afternoon run, thumping out our

well-worn track through the forest. When we arrived back at the house, Trent was still upstairs. Leaving him alone, I showered and changed, made and ate a salad for dinner and fed Bentley.

I sat on the sofa with my feet up, flicking through the text books I'd brought back with me from Boston, reading parts of interest. Bentley sat with me and snoozed with my hand gently stroking his fur.

It was late and realizing Trent wasn't coming down any time soon, I headed to bed. I laid awake for a while, recapping the weekend in my mind. I'd had the best time. Ever. The lines that defined *this*, whatever-the-hell-it-was, just sex and no strings attached, were starting to blur.

Oh, hell. Who was I kidding? They'd long ago blurred.

Trent had stirred something in me. He'd awoken something that had been dormant, sleeping my entire life. When he left would I find that with someone else? Would I even want to?

I didn't remember falling asleep. But I remembered being cold in my bed, in a fitful sleep, until Trent crawled into my bed sometime after three in the morning.

I remembered he was warm, and strong, and he smelled of paint. I remembered him wrapping himself around me, and I remembered him sighing when he held me.

I didn't remember anything else, until my four-legged alarm clock woke me for his breakfast.

After my slave duties to the dog were fulfilled, I showered and went back into my room to get dressed for work. Trent was still sound asleep. The blanket was pulled up to his waist, his well-defined arms were now wrapped around my pillow, and the muscles in his back curved perfectly.

I watched him for a moment. His breathing was even, his lips slightly parted. His blond wavy hair sprawled across his face, and he was so fucking beautiful. And the fact he was in my bed... well, I liked that even more. Sighing, I left for work, wishing like hell I didn't have to.

WORK WAS GREAT. I loved the more personal interaction with patients. I was so used to the never-ending stream of nameless, faceless numbers that tore through Boston General Emergency.

Here, everyone was a mother, a father, a child, a neighbor or a friend to someone. It was personal here, and I didn't just fix them up and send them through to another department. I saw the beginning, middle and end of all treatments here, and I felt a sense of completion.

Validated. I felt validated.

I was humming along to myself, filling out Mrs. MacPherson's papers, because she didn't see very well, when I heard a familiar voice. "Excuse me, doctor?"

I looked up, and there Trent stood, grinning, holding sandwiches. "Can I help you?" I asked him, unable to keep from smiling.

He held up the bags of sandwiches. "Lunch."

I finished the file and told Mrs. MacPherson to wait while I sorted out her medication. I handed the prescription to a nurse to take to the pharmacy, and told her I would be in my office having lunch. Trent and I walked down the corridor, and he explained, "I had to come to town to pick up some things, and I was hungry, so thought I'd swing past to see if you'd eaten... " his voice trailed away.

I stopped at my office, opened the door and walked in. "Thanks. I usually just grab something later, but it sounds good."

I took a seat behind my desk, and he looked around my office. "That's a lot of books," he said, grinning. "Are you smart or something?"

I chuckled and shook my head at him. He opened up the white paper bags and said, "I got you chicken salad on rye. Wholegrain mustard, no mayo."

He knew what I liked, and I knew chances were, he'd ordered ham salad, extra mayo but no tomato. I smiled at him. "Thanks."

After a few bites, he asked if I liked it here. I told him I did and how even I was surprised at how *much* I liked it here.

"Don't you miss the adrenalin, the excitement of a big city ER?"

I shook my head and swallowed my mouthful of sandwich. "Not at all. I thought I would. When I first came here, I had my moments of doubt, but it's been great. It's more personal here... " I shrugged. "Not to mention the sexy housemate that brings me food."

He laughed me off when there was a knock at the door. "Excuse me, Dr. Tierney?" Dani Peters' said as she opened the door. "Mrs. MacPherson's script... " she stopped talking when she noticed Trent sitting across from me. "Oh, sorry... " and of course she blushed and mumbled something I couldn't hear.

I tried not to look at Trent, because from the corner of my eye, I could see he was grinning. "It's okay, Dani, what were you saying?"

She talked to the floor, deliberately not looking at me or Trent, and explained Mrs. MacPherson's arthritis medication was unavailable. "Roxicodone's fine," I told her, and she handed me the script to modify and mumbled a thank you before she almost tripped out of the room.

I looked at Trent, and he tried to hold it in, but he slid down in his chair and burst into loud guffaws of laughter. I threw my scrunched up napkin at him and told him to shut up. "It's not funny," I told him, though I was trying not to laugh.

"Oh, yes it is," he said, wiping tears from his eyes. "I thought you were exaggerating. But she... she looked... " then he mocked the dazed, stupefied look, imitating Dani's face perfectly. Then he started to laugh again.

I couldn't help but laugh, "you're horrible." I packed up our lunch wrappings and discarded them into the trash. I walked around my desk and leaned my ass against it while Trent tried to compose himself.

I shook my head at him. "It's not funny. Every time she talks to me, I can't help but grin at her. She probably thinks I like her."

He grinned. "Don't you?"

"No," I hissed at him. "I smile at her because I know *you'd* think it was funny."

"Aw," he laughed, "I think you'd make a great couple."

I kicked him in the shin, and he started laughing all over again. "She's not my type," I deadpanned.

"Is she missing something?" he asked, waggling his eyebrows.

Yes. Blond hair, dimples, a dick.

I didn't say that of course. I ignored him. "You done?" I asked him.

"Oh," he stood up and patted down his pockets, looking for something. He pulled out a small brown paper bag and handed it to me. "I bought this yesterday at the markets," he told me and shrugged. "But I kinda forgot about it, after what happened with those kids"

I looked inside the bag and found a single strand of

leather. I looked up at him, and he explained, "It's for you...
I put mine around my wrist," he held up his hand, and I
could see the strand of leather wrapped a few times around
his wrist, tied off with a knot. "But I figured, being a doctor
and all, you might want it around your neck."

I was taken aback by this. I was sure it showed on my
face, because Trent was quick to tell me, "It's just junk from
a stall at the market, but I thought... " his voice trailed off.
Then he looked at me and admitted, "I just wanted something to remember what a good weekend it was, and then
those guys said that stuff.... "

"It's great," I told him, pulling the leather strand out of
the bag. I handed it to him and asked him to tie it on for
me. I lifted my chin up so he could see what he was
doing, and I told him, "It was a great weekend, Trent.
Regardless of what those kids called us, I still had the
best time."

The knot tied, he slid it so it was facing the back. His
proximity wasn't lost on me, he was so close we were almost
touching, and when I looked at him, he smiled.

"I had a good time too," he said softly.

I smiled at him, and as much as I wanted to kiss him
right then, I didn't. "Does it look okay?" I asked him.

Then he was all jokes again, "Mmm, your necklace? I
think I'd need to see it without your clothes on to really say
for certain.... "

I rolled my eyes at him and tucked the leather strand
under my shirt collar. "Thank you," I told him. "And for
buying it for me, you might just get to see it without
clothes on."

He grinned and groaned. "I better get going."

"Yes, you better," I told him. "I better get back to work, or
they'll come looking for me."

"Can't be caught having lunch with a guy," he teased, half joking, half not.

"Mmm, there's that," I said and rolled my eyes. "Or if you don't leave soon, they might walk in and find me doing dirty things to you on my desk."

His eyes popped, and I grinned and walked to my door. Trent stood there looking at me, then at my desk. He pushed down on the solid wood frame. "Seems sturdy enough."

I laughed and walked out of my office, and he grinned and followed me. Nurse Watson met me in the hall. "Oh Doctor, there's a gastro in cubicle one."

Trent chuckled as he walked out the door. "Have fun with that."

WHEN I GOT HOME, all I wanted to do was take a shower. Okay, well that wasn't all I wanted to do. What I wanted to do *first*, was take a shower.

The house was quiet, but lights were on, and when Bentley met me on the stairs, I knew Trent was upstairs in the attic. Then I heard, "Hey, be down in a sec."

I yelled back to him, "It's alright. I want to get cleaned up first."

I stripped off and quickly stepped under the water, scrubbing away the day. I washed my hair, scrubbed my body and relished the hot water on my shoulders. It had been a good day, made even better by Trent's visit at lunchtime.

And it wasn't until I stepped out of the shower, dried myself off and wiped the steam from the mirror that I even remembered his gift. It shocked me at first, seeing the leather strand around my neck, but I loved it. It fit very naturally, and at the front, sat just below where my collarbones meet and when I touched it, it made me smile.

I wrapped the towel around my waist, ignoring the permanent semi I seemed to have since I met Trent. I walked into the hall, heading toward my room, at the same time Trent walked down from the attic.

He groaned low and breathy. "Sweet Jesus," he mumbled.

I looked at him and smiled at his reaction. His mouth was open, and his eyes were... dark.

"You okay?" I asked with a smile. "You look a little... hungry."

He stalked up to me and traced his finger along the necklace he'd given me, then his eyes fixed on mine. "I'm fucking starving," he said and pushed me up against the wall in the hallway. He didn't wait for a response of any kind, he just pulled the towel away and dropped to his knees.

He took all of me into his mouth and groaned as he sucked me. I was rock fucking hard in a second, sliding in and out of his mouth, as he devoured me.

"Fuck, fuck, Trent," I groaned.

His hands were on my shaft, pumping me, cupping my sac and pulling. His fingers were rubbing the seam to my hole, and if he kept doing that, I'd be done in under a minute. "Slow, slow," I tried to tell him.

So he went slowly. Savoring every inch of my cock as he took it into his mouth, his hands now held my hips as he fucked me with his mouth. Slowly, so torturously slow, he slid his mouth onto my cock. When I hit the back of his throat, he looked up at me and somehow opened wider, and I felt my cock in his throat.

Up and down, slow and sucking, he took me. He

moaned around me, his flattened tongue licked and swirled and every nerve in my body was wired to my groin.

One of my hands fisted his hair, and the other hand cupped his jaw. I traced the corner of his mouth with my thumb, and I felt where we were joined, his lips around my shaft. I felt myself swell in his mouth, my cock throbbed, and I tried not to come. It was embarrassing how quick he could make me come...

He groaned and swallowed.

And without thinking, my body moved of its own accord, I pulled his face to me, thrusting my cock further down his throat. With a strangled cry, my dick lurched and exploded, and my come poured hot and thick down his throat.

He groaned, and my fingers released his hair, but he continued to suck every drop from my cock. I slumped against the wall. He released me from his mouth, so I could slide down to join him on the floor. My head lolled back, and I tried to lift my hand, but it was too heavy. He chuckled and kissed me, plunging his tongue in my mouth, and I could taste myself.

"Fuuuuuuck," I moaned.

"Mmmm," Trent hummed, licking his lips.

My senses came back together, like quicksilver, coming back to whole. I leaned forward, off the wall, and pulled the neck of his shirt, so I could kiss him. "My turn."

CHAPTER FIFTEEN

I WOKE the next morning naked and wrapped deliciously around Trent, smiling as I remembered his talented mouth doing talented things to me in the hall, and then how I'd reciprocated in my bed.

My oral skills were nowhere near as honed as his, but I was getting better. Trent certainly didn't seem to mind last night, not at all. Neither did I, actually, I enjoyed it. The more he moaned, the more he cursed, the more I liked it. Taking him deep in my throat was a skill that would require practice, but I swallowed his come again, a fact I was both pleased with and proud of. I was learning, and I was liking. Giving pleasure was almost as good as getting it.

Almost.

Thinking of such things while still in bed, naked, with my body pressed against his had my morning wood seeking some attention. I was horny all the damn time, whenever I touched him. God, I only had to think of him, and my heart thumped, and my cock throbbed.

I knew Trent never woke up particularly cheerful, but I thought of a way to make him smile. Pulling the covers up, I slid down under the blanket and rolled Trent onto his back. His cock was beautiful, even flaccid against his thigh, it was thick and full.

Fuck. It made my mouth water.

Even though it was only five in the morning and he was asleep, I cupped his sac and stroked him, before taking him in my mouth.

He moaned and mumbled, as I lapped at him, sucking his cock to life. He mumbled again, lifting his hips, and then he jolted awake when he realized this was no dream. He threw back the covers to expose me, and I deliberately popped my lips off the head of his dick. "Good morning," I said, smirking at him.

"Yes, it is," he said, his voice was thick with sleep.

I turned my attention back to his waiting cock, and he groaned. "Didn't you have enough of me last night?"

"Mm mm," I hummed around him, and his eyes closed as he groaned.

"'Cause I could never have enough of your mouth," he murmured. "Fuck baby, that's so good."

I moaned to encourage him to keep talking. I loved his dirty mouth, hearing his pleasure, what he loved and how he loved it. His hands were in my hair, not pushing or pulling, just holding, guiding.

I pumped the base of his cock and sucked the head, tonguing the frenulum, and his back arched. "Oh fuck yeah, baby, just like that!" Then he groaned, long and low. "Your mouth, so warm, so wet... your tongue. Fuck, your tongue."

Then I added my other hand, pulling lightly on his sac and tracing my fingers around his hole, while still working over his cock with my tongue, and his whole body jerked. "Fuck, fuck, oh fuck, Nathan. Gonna come..." he panted, letting go of my hair, fisting the sheets beside him instead.

I hummed on his cock, letting him know I wanted him in my mouth when he came. With a strangled scream, he bucked into my waiting mouth, shooting down my throat. I swallowed everything he gave me before I released him from my lips.

While he was whimpering and writhing through the waves of his orgasm, I knelt forward between his legs, and took my cock into my fist. I was so hard already, so turned on by him, by what I'd just done to him, that I knew it wouldn't be long until I was coming.

"Oh fuck, Nathan," Trent urged me on. He looked at me, heavy lidded and well sated. "Fuck, you look so hot."

I grunted at him. He groaned, and the sound was wired to my cock.

My head fell back and pleasure rolled in waves through my stomach. My fist was flying over my shaft, and when Trent said, "Come on me," my orgasm erupted.

My cock swelled and throbbed in my hand, emptying onto his stomach. Pulse after pulse surged through me and onto Trent in thick, hot stripes of bliss.

I fell forward onto my left hand, my head hung low as the room spun around me. Trent leaned up and kissed me, his tongue sending spasms down my spine.

"Fuck, that was hot," he sighed.

I still couldn't speak coherently, so I nodded and hummed and fell to my side of the bed. My eyes wouldn't open, but I was fairly sure he wiped himself off with a shirt off the floor. He leaned across me, pulled up the blankets and snuggled himself against me.

"You can wake me up like that anytime," he said with a chuckle. He peeled back one of my eyelids with his thumb. "You in there?"

I grinned at him. He grinned back at me, and I laughed.

We both lay there, smiling, wrapped around each other when we heard the familiar click of dog nails on the wooden floor. I rolled over to see Bentley at the door waiting for me.

I groaned.

Trent laughed. "You started it. I told you he'd expect it."

"Come for a run with us," I suggested.

Trent didn't answer. He just raised one eyebrow with *you've got to be fucking kidding* written all over his face.

I laughed again, and by the time I was dressed in my running gear, Trent was already dozing.

WORK WAS FAIRLY STANDARD, nothing out of the ordinary, and I thought I might even be able to leave a little earlier than normal. Until we got a call to say paramedics were on their way, ETA ten minutes. There'd been a motor-cycle accident, two injured, one with suspected spinal injury, one with a compound fractured leg, both with head injuries and extensive cuts and abrasions.

The nursing staff flew into action, prepping everything necessary, they were on edge. Knowing I wouldn't be home anytime soon, I grabbed my phone out of my office desk drawer and typed a quick text to Trent.

There's been an accident. Don't wait up.

Doctor Varner appeared beside me as I was gloving up. "Guess you're used to this."

Presuming he was referring to my calm and collected manner, I nodded. "Unfortunately, yes." I used to deal with this ten times a day.

The ambulances pulled in, the EMT's jumped out and started reciting their patient's stats. I took the suspected spinal case, and when we wheeled the gurney in, I realized

I'd treated this boy before. It was Toby, the kid who came off his bike two weeks ago. He wore no protective gear then, and he was wearing none now.

Fucking kids. Think they'll live forever.

I managed to stem the bleeding from the head wound. It was a pretty serious gash, concussion no doubt, but my immediate concern was his spinal injury.

The boy mumbled something, and I was quick to ask him if he could feel his toes, but he wasn't very coherent. I checked his pupil dilation, then his torso for discoloration, possible internal bleeding, but thankfully found none. He was breathing okay, had cuts all over him, but nothing too serious.

I grabbed his second toe and pricked the nib of my pen into it, hoping for a reaction. He flinched a little, but it wasn't the reflex I was looking for. I tried the other foot. He coughed and tried to talk. The nurse leaned over and listened to whatever it was he mumbled.

When she straightened up, she looked at me and smiled. "He wants to know if you could stop doing that please," she said, "because it *fucking* hurts."

I barked out a laugh and took a breath of relief. Walking up alongside the gurney, I leaned over the prone boy. "Make a deal with you, Toby. I'll stop jabbing your feet, if you stop riding *fucking* motorbikes."

There were a few laughs, and the immediate stress was gone. I could ascertain he had some feeling in each foot, but wouldn't know more until I ran further tests. I started to clean and suture the head wound, when Dr. Varner called for me.

Leaving a stabilized Toby, I re-gloved and rushed over to find Scott, the second boy, who was critical. He had distended neck veins, a weak pulse and ragged breathing.

"Pneumothorax," I announced, and Varner nodded but was distracted by the protruding bone in the boy's thigh.

"I can't get this bleed under control," he said, rushed. "I think the bone has nicked the femoral."

Fuck.

My mind went on autopilot. Like I could compartmentalize my mind, I heard everything that went on around me perfectly, but could concentrate with 100% focus on what I was doing. I made a small incision between his ribs with a scalpel, at the same time I noticed two men running into the ER.

The two men, both tall African-American men, who I presumed to be friends or relatives of Toby and Scott, were clearly agitated. "Get them out of here," I yelled.

I slid a chest tube into the boy's chest wall, and his breathing eased almost immediately. I looked up, expecting to see security or a warden, removing the two men, but it wasn't. It was Dani Peters.

Both men, particularly the tallest man—who had to be six foot three—appeared to listen to her. Then Chief Peters was there, and he led them out into the corridor with his daughter. My attention was back on the boy in front of me, and Varner.

"I'll need to operate," he said.

One of the nurses answered, "I'll prepare the OR."

But we didn't have time. Scott didn't have time. "No, I'll do it here."

And for a split second, every pair of eyes were on me. "I've done this before," I told them. "I'll get him stable enough to get him to Boston if needed, or even Portland, but I've got to do it now."

And I did. The leg was a mess, the bone compounded and comminuted, and it would require plating and pinning.

Later. Right now, he was bleeding out. I wasted no more time, the surgery was crude, but I found the tear and managed to stop the bleeding.

And about four hours after the paramedics arrived with the two Crusty Demon wannabe's, I pulled off my gloves and bloodied coat and cleaned up.

I was surprised to find Dani, her dad Steve, and the two men, were still in the waiting room. They stood when they saw me, and looked at me expectantly. The tallest man, seemed to sneer. Steve made introductions. "Adam Collins, Lucas Rogers. This is Dr. Nathan Tierney."

"Nathan," Dani's small voice said, "how are they?"

"At first we thought Toby had a spinal injury," I told them, and I could see the color drain from their faces. "But he has regained some feeling in both feet."

"That's good, right?" Chief Peters asked.

"Very. More than likely a bruised spinal cord, but we won't know more until we run some tests. More cuts and bruises than I can count. Twelve stitches to his head, bad concussion, and he'll have a decent headache for a few days."

"And Scott?" Lucas asked.

"Scott suffered a pneumothorax and a comminuted compound fracture of the femor, which tore his femoral artery, causing extensive bleeding."

"In English, Doc," Adam replied sharply.

"Broken ribs caused air to fill his chest cavity. I managed to release the pressure by inserting a tube, and we're watching his breathing. His leg is broken badly at the thigh. The bone punctured the skin and cut the artery that runs down the leg, but I've been able to stop the bleeding."

"That sounds serious," Steve said.

"It certainly is. He's stable right now, but he's in the

ICU. He'll need surgery to fix his leg. The bone was shattered as well, and will require an orthopedic surgeon to pin and plate it. He'll be laid up for a long while, I'm afraid."

"Those goddamn motorbikes!" Adam barked.

Dani put her hand on his cheek. She looked tiny compared to him. "Adam, you can't protect them when they won't listen."

He looked at her softly. "What am I supposed to tell his family?"

Lucas clapped the taller man on the shoulder. "It's not your fault, Adam."

Then Adam looked at me. "Can we see them?"

"They're both asleep," I told them. But with a sigh and a nod, I said, "Two minutes."

Steve stayed with me while the other three disappeared into Toby's room first. "Adam takes on all the local kids," he told me. "He runs the youth club down here. He and Dani have been friends since they were little, makin' mud pies together."

"I think he might like your daughter," I told him with a tired smile. "I could see the way he looked at her."

He laughed quietly. "Yeah, but I think Dani might have a little crush on the new doctor."

I felt my eyes widen, and I shook my head. "Not me. No, Sir."

He laughed quietly and looked down at my blood stained shirt. I shrugged. "Didn't have time for scrubs."

"You're way into overtime, Doc. Go home and get changed."

I shook my head slowly. "No, I'll shower here and keep an eye on these two boys."

His lips smiled under his moustache just as Dani, Adam and Lucas came back. "So be it, Doc. I'll be back," he looked at his watch and groaned, "in a few hours to get details for my reports."

I grabbed some scrubs and showered. I threw my clothes in a heap by my office desk. I'd see if they were salvageable later. It was almost two in the morning when I got back to my office to check my phone. There was a message from Trent.

Guess I'll have to watch porn by myself... (:

I typed out a reply, knowing he'd read it in the morning.

Could have sent me photos at least...):

I checked on the two boys again and instructed the nurses that I'd be asleep in the empty room, and they were to wake me if needed. I took my phone with me, and even though I was tired as hell, sleep didn't come easy. It wasn't that I was worried about my patients.

It was because Trent wasn't with me.

I must have dozed for an hour or so, because I woke with a start when my phone beeped. It was a photo, received at 6:17 a.m., of a hand holding an engorged dick, the photo obviously taken by the man holding his phone in one hand, his cock in the other.

It made me grin.

I recognized the leather strand wrapped three times around his wrist, the star tattoo on his hip, the sheets on my bed, and more importantly, I'd recognize that cock anywhere.

CHAPTER SIXTEEN

THE NEAREST AVAILABLE orthopedic surgeon was in Portland. I made the necessary transfer arrangements and booked young Scott for transport to have his leg fixed. His mother was there early, followed by Adam and Lucas, and I told them he was being shipped out at eight.

Both boys had stabilized overnight, and after running a few more basic tests on Toby, I was confident he'd be up on his feet in no time. When his family arrived, I explained my prognosis and how I would arrange more tests for later in the day. "X-rays have confirmed that his vertebrae have impinged on his spinal cord. He has swelling around the spinal cord around his T4/T5," I told them, and showed them on my body where that was. "That was why we first thought his injuries were more severe. There's no way to determine how long it will take to recover. It's a day to day process." They were solemn and quiet, understandably shaken. "He's a lucky kid," I told them.

I saw Adam talking to both families, and Lucas smiled at me. He was a good looking guy, a bit younger than me, I'd guess. Tall, dark and handsome, the cliché made me smile. "You're here early," he said to me.

"Still here, actually. I never left."

His eyebrows rose. "Jeez, that makes for a long day."

I smiled and nodded. He told me Adam was beating himself up over this accident. The boys were supposed to be in the youth group yesterday, but didn't show.

"He kinda feels responsible for all the kids," Lucas said, and smiled sadly. "Lots of the kids don't have fathers, so Adam kinda fills that role, ya know?"

This surprised me, and I looked at the tall man in a new light. Lucas asked, "So, you're from Boston?"

And he looked at me, his eyes were dark and dancing. Fuck me, I think he was flirting with me.

I gave him a nervous smile, not used to male attention. "Uh, yeah."

"Do you miss it? Belfast's kinda boring by comparison," he grinned at me. "Not much of a social scene here."

My mind flashed to my night of dancing and drinking last weekend in Boston, the hot nightclub full of dancing, half-naked men, and I could feel heat color my cheeks. "No, I don't imagine there is."

Someone cleared their throat behind us, and I turned to find Trent. He was holding coffees and smiling tightly, and it looked wrong on his face. "Hey, Lucas," he said.

"Oh, you two knew each other?" I asked surprised, then I remembered what a small community I was in.

Lucas answered. "I work at the Animal Hospital. My sister Simone's the vet there, and Trent brings... what's your dog's name?"

Trent and I both answered together. "Bentley."

Lucas nodded, and it was a little awkward. I couldn't

help but wonder if they *knew* knew each other. "Um, Trent?"

"Oh," he shrugged and looked at the coffees in his hands. "I knew you wouldn't have eaten dinner or breakfast."

I grinned at him. He'd thought of me. I tried not to show how much I liked it. Lucas's hand on my shoulder broke into my reverie. "Thanks again, Doc," he said and walked away.

Trent looked around. "I watched you talking to them," he said with a pointed nod to Toby's family. "You're a very good doctor."

"Um, thanks?"

He laughed quietly to himself and held out one of the coffees. I told a passing nurse I was going to my office for a break. Walking down the corridor, I took a drink of the coffee and moaned. "I could kiss you right now for bringing me this."

"So, did I interrupt something before?" he asked when we were in the privacy of my office.

"What? With me and Lucas?" I asked incredulously. He shrugged, and I said with a laugh, "I think he was flirting with me..." and Trent looked uneasy.

I liked that more than I should. "Jealous, Trent?"

"No," he answered too quickly.

I smiled. "Of course there isn't anything going on with me and him," I sighed. "My time's otherwise occupied with someone else."

Trent seemed to breathe easier, and he smiled. "Anyone I know?"

"I don't know," I said, playing along. Pulling my phone from my top drawer, "I have a photo of him...wanna see it?" I held the phone up, displaying the photo of his cock. He chuckled, and I told him, "Cruel. Cruel, for teasing me like that."

He grinned at me and looked me up and down. "Mmm, I have to say, you could wear your doctor's outfit anytime."

I looked down at my scrubs. "Oh, I spilled a little something on my clothes," I told him and pointed to the bloodied shirt on the floor.

"Oh, Jesus!" he said, looking back at me with wide eyes.

"Mmmm, it wasn't pretty."

He was quiet for a moment. "You look tired."

"I am, thanks to you."

"Me?"

"Yeah, you've made me get used to sleeping," I said with a laugh, followed by a yawn. "I used to be able to work double shifts no problem... now I need you with me so I can sleep."

He smirked, but he was quiet, and I realized I'd probably crossed the in-this-just-for-the-sex line, but I was too tired to care.

Trent stood up. "Better let you got back to your patients." I put his empty paper coffee cup in the trash, and he walked to the door.

I stood up and stretched. He sighed as he walked back to me, and touched my neck. "This suits you."

My hand flew to where he touched me and I felt the leather strand around my neck, clearly visible with my scrub shirt. I'd forgotten about it.

"Makes you look hotter," he said with a chuckle. Then he opened the door and whispered, "Don't forget. Keep the doctors outfit on." He winked and snickered to himself as he walked out, leaving me to follow.

Chief Peters and Dani were there now, and he stopped Trent, asking, "Did you hear your housemate saved two lives yesterday?"

Trent looked at me and smiled. Then he nudged Dani

with his elbow and whispered, though we all could hear him perfectly, "Yeah, they say he can work miracles with those hands."

Dani blushed and I wanted to kill him. I glared at him, and he grinned. The Chief looked between us suspiciously. Great. So ignoring my *housemate* completely, I told the Chief there was an old Chevy parked illegally out the front.

Trent laughed as he walked out, and Steve shook his head at us.

The nurses spoiled me with sandwiches, muffins and coffee, saying it was only fair if I had to work nearly thirty hours straight, it was the least they could do. I was certainly not going to tell them not to bother.

I noticed Dani spent a lot of time with Toby. Every time I checked on him, she was there. And when Adam came back in the afternoon, I also saw how he watched Dani. It was clear he adored her, and it was clear she was oblivious. I knew she looked at me. Hell, even the Chief told me she had a crush on me, surely Adam saw it too.

I tried to keep my distance from her, but it was a small place. She did more sitting with Toby than work, so it was a little difficult. Every time she looked at me and blushed or gushed, it was awkward. But Adam didn't see how uncomfortable it made me, he watched her, how she touched my arm, how she smiled at me. He didn't see how I recoiled from her touch, cringed at her attention, and how I tried to avoid her. Apparently, neither did Dani.

Dr. Varner started his shift early, surprised to learn I never went home. I reassured him it was my choice to stay, and it was really no big deal, but I'd be glad to go home.

Before I left, I approached Adam to tell him about Scott. "I phoned Portland. The surgery went well, I believe," I said, and he sighed in relief. "He has a rod, with pins and plates, inserted along his thigh bone. He can expect a few months of physical therapy."

"Will he be coming back here?" he asked. "His family can't get to Portland to see him."

"In a few days, I think," I told him and smiled. "They'll try getting him up on his feet before they let him go anywhere."

"Up on his feet so soon?" he asked disbelievingly.

I nodded. "Assisted of course, but they don't waste time these days."

He sighed again, and his head fell back against the hall wall. He looked as exhausted as I felt. Dani walked in and smiled and stumbled when she saw me. Adam closed his eyes, not able to watch her fawn over me. "Everything okay?" she asked.

"Dani," I said very seriously. "Your friend here needs a hug," I told her, and Adam's eyes flew open. I walked toward my office and called out, "Doctor's orders."

When I got to my office door, I could see she had her arms around him. Smiling, I collected my satchel, phone and keys, and went home.

I walked inside, threw my bag on the table, toed my shoes off and headed to the kitchen, exhausted.

Trent walked in from somewhere. "Hey, 'bout time you came home."

"Mmmm," I agreed with him and opened the fridge, looking for something to eat.

"You sit." Trent ordered, steering me to a chair and busying himself. He dished out something, heated it in the microwave and when the smell made my stomach growl, it was ready.

"My infamous vegetable stew," he announced and put the bowl and some bread in front of me.

I smiled at him, too tired and too hungry to make some smartass comment, and tasted it. It was good. Really, really good. "Mmm," I moaned as I ate. "This is soooo good."

He grinned. "Leftovers from last night. You need food in your belly. It'll help you sleep."

I chuckled. "Thanks, Dr. Jamieson."

He snorted. "If I'm a doctor, do I get scrubs like yours?"

I swallowed down my food and pulled at my shirt. "You like these, don't you?"

"I'd like to take you out of them," he said with mischief in his eyes. "But you're too tired."

I took another spoonful of stew and nodded as I chewed and swallowed. "I want a shower."

"Now *that* I can help you with," he quipped, and I laughed.

He was quiet then, watching me devour his food. When I finished he was quick to offer me more, but I shook my head and patted my stomach. "I'm done, thank you. It was delicious."

He smiled again, took my plate and put it in the sink. "Come on, Doctor," he said and pulled me up from the table. "I'm wasting an opportunity to get you out of these scrubs."

I laughed, tired, and he grinned all the way up the stairs. In the bathroom, he started the water and turned to face me. He eyed me appreciatively and hummed when he took my shirt off, then pulled on the cord at my waist, opening my pants, and they fell to the floor. I leaned on the bathroom counter to take my socks off and Trent took my face in his hands, pulling me up to kiss him. Softly, sweetly, his lips pressed to mine.

His thumbs scraped the scruff along my jaw. "Don't shave," he told me, then rubbed his smooth cheek along my rough one, and he hummed again.

I stepped into the shower, and the hot water flowed over my tired shoulders and down my back. Trent asked me about the two boys and how they were doing. I told him as I washed my hair. He didn't leave the bathroom, he stayed and talked to me. And as I talked to him through the shower door, I realized I'd missed him.

He was keen not to be too far from me, and I wondered if he'd missed me too. It had only been a day and a night, but still... I didn't dare mention it.

When I turned the water off, he handed me a towel. I stepped out onto the mat and dried my hair first, standing completely nude in front of him, and I wasn't fazed at all. I wanted him to look at me. I wanted him to want me.

I dried off and wrapped the towel around me. I looked in the mirror and I saw the dark circles under my eyes. Trent's hands were on my shoulders, he was standing behind me. He massaged my tired muscles, and I found myself leaning over with my hands on the counter, relishing him manipulating the tight knots in my shoulders.

I looked up into the mirror, and he was watching us. The position we were in wasn't lost on me, so I leaned my ass back a little, meeting his groin.

"Fuck, Nathan," he hissed.

"Don't tease me," I warned him playfully. "You know I want you to."

He pulled away from me, and I groaned.

"Nathan..." he started like he was about to say something important, but stopped. "You're too tired anyway," then he slapped my ass. "To bed with you."

He was right. I was tired. I was exhausted. I dragged myself into my room, threw the towel over the chair and fell into bed naked. I laid on my back, and I felt the bed dip with his weight. I was tired and already half asleep. My eyes were closed, but I still told him, "Sorry for pressuring you about sex. It's just that I want you to do that to me, I don't care if I'm not ready." I tried to open my eyes to see his face, but my eyelids wouldn't work. I tried not to mumble, "I'll stop asking you. It's not fair that I make you feel like you have to say no all the time."

The last thing I remembered before sleep took me was the feel of his fingers on my cheek.

CHAPTER SEVENTEEN

I WOKE up stiff and sore from lying down too long. The alarm clock told me it was 4:36 a.m., and Trent was asleep beside me. I'd been asleep for close to ten hours.

I rolled onto my side and watched him sleep. I wondered what dreams he had, what might have been going through his head, and I wondered if he dreamt of me.

Because I dreamt of him.

I wondered what he thought of me, what he felt for me. I wondered what went on behind those carefully constructed walls.

I wondered if I'd ever know.

I noticed how his lips moved slightly, the purplish tint to his closed eyelids and his soft snores. I touched his face ever so gently. He was so peaceful, beautiful when he slept. I touched his neck, his shoulder, tracing my fingers lightly and barely there, and he mumbled something I couldn't understand.

I smiled at him, even though he was sound asleep and couldn't see me. He rolled over, and I slid my arm around his waist and snuggled against him. I just lay there, feeling his back against my chest, his wayward hair tickling my nose, the feel of him in my arms, until Bentley let me know it was time for breakfast.

Going for a run ironed out the kinks in my sore muscles, and by the time we got back, I felt good. I shared my breakfast, as I did every morning, with my grateful running buddy. I apologized to him for missing breakfast yesterday by means of an extra piece of toast.

"You're spoiling my dog," Trent said from behind me, his voice croaked from sleep.

I grinned at him and replied with my standard response to his gripe about me spoiling his dog. "He doesn't mind."

Trent snorted, and flipped the coffee machine on, and rubbed his eyes. He never woke up particularly well. I wanted to ask him how the house painting was going, but couldn't bring myself to. I didn't want him to tell me it was nearly done. I didn't know what that would mean... if it meant he was leaving.

I'd rather not know.

So I ran my hands over his shoulders, down his waist and across his stomach. I murmured into his neck, "I'm going to shower." Then I trailed my hands down over the elastic of his sleep pants and took the weight of his cock in my hand and whispered to him, "I don't have to leave for forty minutes."

He followed me up the stairs, stripping as he went.

In the shower, I soaped us up and pushed the shower head away. Using the shower gel as lube, we started with mutual hand jobs. I knew what he liked. I pumped his shaft with one hand and played with his balls with my other. He groaned with his head back, as I worked him over.

His hands were on me, pumping me with equal fervor. He slid one hand up and down, squeezing the shaft and twisting his palm over the head of my cock as his other hand tweaked my nipples.

But he started to get lost in what I was doing to him. He leaned his back against the wall and started thrusting his hips toward me. I stood with my feet between his and started to rub our cocks together. I took both our dicks in my hand, pumping us both at the same time.

He moaned deep and low, and continued to thrust. His cock slid against mine, silky and hot, and his head was back on the tiles, his eyes were closed. He moaned again, "Fuuuu-uck, baby."

Strands of wet hair were stuck to his forehead, and his lips were red and parted. "You look so hot right now," I told him, and pumped our cocks harder.

Reaching with my other hand, I cupped his balls, and he groaned. When I used a finger to tease his hole, he somehow leaned up, encouraging me. So I did it. I slid the tip of my finger in his ass.

"Oh, fuck!" he cried. "Yes... Nathan."

So I pushed just a little farther, still pumping our cocks. His thighs were opened wide, and I was standing between his legs as he propped himself against the tiles. The deeper I pushed my finger, the deeper he moaned, and the more it turned me on.

I slid my finger in and out, pushing back in a little farther each time at the same pace I pumped him, me... us. I wanted to see him come like this, I wanted to feel it from inside him.

"Come for me, baby," I urged him. "I want to feel you come with my finger in your ass."

"Oh, fuck. Oh, fuck," he said. His body started to shake, and he was so close.

"Come on me, Trent."

And he thrust wildly, his cock in my hand, his ass on my finger. His head pushed back, his hips pushed farther into me, his neck was corded and his teeth were clenched, and he came hard.

I felt his ass clench on my fingers, his cock throbbed, spilling his release as he groaned. I felt his hot come spurt from his dick onto my hand, but I watched his face instead. He was so lost, he didn't feel my finger slide out of him. I used both hands to keep pumping us, milking every drop from him.

His pleasure gave me pleasure, watching him come, feeling him come, my cock rubbed against him, and my orgasm ripped through my body.

I exploded in my hand, onto him, streams of my come spurting thickly onto his stomach. He watched me come and his fingers quickly swiped at my release on his skin. Looking in my eyes, he brought his fingers to his mouth and lapped at my come with his tongue.

"Oh, fuck," I mumbled, my head falling back. My eyes closed, and my head spun, then I felt the water on me again.

Trent maneuvered the shower spray back over our heads, and the water fell over the both us. He rubbed his hands over my body, and I pulled his face to mine and kissed him.

I had no idea when the water went cold.

THE REST of the week was the same.

Trent was all fun and laughs. We couldn't keep our hands, or mouths, off each other. We brought each other to orgasm a range of different ways, though he still wouldn't penetrate me. He fucked me with his fingers, but wouldn't fuck me with his cock. I tried not to pressure him, but it was difficult not to beg him for it when he had me so worked up. He looked torn, like he wanted to, soooo bad.

But he didn't.

He slept every night in my bed. He wore my scrub pants, claiming they were now his.

Work that week was great. Toby, the boy with the bruised spinal cord seemed to be recovering nicely. He still had spasms, but he had full feeling in both feet. Scott was expected to be transferred back to Belfast on Monday.

Adam and Lucas visited Toby every day. Adam seemed a little warmer to me since I told Dani to hug him. I think he understood it was my way of telling him I wasn't interested in Dani's advances.

I only wished Dani understood that too.

She still blushed, stammered and stumbled when she spoke to me. And so help me God, when Trent stopped by for lunch on Friday, he walked in just when she was touching my arm and giggling.

His eyes were huge and bright as he grinned like the devil. He chuckled and winked at me when she wasn't looking, and I kicked him in the shin. He played along, almost encouraging her. When I got home, he still thought it was funny.

I walked into the living room, and he burst out laughing when he saw me. "Leave the poor girl alone," I told him, sitting next to him on the sofa. "It's not funny, Trent. I'm going to have to tell her."

"Tell her what?" he taunted.

"That I'm not fucking interested!" I threw my hands up. "Jeez, I try to be nice and diplomatic about it, but she just doesn't get it."

Trent laughed again. "It's because she's got diminished learning capabilities."

I hit him with a cushion, but I couldn't help but laugh. "It wasn't very funny when it was Lucas who was flirting with me, was it?"

His smile died a slow death, and mine widened. I waggled my eyebrows at him. "Didn't think so."

He was quiet for moment, then he looked at me smugly. "You should ask him out."

"What?"

He smirked. "Yeah, you two would make a cute couple."

My heart fell to my stomach. My mouth fell open, and I didn't know if he was joking or not. I was stuck for something to come back with that didn't give me away. If I told him I would, or if I told him I wasn't interested in anyone else, it implicated me in this emotionless farce I tried so hard to keep up.

He didn't want to know how I felt about him.

So I said nothing. I closed my mouth, hid my hurt and asked about his day instead.

THE WEEKEND WAS FILLED with the usual hiker and backpacker injuries, sprained ankles, cuts and abrasions, rashes and one case of dehydration. How a hiker could suffer dehydration when it rained all day was beyond me.

Apart from a lack of common sense, or in some cases just sheer stupidity, I guessed I'd seen enough not to be too surprised about much. The good thing about the torrential rain over the course of the weekend was that it kept kids off motorbikes.

It also meant for cozy times on the couch and in bed

with my favorite painter. It was getting harder for me to not say something to him. I wanted so badly to tell him that this, *whatever-the-hell-it-is*, meant more to me than just a physical release.

That *he* meant more to me than that.

And there were several times over the weekend where I nearly did. Like on Saturday night, after work, we'd had a few beers and were just being cozy on the couch. We both had our feet on the coffee table, and I had my head on his chest, my hand on his stomach and we watched TV and talked.

His arm was around my shoulder, his hand tracing circles on my side, and he kissed the top of my head.

That wasn't something you did to someone you didn't care about.

And he froze. I felt him freeze, just for a second, when he realized what he'd done. I was about to say something, the words were on my tongue, but he made a joke about scented shampoo and laughed it off.

And my words went unsaid.

Then on Sunday night it was late when I came home from work, and he was already wearing the scrubs he'd claimed as his own. He said they were the most comfortable lounge pants, and he had the shirt on because it matched.

I laughed at him and gave him my stethoscope to complete his look, and he proceeded to play doctor. He examined every inch of my body, starting at my toes and working his way up. He tested different reflexes by different touch, fingers, lips, tongue.

He was very thorough.

Afterwards, he had my stethoscope pressed to my chest, and he listened. His eyes shot to mine, and his voice was one of wonder. "I can hear your heart so clearly."

I almost broke.

I almost asked him what he heard, what it sounded like, or if he knew it only beat for him. My mouth opened, and I almost told him, but he quickly put it to his own chest and made jokes that his heartbeat was healthier and how diet and exercise meant nothing.

It was as though he wanted to let himself feel, but stopped just short of starting. Some of the things he did and said were proof he felt something, but he quickly dismissed anything serious with jokes.

I'd been in Belfast for over three weeks now, and I couldn't help but think we were running out of time. I knew I needed to say something to him, I just wondered what the catalyst would be to make me actually say it.

Unfortunately, I didn't have to wait long to find out.

Because on Tuesday, my happy little world went right to fucking hell.

CHAPTER EIGHTEEN

ON THE MONDAY after Scott was transferred back to Belfast, I found myself immersed with the families of the two boys. I liked them. They were good, honest, friendly people. And I was *in* with them.

In their eyes, I'd saved two of theirs. And that made me, a newbie from Boston, good with them. Monday was a good day, and that night at home with Trent, it got even better.

I fell asleep with him in my bed, happy and sated, thinking life didn't get any better.

I should have known better than to jinx myself.

Tuesday started out just fine. Leaving a still-sleeping Trent all fucking gorgeous and rumpled in my blankets, I took Bentley for my morning run. I fed him breakfast and showered. When I was dressed for work, I leaned over Trent, kissed his cheek and squeezed his ass in my hand.

He groaned. I grinned, and as I walked out the door, he threw a pillow at my head.

I was still smiling at work, and not even vomiting patients and screaming babies could dampen my spirits.

That was until I was just about to leave.

Dani Peters had been eyeing me all day. I'd managed to avoid her for the most part, but at the end of my shift she cornered me. For someone who couldn't look at me without blushing and stammering, or tripping over thin air, she was quite tenacious.

We were standing in the hall, across from Scott's room where her friends were, where Adam was. "Nathan," she started, still not looking at me. "I don't normally do this, but I was wondering if you'd like to have coffee sometime?"

I sighed. Fucking hell. "Dani, I um, I don't think that's a good idea..." I trailed off awkwardly.

"Oh," she said, and she looked like she was about to throw up.

"No, Dani, it's not like that," I said quickly, wishing like fucking crazy a black hole would open up and swallow me.

She looked at the ground, and I swear if she started to cry, I would have stabbed myself in the leg with my pen to get away from her. But she said softly, "I just thought you might have liked me... you're always so friendly and always smile at me."

And I could have punched the ever living shit out of Trent for making me smile every time I saw her. It wasn't like I could admit to smiling at her because we made jokes about her mental capabilities. So I went with a different kind of honesty. "Um Dani, I'm gay."

She looked at me and blinked.

And I blinked.

She looked rather shocked.

But she wasn't as fucking shocked as me.

Oh. My. God.

I'm gay.

I. Am. Gay.

Fuck. I am. I knew I was. I think I'd known for a little

while, since our trip to Boston. I'd tried not to define whatever-the-hell-this-is and just *feel*. But there was no denying it. I was definitely not straight. Nope, crossed that off the list the day I got here. Possibly bi-sexual... could I ever have sex with a woman again? The thought alone made me shudder.

Nope.

Did I want to do incredibly dirty things to another man? A blond haired, blue eyed man in particular?

Fucking hell, yes.

Definitely gay.

A smile spread across my face. I looked at Dani, and she looked at me for the first time without having a brain aneurysm.

"Oh," she said again.

"Dani, you should look a little closer to home," I told her. She looked at me thoroughly confused. So I clarified, "I think Adam likes you."

"No," she rebuffed quickly. "Adam doesn't think of me like that."

I told her quietly, "Dani, that man is in love with you."

She looked from me to the man we could see in Scott's room then back to me. "Adam?" she asked softly.

I smiled and nodded. "Dani, I've got to go," I told her, and left her to stare at the man through the door.

I raced home to tell Trent about my little epiphany. I couldn't wait to tell him. It felt like a weight had been lifted from me, a conviction that warmed my very soul.

"Trent?" I called out when I was through the front door, but there was no answer.

I took the stairs two at a time. "Trent?"

And he stuck his head out from the attic door. I grinned at him, and he smiled at me. "You'll never guess what I did today."

He wiped his hand on his shirt and grinned at my excitement. "What did you do?"

"I said three *very* special words to Dani Peters."

Trent blinked and shook his head. "What?"

"Those three little words that no girl ever wants to hear." I grinned at him.

"That *no* girl ever wants to hear?" he repeated slowly, still unsure.

I nodded. "Dani, I'm gay."

His mouth popped open, and his eyes went wide. I nodded at him. "I told her I'm gay, because I am. Trent, I'm gay," the more I said it, the happier I felt. Tears sprang to my eyes, and I didn't know why, but I started to cry. "Trent, I think I came out today."

And he hugged me, so fucking hard. He held me, and I laughed, cried and laughed some more. My tears fell and they were happy tears, sad tears and tears of relief.

The part of my life that had been missing, the unidentifiable part of my life that had been missing, wasn't missing anymore.

"All my life Trent, something's been missing," I told him as he held me. "There has been a cloud hanging over me. I never knew what it was. I always thought I was never meant to be truly happy. I've lived a mediocre life for twenty-seven years, not feeling anything."

Trent pulled me back and wiped my tears. "Don't cry, baby."

I looked at him, and looked into his eyes, I steeled my resolve to tell him. "The part of my life that was incomplete isn't incomplete anymore. Because of you, Trent."

He shook his head. "I didn't do anything."

I took his face in my hands. "Trent, you... you brought me back to life. For the first time ever, I feel something.

You've made me *feel* something. The part that's been missing isn't me being gay, Trent. The part that's been missing is you."

Taking a deep breath, I told him, "You... I'm in love with you."

Finally. Relief coursed through me, like I could finally breathe. The words were finally out, and I couldn't take them back. Completely elated, I pulled his face to mine and kissed him.

But his lips didn't move.

He shrank back from me and shook his head. "No," he breathed. His face was pale, and he looked horrified. "You don't love me."

All I could do was stand there, and watch him as he backed away from me and ran down the stairs, away from me. It was all I could do.

Because my heart had stopped beating.

And I think a part of me died, right there in the hall.

I stood there, not breathing, not thinking, not feeling. I wasn't sure what the Hell just happened.

Twenty fucking minutes ago, I'd come out. *I'd come out...* I realized I was fucking gay, and the only person on the planet who understood, who I wanted to be with, just walked out on me.

I told him I loved him. Fuck.

I told him I loved him, and he left. He didn't just leave... he ran.

My head started to spin, and I stumbled to my room. The walls pulsed, throbbing as if alive, pounding, thumping and aching. Falling to my knees, I rested my head on the side of my bed and tried to breathe.

Oh, fuck it hurt. I held my stomach because it fucking hurt.

I'd just come out. I just told someone I worked with I was gay. Dani. Fucking Hell.

I dragged my body onto the bed, watching the light fade out of my room. I wished for darkness, numbness. I wished for silence inside my head. But my mind didn't stop. Neither did my heart. It ached. And my stomach twisted.

And I knew I only had myself to blame.

Sleep did not come. Not at all. Trent came back inside some hours later. I thought he might have stopped at my door, but he didn't. He walked quietly, sneaking past my room, and I heard the quiet click of the attic door.

I laid there, staring at the wall. Sleep wouldn't come because Trent wasn't with me...

By 4:30 a.m., not knowing what else to do, I got dressed in my running gear and went downstairs.

Bentley woke and stretched. I didn't wait for him, but he followed. It was dark and misting rain, but I ran anyway. For miles I lost myself in the constant beat of my footfalls, and the cold sting of the falling rain on my face helped with the much needed numbing. Eventually, my mind cleared. If only for a little while.

When I got back to the house, it was daylight, but there was no sign of Trent, and I was glad. I showered quickly, got dressed and ready for work. I didn't get Bentley breakfast. I didn't have coffee. I just wanted to leave without seeing him, but I got to the door, and his voice hit me like a wrecking ball.

"Nathan?"

I didn't look at him. I couldn't. I took another step toward the front door. My voice was hoarse and quiet. "I have to go to work."

"Can we talk?"

My mouth opened and then closed, but no words came out. So I shook my head no and walked to my car.

I willed myself not to turn and look at him, like I willed myself not to fall apart. I prayed it would be a busy day at work, where I wouldn't have time to think.

I arrived at the hospital with no recollection of the drive there, and I walked down the now familiar white halls to my office in a daze. I put on my coat, told myself to pull my shit together and headed out to start my day. I intended to find Dani, to say... something....

But I saw Lucas, and something wasn't right. He was somber, and there were people around him. Some faces I knew, some I didn't, but none of them were the smiling, happy faces from two days ago.

One of the nurses told me that Graeme Rogers, Lucas's father, was admitted during the night with chest pains.

Alarmed, I asked her, "Where is he now?"

She frowned and answered quietly. "He had a massive heart attack. He didn't make it."

I could feel the blood run down my spine. Fucking hell. Not today. Not today. Please, not today.

I looked back at Lucas and his family. There were two women there, one I presumed to be his mother, the other his sister Simone, the vet, and so was Steve Peters.

"The Chief and Graeme were best friends," the nurse beside me said, in explanation.

Some days, like most of last week, I loved my job. When I saw kids like Toby and Scott suffer some serious injuries, then saw them laughing and smiling with their families later, it reminded me why I love what I do.

And some days, like today, I fucking hated it.

"They've been told?" I asked.

She nodded. "Doctor Varner told them. He's with them now."

And she was right. Behind half of the town standing in the small room, I saw his coat.

So picking up some waiting files, I started on the people waiting in the ER. It wasn't until some hours later, that I was supposed to break for lunch, but my stomach wasn't up for it. Deciding to spend ten minutes of downtime in my office, I headed down the corridor to find Lucas, Adam, Dani and a few others, leaning against the wall.

I stopped, and putting my hand on Lucas's arm, I told him, "I'm sorry for your loss."

He nodded as the emotional dam broke, and he started to cry. He looked heartbroken and alone, and as tears fell down his cheeks, I did the only thing that felt right. I hugged him.

He clutched my coat and sobbed as I patted his back. It wasn't an affectionate embrace, it was one of comfort, and because he needed it. And quite frankly, it was a little comforting to me too.

I noticed Dani and Adam's heads both turn to the door, and they stared for a long second behind me. I let go of the grieving man in my arms, and he was taken by his sister. When I turned around, I saw the back of someone's head as they walked away.

A wavy, blond-haired head.

Trent.

Dani looked at me with sad eyes and whispered, "I think he was bringing you lunch."

"You want me to go grab him?" Adam asked. I realized they were holding hands, and I gave them a small smile.

My heart sparked at the thought of Trent coming to see me, but I was pretty sure I didn't want to hear what he had to say. I just couldn't face his *it-was-only-physical-for-me* right now. "No, thanks. Don't feel much like eating," I told them. "If there's anything I can do for the Rogers family, please let me know."

I spent the next twenty minutes in my office with a pounding head and a heavy, heavy heart.

It was a long afternoon. By the time I headed home, it was late, and I was exhausted. I pulled up at the house and saw it was all dark, except the kitchen light. I dumped my satchel on the table and with leaden feet, I walked into the kitchen.

He was there. Waiting for me. And I wanted to turn around and walk away, but my feet wouldn't let me move.

He spoke first. "Nathan... please, I... " he trailed off, seemingly as lost for words as me.

I decided to let him off the hook. The responsibility for my broken heart rested firmly on my shoulders, not his. It was unfair of me to blame him when he said from the very beginning that whatever it was between us, was only physical for him.

"Trent, please don't. Just forget what I said. It's fine."

"Nathan, you came out! At work!" he said, his hands pulled at his hair. "I feel responsible for pushing you, and to make matters worse, I let you go through that alone." His voice was so quiet. "I'm sorrier for that than you could possibly know."

I snorted. I wanted to tell him it was all okay, that I loved him, and I wanted to scream at him to go to fucking hell.

But I did neither.

"You came to see me today?"

He looked at me, and there was fear in his eyes. Fear. He looked away and swallowed, twice, like he was trying to find the right words. "I saw you with Lucas."

"Trent, his—" I started, but he cut me off.

"Nathan, the house is done."

I blinked, not understanding. I was so fucking tired and confused. "What?"

"The house. The painting," he said, still not looking at me. "It's done."

Oh.

I wanted to ask him what that meant, but my mouth wouldn't work.

He cleared his throat. "I'm leaving."

My voice was so quiet and so removed, it sounded like someone else's. "When?"

"Tomorrow," he whispered in return. "In the morning. When your family comes this weekend, they can have my room."

His words swirled in my head. I could hear them, but I was so tired, and I didn't under-fucking-stand.

I blinked, and I think I swayed a little. Then it was his voice I heard again. "Would you fucking eat something? Please? Do that for me?"

He grabbed something, and I heard the microwave. Then I was sitting at the table, and there was a bowl in front of me. His voice sounded broken, "It's soup. Please... "

Then he was gone.

I tried to eat. It smelled good, but three mouthfuls later, I pushed it away. I just wanted to sleep. I fell into my bed, fully dressed, and too tired to care. It still smelled of him, the sheets, the pillow, *his* pillow.

I took a deep breath of him. The next thing I knew it was morning.

I was surprised Bentley hadn't woken me demanding

his run and his toast. I shuffled down the stairs to tell him there'd be no running today. I just didn't feel like it.

But he wasn't there.

His bed and his dish were gone. Everything of his was gone.

I looked out the window to where Trent's truck was always parked, but I knew it wouldn't be there. Just like I knew when I checked his room, the bathroom, the attic, there'd be no trace of him.

And there wasn't.

His bed was stripped, and his toiletries were gone. I felt sick walking up the narrow stairs to check the attic, but I needed to see it. I knew it would be empty. I knew everything would be gone, but I needed to see it.

My masochistic heart needed to see it.

I opened the door and walked in. The vastness, the emptiness, numbed me.

If it weren't for the faint smell of acrylic paint, it would be as though he was never there.

I turned to walk out, and that was when I saw it. Leaning against the wall, near the door was a painting. It was square, each side about thirty inches, and it was a dozen shades of red. It was a mass of disjointed swirls, textures and layers. It was sort of beautiful... and sad.

He didn't just accidently leave it behind. He knew I'd come up here, he left it for me to find.

He'd given it to me, his parting gift—a farewell note.

I picked it up, carried it downstairs and placed it on the table. The different shades of red were striking. There was no pattern, but it was almost poetic.

This was how he told me goodbye. A fucking painting I didn't understand and couldn't interpret.

Well, fuck him.

Fuck. Him.

My anger surprised me, but it was welcome. Mad was better than hurt and heartbroken. And I was fucking mad at him. So he made me realize some things about my life, I'd probably have died of old age not knowing without him. I'm gay. So fucking what. I was sure I'd have figured it out eventually. Someone else would have come into my life and shown me... surely.

I stomped upstairs to the bathroom and into the shower. I scrubbed harshly at my body, washing away the fucking hurt, and by the time I was dressed and on my way to work, I had a new resolve.

I would go about my work like I always had. Patients first, always.

And me, life and love last.

I could just put my broken fucking heart on a shelf and never deal with it, just like I did before I met him. It worked for twenty-seven years, and it'd work just fine for another twenty-seven.

At least that was what I told myself.

And for an hour or two, it worked just fine.

Until I heard my name being yelled from the ER—a familiar voice, with a southern accent.

I ran out to see a man with blond wavy hair, who'd been crying. He was holding a golden retriever, and there was blood dripping onto the floor.

CHAPTER NINETEEN

TRENT.

Trent was standing in my ER, holding Bentley. The dog was clearly injured, his fur was damp with blood, and his front right leg was distorted, hanging loosely.

Trent looked awful. He'd been crying, and I could tell he hadn't slept.

But it was Bentley...

"Can you fix him?" Trent asked, on the verge of new tears.

"What the hell are you doing here?" My tone was harsher than I intended.

"I came back..." he mumbled in a whisper.

"No, what are you doing *here*? This is a hospital!" Now there were three nurses and Steve Peters beside us.

"I tried the vet's, but it was closed," he said, looking around the curtained cubicles. "Can you fix him? I didn't know where else to go."

"I can't fix a dog," I told him.

He looked at me, and his eyes went wide, full of hurt and knowing.

"I'd lose my license," I explained.

Then Nurse Watson, Carla, said, "Well, Dr. Hine X-rayed his cat. He didn't lose his license."

The other nurses nodded, and then the Chief said, almost conspiratorially, "Because no one reported him, that's why."

The other two nurses, Helen and Marta, both looked at each other, and Helen said, "I'm not gonna tell anyone."

Marta shrugged. "I won't tell anyone."

Trent shuffled his bleeding dog in his arms, the weight starting to affect him. "Nathan, please..."

Fuck. I couldn't believe I was even considering this. I looked at Trent, the man I loved, the man who left me. And I looked at his dog. Bentley. My breakfast buddy.

"Come this way." I ushered Trent down the corridor into radiology, and told him to lay the dog on the table. When he did, Bentley tried to get up. Trent coaxed him back down and patted his head to calm him. Trent was obviously upset, his hands were shaking, and his eyes were teary.

He looked at me, and he breathed the words, "I'm so sorry."

I couldn't do this right now. "Trent, go to my office and grab my cell." He blinked at me, not moving. "NOW," I yelled, and he ran out of the room.

Nurse Watson was with me. "Carla, you don't need to be implicated in this. You should go."

"Implicated in what?" she said with a smile. "Don't know what you're talking about, doctor."

I smiled at her, and Bentley tried to get up again. I held him down. "Hey, little buddy. Stay there, I'll get you fixed up, okay?"

Trent came back in and handed me my phone. "Hold

him down," I instructed him, indicating to Bentley. Quickly scrolling through contacts, I found my brother's number. "Brendan?"

"Hey, what's up? I'm kinda busy," he said.

"Can dogs have human sedatives?" I asked him quickly.

"What?" he asked. "What the hell do I know about human sedatives?"

"Name some sedatives you'd use on a dog."

"Nathan, what the fuck are you doing?" my brother asked.

"Bentley's injured," I told him. "His front right leg's broken, and he has lacerations..." I looked over the dog, "everywhere. He's bleeding pretty badly, but I'll know more about the break when I get these x-rays done."

"*You're* doing them?" he almost yelled. "Please tell me you're not doing this in a hospital."

"Brendan..."

"ARE YOU FUCKING CRAZY?" came his loud response, and everyone in the room heard him. "You'll lose your goddamn license, Nathan!"

Trent's eyes were on me. He knew the risk I was taking.

"Brendan! Sedatives, please," I begged.

"Um, any benzodiazepines. Like diazepam-"

"Diazepam. Yes!" I called out, and Carla darted out of the room to get it. I looked at Trent, "How much does he weigh?"

It was Brendan who answered. "Four mg's should do. Nathan, I hope you know what the fuck you're doing."

I clicked off the call and threw the phone on the table. He could lecture me when he got here tomorrow. And he would. I had no doubt.

Carla was back quickly. I told Trent to hold Bentley's

head, and found the best vein I could in his good leg, I gave him the measured dose.

It was only then we all took a much needed breath. And I realized the Chief was in the room with us.

I looked at him questioningly, and he gave a pointed nod to Trent. "Mr. Jamieson here overtook me on the highway, drove through two stop signs..." he said with raised eyebrows. "I thought I'd follow him to see what the emergency was."

Then it was Trent who spoke. Looking straight at me, he said, "I was already coming back." He looked so miserable. "Bentley's collar must have snapped, because he jumped around in the back, barking at a passing truck and just fell out."

And from his injuries, I'd guess Trent was driving fast.

"Nathan, I'm so sorry," he said, and fresh tears filled his eyes. Unable to bear his tears, I cupped my hand to his cheek, and he leaned into my hand. "I'm so sorry," he whispered again.

I didn't say anything in response. I couldn't. I pulled my hand away and stepped back from Trent and focused on the task at hand instead. I maneuvered Bentley so I could X-ray him, and it was then I saw that Carla was smiling at us. I glanced quickly at Steve, and his lips were in an 'o' shape. I think he just realized he'd witnessed a moment between Trent and I.

I gave my stethoscope to Trent. "Listen to his heart rate. Tell me if it gets faster."

He looked bewildered, but did as instructed. "How fast should it be?" he asked.

"I have no idea," I answered him honestly. "Just tell me if it changes."

I laid Bentley's leg out as I would a child's. I worked the

x-ray machine, and while I was waiting for them to process, I started cleaning the open wounds.

As I was tying off the sutures in Bentley's chin, Carla came back with the X-rays. I asked Steve, who was still in the room with us standing guard at the door, to grab them and put them on the light board so Carla could keep cleaning the dog's lacerations. He did, and I could see the break clearly.

"I have to set his leg," I told Trent. "If you want to step outside...?"

Trent pulled the stethoscope off, and his eyes were determined. "I'm not leaving," he said. Then he spoke quietly, "I'm not leaving again."

I knew what he was referring to. But I couldn't do this now. Or here.

Gingerly, I felt out the broken leg in my fingers. "How's his heartbeat?"

Trent blinked and wiping his eyes, he looked back at his dog. "Um, good? It hasn't changed, I don't think."

"Well, he's fit and healthy." Then with a smile, I said, "Because he runs every morning."

Trent smiled sadly, and his eyes watered again. "But he has toast for breakfast."

He looked at me, and I at him. "He doesn't mind," I said, and Trent smiled genuinely this time.

And I snapped Bentley's leg, realigning the bone.

Trent paled, the color drained from his face. Steve quickly grabbed him before he fell, took him by the arm and led him out the door. "We'll just wait in the hall," Steve said. "I'll make sure no one comes in."

I finished bandaging the leg while Carla cleaned up the cuts and scrapes. She bathed him the best she could so I could suture a few more gashes. We worked in amicable silence, and when we were done, I opened the door. Trent looked up at me. He'd gotten some color back in his face, and he asked, "Is he okay?"

I nodded. "You need to take him. If anyone else sees him here, I *will* get reported."

He nodded quickly. "Thank you... I, I need... could we..."

I cut him off. "Trent, do me a favor and get Bentley out of here. He'll be sedated for a while yet. Keep him off his leg, keep him warm and keep an eye on him." Then I added softly, "If you don't want to stay at the house I'll understand, but you're welcome to... if you need somewhere to stay."

"Of course I'll stay," he said quickly. "I'll wait up," he said quietly, then looked at the Chief, who was watching us.

It was awkward between us, so much needed to be said.

"I'll be home as soon as I can," I said, looking back to the radiology room. "I'll be disinfecting every inch of that room three times over for the next few hours."

He offered to help and I told him to leave. I was still mad and very fucking hurt, and I'd just jeopardized my entire career. Trent gently picked up Bentley, and I knew he wanted to say something, but he didn't. Carla, Steve and I watched him leave. When he was gone, Steve rocked back on his heels. He cleared his throat and said, "Always knew there must have been a reason why you turned down a date with my daughter."

I snorted, and Carla giggled. Then the Chief said, "If you want to make sure he stays, I could put him under house arrest?"

I laughed. "I'll keep that in mind."

IT WAS LATE when I got home. The house was mostly dark, but I could see a flickering light. Tentatively, I walked into the living room, unsure of what I would find. But he was there. He'd lit the fire, and Bentley was lying down on his bed in front of it. I looked at Trent, and he looked uneasy, nervous... sorry.

I had to clear my throat so I could speak. "How's Bentley?"

Trent's voice was quiet. "He's been awake, but he went back to sleep. Thank you, again, for doing what you did. The vet was closed, and I didn't know what else to do. "

Then I remembered. "Lucas and Simone are away," I said. "Their father passed away."

He looked at me, and there was a brief flash of recognition in his eyes. "I saw you hug him... I saw you and Lucas, and I panicked. I thought... I thought..." he took a deep breath and exhaled loudly.

"Trent—"

"Please let me finish, Nathan." He swallowed and took another deep breath. "I saw you with him, and I thought you'd be better off with someone like him, rather than someone who's closed off like me. I made the decision to leave right then and there. I'm sorry. I'm sorry for everything. I knew this was different from the very beginning. I should have stopped it then, but I didn't. I was selfish, and I'm sorry. I never meant to hurt you. The last thing I wanted to do was hurt you."

I put my hand up. "If you've come back to twist the knife a little further, please don't."

"No!" he said quickly, "No, that's not why I'm here."

"Then why *are* you here?" I asked him sharply. "*Why?* You. Left. Me. Remember?"

He tried to speak, but I wouldn't let him.

I jabbed my finger into my chest. "I came out, for fuck's sake. I came out! Fucking hell, Trent," I said, throwing my hands up. My anger came back with a surge. "My entire world gets turned on its head. I realized I was gay, I fell in love with a *man*, I was prepared to give *him* everything, and what did I get in return?"

His face fell, but he stayed quiet.

"A fucking painting," I said, motioning to the canvas painted in different reds—the *farewell note*—he'd left for me, it still sat on the table. "I mean, it's great, don't get me wrong," I was being sarcastic now, and I couldn't seem to stop myself. "But gee, I could think of something that would have been more appropriate. Like a goodbye! What the *hell* was the painting supposed to mean anyway?"

He opened his mouth and closed it again before he spoke. His voice was so quiet, it was barely a breath. "... it's my heart. I left it with you."

And my breath, all my fight, all my anger, left in a whoosh.

He gave me his heart!

He saw my resolve stumble, and he started talking, desperately. "I know I don't deserve it, but I need you to listen. Please?" His eyes were wide and honest, and his chest was heaving, rapid breaths. "Please, I need to say this without getting it wrong. I *couldn't* leave. I tried. I did, but it got harder to breathe every mile I put between us. I had to pull off to the side of the road, I couldn't breathe."

His breathing was becoming labored now. He was taking deep breaths, but it didn't seem to be working. He was almost gasping.

"Trent calm down, please."

He shook his head. "All my life I've been on my own. Since I was sixteen Nathan, I've had to look out for myself.

I'd never been close to anyone, not since my parents died... my aunt and uncle didn't want me because I was gay." He pushed the palm of his hand against his ribs, like they hurt. "There was a guy in Texas, I thought I loved him... I told him I loved him, and he... he...."

He was gasping. His words were all running together because he was trying to talk too fast, and he wasn't breathing properly.

"Since then, I've only ever used people for sex... never anything more. I never let anyone else in. I couldn't risk being hurt like that again... then you came along, and I knew it was different from the start."

I tried to listen to him, but he was breathing too hard, as though he was about to hyperventilate. He was having a panic attack.

I found myself walking over to him. I put my hand on his shoulder, and it seemed to help calm him. "Trent," I said his name calmly. "I need you to calm down. Take some deep breaths for me." He gulped at the air, and he closed his eyes tight. I tried to soothe him, "Trent, it's okay. Just breathe."

"Remember when you told me," I said as I took some deep breaths to help regulate his breathing, "you told me to breathe. You calmed me down, remember? When we first met, and I freaked out?"

He nodded and tried to smile. After some deep inhales his breathing seemed to steady a little.

Then he said, "I'm just so sorry, Nathan. You told me how you felt, and I fucked it up by leaving." Then he said, "It's been so perfect, here with you. Just like a real relationship from the very start. I told myself for years I'd never have that." He swallowed hard again and took another deep breath. "I've never wanted something so bad."

"What are you trying to say, Trent?"

He looked like he was about to be sick. His voice was so quiet, I almost didn't hear him. "I'm scared."

And from the look in his eyes, I didn't doubt it. He looked scared. I wrapped my hand around his neck and pulled his face into my neck. His breathing started to accelerate again, and I whispered, "Breathe."

And he did. His hands went to my waist, fisting into my shirt, his forehead was against my collarbone, and I could feel him shaking.

Quietly, I asked him, "Did you come back for me?"

He nodded yes.

"Is that what you're scared about?"

He nodded yes.

"Are you scared for your heart?"

He nodded again, and he started to cry.

"Trent, you hurt me," I told him honestly, and I felt his body recoil from my words. I held him tighter. "Look at me."

I could tell he didn't want to, but reluctantly he lifted his head. There was defeat and resignation and tears in his eyes. I told him, "When I told you how I felt and you walked out, it felt like a hole had been punched through my chest. I didn't know what else I could have done to make you want me. I told you I had feelings for you... all those times I asked you to have sex with me... "

His eyes closed and tears fell down his cheeks. "It was never you," he sobbed quietly. "All those times, every single time you wanted me to, it was never you that wasn't ready." His eyes opened, and he looked *into* me. "It was me. I knew. I just knew if I did that, with you, then it wouldn't be just sex anymore. I knew I was falling for you, and it scared me. "

"Why didn't you tell me?"

He sobbed, and his tears fell freely. His voice was so, so quiet. "Because everyone I love leaves me."

His pain was killing me, so I held him tighter against me. "So you thought you'd leave me first, before I could leave you?"

He nodded against me and cried harder. "I'm sorry," he sobbed, over and over. "I'm so sorry."

I took his face in my hands and wiped his tears with my thumbs. "No more apologies. No more tears." I kissed his cheeks and tasted salt water.

"Don't ever, ever leave me again," I told him, and his eyes opened wide. They were blue, red and puffy, and they sparkled with disbelief and hope.

"Where else am I gonna go," he said shakily. "I couldn't get any farther than Littleport. It nearly killed me. It nearly killed Bentley."

I smiled sadly at him. "You silly man. Next time, talk to me."

"Next time? You mean you forgive me?" He was almost pleading.

"Of course I forgive you," I told him, and he exhaled in a huff and smiled. "I love you, Trent Jamieson."

He started to cry again, but these were happy tears, tears of relief. I held him for the longest time. His breathing was back to normal, so I kissed him, softly, sweetly. Our bodies started to sway. We were dancing almost, there was no music, no lights, just us, the fire and a sleeping dog in a darkened living room. And I was holding him, and he was clutching me like he never wanted to let me go.

He didn't say he loved me, not in so many words.

But I knew he did.

I felt it in his tears on my neck, the way he gripped onto me, holding me, and when he looked at me, it was there in his eyes. I saw it.

And without words, his lips pressed to mine, and he

loved me with his kiss. It was sweet and tender and sure. His eyes were closed, and he was so lost in kissing me. It was there in the way his hands touched my face, the way he caressed me.

And we danced like that for a long while. Slow dancing to no music, moving and kissing, never parting, not even for a second. I felt his desire, his growing erection, pressing against me, and I knew he could feel mine, but there was no grabbing or pulling, there was no urgency.

But I needed him. I needed for him to claim me as his own.

My feet stopped moving, and my hands cupped his jaw. I whispered against his lips, "Make love to me."

He made a strangled whimpering sound and nodded. He kissed me harder this time, more purposefully, with more desire.

Then he took my hand, and without another word, we walked upstairs and led me into my room. He unbuttoned my shirt slowly and kissed every inch of skin he exposed. His hands trailed over my chest, my shoulders. When he undid my pants, he pushed them over my hips and allowed them to simply fall to the floor. Ignoring my hard-on, he cupped my face in his hands and kissed me.

Languidly, lovingly, his tongue tasted me and teased me. It was different this time. *He* was different this time. I knew this was it. I knew what I was about to give him. More importantly, I knew what he was about to give me.

Love.

Seconds, minutes, hours later, I was lying down on my bed, naked, exposed and wanting, needing. He was between my legs, equally naked, but he was more exposed than me. Even though it was him that had his hands on me and his fingers inside me, it was me that held his heart in my hands.

He was giving himself, his heart, for the first time. Just like me. And when he pressed his condom sheathed cock against me, it was me that comforted him. He was trembling, nervous and vulnerable, and when he slipped the head of his cock inside me, I cupped my hand to his cheek. His eyes bored into me, and there was no disguise.

Not this time.

There was the burn of him stretching me, but he'd prepared me well. He was patient and slow. Loving. He was trembling and his breath gasping, but he didn't rush, as much as his body protested. Leaning on his elbows, his nose touched mine. He kissed me, consumed me, gently, perfectly.

Then he was inside of me, all of him, every inch of him. When he slid back out and pushed in again, his eyes rolled closed. He groaned low in his throat, and he moaned my name every time he moved.

His hands were on my face, his thumbs on my lips. Slowly, he thrust, and my hips rose. He pushed into me, so far inside of me. I cradled him in my arms, with my legs, and his eyes told me he loved me. I could see the words he couldn't say.

"Nathan," he breathed.

"I know," I whispered against his skin.

He nodded, and closed his eyes, tears slid down his cheeks. His entire body was trembling, and he pushed himself further inside me, pulling out and sliding back in, he told me with his body that he loved me.

I pushed my hips up, somehow needing more of him, and I kissed him hungrily. His hands curled under my shoulders as he thrust deeper, longer, and harder. When he plunged his tongue into my mouth, his whole body convulsed violently.

He cried out as he came, and I held him together while he fell apart. He sobbed as he stilled over me and inside me. I felt his cock spilling, surging into the condom.

His face buried into my neck as his orgasm subsided, and his breathing hitched as he tried to contain his emotions. I pulled his face into my hands, and made him look at me. "I love you," I told him.

He nodded, and his eyes closed. He pulled out of me, discarded the condom and came back with a warm, wet cloth. He cleaned me, cared for me, without a word, and the emotions of the last two days bore a sleepy weight on me I just couldn't fight.

Trent burrowed himself against me, his arms wrapped around me, holding me too tightly. Sleep came quickly, I was so warm and content as he kissed my hair and my face.

I knew I must be dreaming when the words, "I love you," were whispered in my ear.

CHAPTER TWENTY

I NEEDED TO PEE. I really needed to pee. But I'd woken up from the best sleep ever, warm and completely encased in Trent. He slept soundly, his arms were around me and his face was just an inch from mine.

He was half laying on me, his thigh hitched on my waist, pressing on my bladder, hence the need to pee. But I didn't want to move. Ever.

Unless I wanted to wet the bed, I didn't have much choice. So I rolled onto my side so his leg was now resting on my hip instead of my bladder. He stirred and mumbled, but his hand held onto me, and he nuzzled himself into my side. I brushed the hair from his face and kissed his forehead, and he sighed.

I moved his leg and pulled away from him, but he protested in his sleep. "Mm mm."

"I need to pee," I told him, finally peeling myself out from his grasp. I quickly put on some boxer briefs and headed to the bathroom. I was a little sore, but it only reminded me *why* my ass was sore, and it made me smile.

While I was up, I decided to check on Bentley. He

woke to the sound of me approaching him, and I gave him a quick pat, mindful of where he was cut and sore. He stood up, shook himself a little, but he wasn't his usual bouncy self.

"Need to pee too, little buddy?" I asked him.

I coaxed him out the door, and he limped on three legs, favoring his bandaged right leg. I knew dogs were tough little critters and had a high pain tolerance, but it was still hard to see him struggle.

After he relieved himself, I picked him up and brought him back to his bed by the now-just-embers fire. I threw some kindling and smaller logs into the fireplace and wished it well. I didn't stick around to see if it lit, there was only one place I wanted to be.

I slid back into bed, and Trent shivered and shuddered when I slipped in behind him and pressed my cold body against his warm one. He groaned, "...cold."

"You're warm," I whispered back.

He turned so he was facing me and wrapped himself around me. He rubbed my back, his thigh hooked over mine and he warmed my body with his own. His face was so close, the tip of his nose was touching mine, and his eyes were sleepy, but open.

He moved his hand, laid it gently on my face and lightly traced his thumb along my jaw. His eyes showed me his insecurity, his vulnerability, like he was waiting for me to tell him goodbye.

I didn't know much about relationships, or couple dynamics, but I could safely presume his insecurities and abandonment issues were not something that would magically disappear overnight. It would take time and reassurance. So I kissed him lightly to let him know I had no regrets.

"I'm not dreaming, am I?" he asked. "I'm here, in your bed, with you, aren't I?"

I smiled and nodded. "Sure are."

He gave me a small smile and closed his eyes.

I took his hand that was pressed against my cheek and kissed the palm and held his hand in mine. "Right where I want you to be."

He looked at me then and quietly, he said, "Thank you."

"For what?"

"Everything," he answered simply. "For everything."

"Thank you, Trent," I echoed his words. He looked at me with wide eyes, and I smiled at him. Pulled him closer so my face was against his hair, I just held him. I kissed the side of his head and whispered, "Thank you."

We lay like that, wrapped around each other for a long while. It wasn't sexual, not this time.

After snuggling down into me, Trent's face was against my chest. He sniffed me, twice. "Why do you smell like a wet dog?"

I laughed. "I took Bentley out for a pee and carried him back inside."

He pulled away with a start, alarmed. "Is he okay?"

"He's just fine," I reassured him and pulled him back against me. "I put him back on his bed."

I felt him chuckling against me. "You're gonna spoil my dog."

I laughed again and squeezed him in my arms. "He doesn't mind."

Still laying half over me, Trent leaned up on one elbow and looked at me. For a moment, he said nothing. He just looked at me. He cleared his throat, then speaking softly he asked, "How do you feel this morning? Are you sore?"

I smiled again at him and shook my head. "Not really," I answered him honestly. "I've never felt this good."

He gave me a cross between a disbelieving eyebrow and a smug smirk.

"Come on," I said, throwing back the covers. "I need to get Bentley some toast before he tries to come up the stairs to get me."

I pulled on a shirt, Trent put on the clothes he was wearing last night, and we headed downstairs. Before Bentley could get up, Trent was quick to sit beside him. Bentley was happy to see him, and Trent told him, "Nathan will get you some toast now, okay?"

I smiled at this, but he didn't see. He was already fixing my poor attempt to start the fire, so I headed to the kitchen to fix breakfast.

When I brought a tray of toast and coffee into the living room, Trent had resurrected the fire and was looking over his dog. He looked up at me, and there was sadness in his eyes.

"I really fucked things up yesterday, didn't I?" he said. "If I didn't leave, Bentley wouldn't have been hurt and neither would you."

I placed the tray down on the floor, sat next to him and handed him his coffee. "No you didn't, Trent. And there's no point in beating yourself up over something you can't change." I tore the toast into pieces and gave the dog a piece at a time. "Bentley and I will be just fine."

Trent looked at the coffee in his hand, and I knew he was about to finally explain.

"There was a guy in Texas," he said softly. "His name was Santiago. I was young, still in college. I thought it was the real deal, ya know? I thought it was love... but I know now it wasn't." He looked at me then before he continued talking. "We'd been together for a while. My aunt and uncle told me I could leave if I was '*that way inclined*', so I stayed at Santiago's."

He was looking far away, into his memories. "I asked him to come to my graduation, but he said he was busy... God, I was so stupid." he stopped talking to take a sip of his coffee, and I saw his hands were trembling.

As much as this was hard for me to hear, it was harder for him to talk about. But he needed to say it. He needed to get it out. I sipped my coffee and looked at him, expectantly.

"When I got home, he had... *company*. I asked him what the hell he was doing. I was so young and naïve... I told him it was okay because I loved him... and he laughed at me."

"Oh Trent, baby." No wonder he was so scared. My heart broke for him.

"I hit the road the next day," he said, "and basically just went wherever I wanted. I had told myself I'd never be that guy again. I spent years convincing myself I didn't need anyone. I spent about a year in New York and hooked up with this guy... I kept it casual, of course. He was a nice guy, don't get me wrong, but he wanted something from me that I couldn't give."

Love. He couldn't give love.

I rubbed his foot with mine, so he knew I was still on his side.

"Then I came across this little fella." He nodded to Bentley, who was dozing by the fire. "I rescued him because some lady didn't have time for him. She was gonna have him put down. Can you believe that?" he asked, shaking his head in disgust. "King Bentley was the first living thing I'd loved in about eight years."

Oh, fuck. My poor, sweet Trent.

"After a while, I hit the road again, and we came here."

He looked at me then, with honesty and pleading in his eyes. "Nathan, I'm not leaving again. I promise. The first time I saw you, when I came down those stairs, and you were patting Bentley, I knew."

He put his coffee down and scooted over to me, putting his hand on my leg. "Nathan, I just knew. I tried to keep it casual, thinking it'd just be physical and then I'd be going again, but I couldn't get you out of my head. Every time I saw you, my heart would take off and my palms would sweat. I knew it was different."

I squeezed his hand and smiled at him. Then he said, "And that first time I slept in your bed... it was like my body knew what it needed. It was the best sleep I've ever had."

"Me too," I told him.

"When you took me to the Museum of Fine Arts in Boston, Nathan," he said, shaking his head, "God, it meant the world to me. And taking you to that nightclub, seeing you so free, seeing all the guys who wanted you... made me only want you more."

Then he looked to my neck. "I bought you the necklace," he took a breath and spoke softer. "I wanted there to be some part of me on you," he said almost apologetically. "I know that sounds all kinds of fucked up."

"No it doesn't," I reassured him. Touching the leather cord around my neck made me smile. "I wear it because you gave it to me."

"I tried to fight what I felt for you. I was so stupid." He nodded, and then his face twisted. "You give me peace, Nathan."

"Peace?" I asked him quietly.

He nodded. "It's a peacefulness I feel when I'm with you. A calmness... I can't really describe it. I'm not very good with words..." he trailed off, and I was reminded of his paintings.

He expressed himself through his art.

"You express emotions through your art, don't you?" I asked him. "Like the painting you gave me?"

He looked to the ground, but he nodded. "I wanted you to have it," he shrugged, "the painting. You already had my heart. I'd left it with you."

I leaned forward and kissed his forehead and whispered against his skin, "Thank you." I leaned back and told him, "It's beautiful. Now that I know what it represents."

He looked away again. "I wanted to tell you. So many times. I wanted to tell you, that I've never felt like this," he swallowed loudly. Then he finished quietly, "I've never... wanted someone to love me like I want you... to love me."

He was so unsure, still. "Nathan, yesterday was *horrible* and *wonderful*. All I did was cry," he said with an embarrassed laugh.

I nodded and touched his face. As much as I wanted to kiss him right now, I didn't. If he didn't speak now, I didn't know if he ever would.

"It was horrible because I knew I had to leave you, but I couldn't. It was horrible because Bentley got hurt and when he fell out of the truck, I thought I'd killed him. I was so scared. Then you fixed him, and it was wonderful... you were wonderful. And then last night... Nathan, last night was the best night of my life."

"Mine too, Trent."

He looked at me and gave me a half smile. "I'm sorry I didn't make you come. I was so lost in what I was feeling. Finally being able to give that part of me to you."

"Trent, to be honest, it didn't even occur to me that I

didn't come," I told him honestly. "I was so overwhelmed with what I was feeling... it was perfect. It was so perfect."

This time I did kiss him. Sweet and soft I kissed him, with my hand on the side of his face. When I leaned back, a shooting pain in my ass fired through me, and I flinched.

"Are you okay?" Trent asked, alarmed.

I chuckled. "I'm fine, but I don't think sitting on a hardwood floor for any length of time is a great idea for me."

Trent jumped to his feet and pulled me up. "I'm sorry, baby," he said, "I should have thought of that."

I brushed his concerns off. "Really, I'm fine," I told him, because I was. I slid my arms around his waist and kissed his neck. "I'm more than fine, Trent. Thank you for telling me. Thank you for letting me in."

He kissed me and put his forehead on my chin so he was looking down at our feet. "I don't know what I'm doing. And more than likely I'll fuck something up," he looked up at me then. "But I'm in this, whatever the fuck it is. With everything that I am."

I grinned and kissed him. "I don't know what I'm doing either, to be honest. We're both new to this, whatever the fuck it is, but just so you know, I'm in this too. With everything that I am."

He laughed, and it was the most beautiful sound in the world.

"First things first," I grinned at him. "We should get changed before my family gets here."

His eyes widened, almost comically. "Oh shit, I forgot."

Smiling, I pecked his lips. "They already like you."

"I have to grab my bags from the truck," he said quietly. My eyes darted to his, and he was quick to explain, "I only brought my paintings in last night," he said, pointing his chin toward the canvases stacked against the wall. Then he said, "I left my bags because I didn't know if you'd want me to stay."

"Then I will help you bring them in," I told him, and he smiled. When we'd collected his luggage, we took it back upstairs. He paused at the door to my room, unsure of which room to put his stuff in.

"Your family will need my room," he said, matter-of-factly, as he walked inside. "So, I'd better put my stuff in here for now."

I walked into my room, dropped his bags in the closet and pulled him into my arms. It was like it was official, for real now, with his stuff in my room... *our* room. "You'd *better* put it in here," I said against his lips. "You can leave it in here, too."

I SAT on the bed and watched him unpack. He threw his shirts in with mine, and his jeans and pants got tossed in too. In the top drawer, he pushed all my neatly folded underwear to one side and dumped his pile of underwear in the now vacant side. His shoes got tossed to the floor of the closet, and when he was done, he smiled.

He had no personal mementos or photos, not that I saw. He really had been so alone for far too long.

That changed today.

I pulled him onto the bed with me, my lips fused to his, my tongue in his mouth. I broke my mouth from his, only to pull my shirt over my head.

When I started to remove my boxers, Trent stopped me. "Nathan," he said, pulling away from me. "You're far too sore for me to-"

"To what?" I cut him off. "For you to suck me?"

His eyes nearly popped out of his head, and he barked out a laugh. "Nathan!"

I undid his jeans, pushed them over his hips and pulled his shirt over his head. I grinned at him, "I'm pretty sure it won't hurt, Trent."

He shook his head and laughed, and wasted no time in obliging. "Well, I do owe you an orgasm," he said casually. My dick was already hard, and his lips slipped over me, taking all of me into his mouth.

My head fell back onto the pillows, and I groaned. He slid up and down my shaft, using his lips, his tongue, licking and sucking me. When his nose nuzzled into my pubic bone, he slid his arms under my hips and swallowed around me.

"Holy shit!" I yelped and tried to not buck my hips, but he was consuming me. The pleasure was so intense and focused on my cock. He has a very fucking talented mouth.

"Oh, fuck," I groaned.

He replaced his mouth with his hand. "Look at me, Nathan," he whispered huskily.

So I did, and he had his fist around the base of my cock and was flicking the head with his tongue. He pumped me and tongued the slit. "Mmmm," he groaned. "You taste so good."

"Oh fuck, Trent."

"I want to taste more of you," he murmured. "Empty your cock in my mouth."

I gasped at his words. He smiled before opening his mouth and taking my engorged cock in between his lips. He pumped and sucked and licked and groaned and I was raising my hips to give him more.

My hands took to his hair and his face. I felt his hollowed cheeks and where his swollen lips were wrapped around me. My thumb traced our joining, my cock and his mouth. He groaned, and I was gone.

With a final lurch, pleasure detonated within me and the fallout of my orgasm obliterated every cell in my body. He swallowed and drank the come that poured into his mouth, and I couldn't see or hear, my senses were overwhelmed. All I felt was his mouth on me, his lips, his tongue lapping at me, as the last of my orgasm emptied into his mouth.

He pulled me up off the bed and into the shower before I could focus or even stand unassisted. Trent chuckled and washed me, and when we got out of the shower, he kissed me. It was a quick kiss, just a peck on the lips really, but the way he smiled and how his eyes shone, just about set me flying.

There was a happiness that was shining out of him. He smiled at me, and I grinned back at him. "You know, you're beautiful," I told him.

He took my chin in between his thumb and forefinger. "Not too bad yourself, doctor."

I kissed him, and he rubbed his hand along my cheek. He groaned against my lips, "Mmm, please don't shave today. This," and he rubbed his thumb along my jaw, "this should stay."

"Oh, darn it," I rolled my eyes and scrubbed at the scruff on my neck. "And I was going to ask you to shave me."

His head lolled back, and he groaned. "Please don't tease me with shit like that." He chuckled, "You have no idea how much I'd like to do that."

I waggled my eyebrows at him. "I'll remember that for work on Tuesday."

He nodded excitedly, and I laughed at him. Tying the towel around my waist, I walked to my room, *our* room, and got dressed. I put on an old pair of jeans, v-neck and flip flops, perfect lazy day clothes.

Great. Now I sounded gay.

I snorted and Trent looked at me, curiously. I laughed and asked, "So, now that I'm gay, I have this excellent in-built dress sense, right?"

Trent shook his head at me and laughed, as we heard a car come down the drive. We made our way downstairs, and I saw Brendan's Jeep coming toward the house. I went to open the front door as they pulled up, and Trent stopped me. "Um, Nathan?" he asked quickly, nervously. "How do you want me to act around them?"

"Just be yourself," I told him, a little unsure of what he meant.

"No, how are *we* acting around them?" he clarified, motioning between us.

Oh.

"Well, I was going to tell them I went and got myself a boyfriend, if that was alright with you?"

His slow spreading smile was my answer. I opened the door, Brendan and Kat were looking around at the house and the forest, taking in the beautiful scenery before them. Smiling, I stepped outside to greet them.

CHAPTER TWENTY-ONE

I WALKED out onto the patio as Brendan and Kat looked around them, taking in the walls of green trees surrounding them. They both wore huge smiles. "This place is pretty fucking awesome," my brother declared loudly, and his wife whacked his arm.

"Don't swear," she chided him, still smiling at me. "He means it's very beautiful."

They grabbed their bags from the back seat, and Kat snarled at her husband. "Jeez Brendan, you could at least offer to carry my bag."

He stopped dead and stared at her. "Cut me a break, Woman! I offer to carry your stuff, and I get crucified for being chauvinistic. I don't offer to carry your stuff, and I still get crucified."

Trent, who now stood beside me, mumbled, "Thank God, I'm gay."

I laughed, causing Brendan and Kat to look up at us. Trent chuckled and met them on the stairs. He asked Kat, "Can I carry your bags for you?"

"No, thank you," she replied sweetly. "I'm perfectly capable."

Brendan looked at him so seriously. "Don't even bother, my friend. You'll never win."

Kat kissed my cheek, smiling like she'd won that one, and we walked into the foyer, just as Bentley limped out to greet us.

Brendan put down his bags and pointed to the bandaged dog, then to me. "You and me, we're gonna talk about this."

I rolled my eyes at him and crouched down in front of Bentley. "It's okay, little buddy. He looks big and scary, but he's a softy." Then I looked back up at Brendan and told Bentley, "He'd have done the same thing."

"Fixing people in a vet clinic is one thing, Nathan," he huffed. "Fixing a dog in a hospital is something else entirely!"

Kat's eyes bulged. "You did what?"

Trent interrupted. "It was my fault. I asked him to."

"It wasn't your fault," I said, looking at Trent. "It was my decision."

"It was a stupid decision," Brendan grumbled pointedly at me. "You know how much I love animals Nathan, but to risk losing your license?"

"And if I had to Brendan, I'd do the same thing again," I told him truthfully.

He looked at me like I'd lost my mind. "This country air has fucked with your head," he added, and Kat whacked him again.

Ignoring his rant completely, I asked him, "Did you tell Dad?"

Brendan blinked. "I'm not *fucking* crazy!"

Kat whacked him again. "Stop hitting me," he whined.

"Stop swearing," she replied, mocking his tone.

Brendan huffed at her, then looked to me. "Mom, Dad and Alana stopped in town to pick up some *brunch*," Brendan said, using my mother's tone and rolling his eyes. "They'll be here soon. Who the hell uses the word brunch?"

"Your mother does," Kat answered. "Leave her alone."

Trent looked at me, a little unsure at how to take my brother and his wife.

I smiled at them. They were still the same, volatile, hot and cold—though more times hot than cold—and completely right for each other. "Come on," I said. "Leave your bags there, I'll show you the back yard."

We walked out onto the back patio, and we watched Bentley navigate the steps with his bandaged leg. "Maybe I should make him a ramp or something?" Trent thought out loud.

"Dogs are resilient," Brendan told us. "He'll be running around on that leg in a day or two."

"Could you check him over?" I asked. "Just to be sure?" Bentley sniffed around on the grass, tail up, looking rather happy.

He nodded and then looked out into the huge backyard. "It's huge! Is that the Bay?" he asked, pointing down the yard. I nodded, and he shook his head. "No wonder you love it here. It's in the middle of the freakin' wilderness."

I couldn't help but smile. I do love it here, but it wasn't strictly the forest and water that I loved. I glanced at Trent, and his lips were fighting a smile. When I looked at Kat, her eyes darted to mine, and then she looked away, smiling. She saw the look between Trent and I. I considered just coming right out and saying it that we're together, that I'm gay, but figured I should wait until everyone was together and explain it gently.

As I walked down the stairs to the back yard with the others following, we heard another car coming down the drive. "That'll be Mom and Dad," Brendan said, so we headed toward the front of the house. Trent was nervous, and although I doubted my brother or his wife would notice it, but I did. I wanted to hold his hand, I wanted to reassure him that it was all fine, but I couldn't.

Not yet.

Maybe I'd tell them at lunch. I had to tell them today, because Trent would be in my room tonight. Maybe I'd tell them at dinner. Delicately, clearly and calmly, that was how I'd tell them.

They pulled up and got out of the car, all smiles, hugs and hellos. Alana bounced out of the back seat and hugged the life out of me, my mom and dad were next. There were friendly hellos to Trent. He smiled and made general chitchat, and he was quick to offer to carry something.

We grabbed their bags, while they took in the surrounding trees and scenery. Mom had her hands full of paper bags from the deli. Brendan helped with those, taking them inside.

We took their luggage upstairs, dropping them in their allocated rooms. I didn't want them to realize the sleeping arrangements, especially mine and Trent's, until I was ready to tell them, so it was a brief, probably rude tour. "Brendan and Kat first door on the left, Alana second door on the left, bathroom through that door, Mom and Dad last door on the right," I told them, probably too fast to be considered polite.

I was quick to head back downstairs, knowing they'd follow me. "Who wants coffee?" I asked.

Mom, Dad, Alana, and Kat were talking near the back door, and Brendan was now outside giving Bentley a quick once over. I was in the kitchen with Trent getting plates for the pastries and he asked me quietly, if I was okay.

I nodded. "Just nervous, that's all. I'm going to tell them. Today."

He was obviously surprised. "Are you sure?" he whispered. "You can't undo this, Nathan."

I looked him in the eye. "I'm very sure."

We took the plates out to the table on the back patio so my family could enjoy the view while they ate. Everyone helped themselves to the pastries and were talking happily, and my nerves settled. Then Brendan came back outside after washing his hands, sat down and helped himself to some brunch.

My father asked what happened to Bentley. "He was on the back of my truck when his collar broke," Trent explained. "He fell off."

My mom put her hand to her chest. "The poor thing."

"Did the vet do an adequate job?" Dad smiled when he asked Brendan. If only he knew....

Brendan smiled tightly, and his eyes flickered to mine. I told him with my eyes he better lie convincingly. He looked back at Dad and said, "Yes, it would seem *the vet* did an excellent job."

My father looked at me, then at Brendan and back to me. He simply put his coffee down and smiled. "Do you boys remember the time the vase in the dining room mysteriously broke all by itself and the time the bumper on my car got dented, all by itself?"

Fuck.

"Well, you boys couldn't lie then, and you can't lie now," my father said.

Fuck. Fuckityfuck.

My father was an astute, perceptive, intelligent man. Fuck.

"I'm not lying," I lied.

Dad rolled his eyes dismissing me, and looked at Brendan. My brother folded. "Hey," he said, putting both hands up. "I'm not involved in any way."

I stared at my brother. Traitor. "What's *wrong* with you?"

"What's wrong with *me*?" he scoffed over the table. "I'm not the one who treated a *dog* in a hospital!"

Five sets of eyes popped simultaneously, someone gasped... I didn't see who... because I was looking at my dad. He stared at me, turning an odd shade of pale. It seemed to take an eternity for him to be able to speak. "Nathan..." he said quietly.

I could handle yelling, visible anger and seething ire, but it was the quiet disappointment I couldn't handle.

My father was one of the most renowned and respected doctors in Boston. To have his son's medical license revoked or to be fired, disgraced because he treated an animal in a hospital, would be devastating to him.

I couldn't look at him. Everyone else stared at me, and I swear I heard Trent's heart beating double-time from the seat next to me.

"Nathan," Dad repeated quietly.

My father had always had a way of staying quiet whenever we did something wrong, making us talk just to fill the silence.

I looked at Trent, and he was sipping his coffee, looking anywhere but at me.

And I panicked.

I blurted out the one thing I'd been trying to not say. "I'm gay!"

Trent choked on his coffee beside me. Everyone else stared, gaping at me, and Brendan laughed. "You need to work on your diversionary tactics, Nathan," he said, snickering.

"Fuck. That wasn't what I meant to say," I muttered, looking at my slack-jawed family. "I mean, I was going to tell you, but that wasn't how I was going to say it."

I looked at my dad. He was looking at my mother, and when I looked at Brendan, his smile was gone. My brother slowly leaned forward in his seat, glared at me, then at his wife, then back to me. "Did she put you up to this?"

"What?"

"Kat put you up to that, didn't she?" Brendan asked. "How much is she giving you?"

I shook my head at him. I didn't know what he was talking about. I looked at Trent. He was wide-eyed and darting glances to everyone at the table.

"Goddammit!" Brendan cursed and abruptly got to his feet. His chair skidded on the decking, and Trent tensed beside me, his feet moved as though he was ready to stand, ready to fight.

I grabbed his hand, instinctively, but before I said a word, Brendan was pulling notes out of his wallet. "Two-hundred bucks, Nathan! Two. Hundred. Dollars," he said again, counting out twenty dollar bills onto the table.

I was really fucking confused. I looked at Kat, and she was smiling. She explained, "I told Bren after we saw you two weeks ago, you were gay. I told him I hoped you came out soon," she smiled sweetly at me. Then she said, "He said 'no way'," she imitated his voice perfectly. "I said 'yes way'. Then he said 'I bet you two-hundred dollars he's not gay'."

I stared at her. Then at my mom and my sister. But Kat

stood up, walked over to me kissed my cheek and told me softly, "It's so good to see you happy. And about time."

I finally breathed. Trent wiggled his fingers in my hand, and I realized the vice-like grip I had on his hand was probably a little too tight. But I couldn't let go of him completely. So I just loosened my grip a little.

Then my mom pulled me out of my chair to hug me. I hugged her with one arm. Now everyone saw I was still holding Trent's hand before I dropped it to really hug my mom. Mom kissed one cheek, then the other and she wiped tears from her own. "Oh, Nathan," she said, smiling. She hugged me again and whispered, so only I could hear, "I'm so proud of you."

I nodded, numbly, and she let me go. I still didn't have time to fully register what I'd just unloaded on them before Alana hugged me. "About time, Nathan," was all she said.

I looked at her, stunned. She smiled and shook her head, knowingly. "You knew?" I asked her.

"We all... *wondered*," she said softly. Then she shrugged, "Well, not Brendan. But he's an idiot."

I looked at my brother then, and he was now in a state of disbelief. I slowly sat back in my chair and reached blindly for Trent's hand. I deliberately didn't look at my father.

After the longest time, Brendan finally closed his mouth. Then he opened it again. "But you've been with women," he said.

I snorted. "And it was..." I tried to think of the right word, "wrong." Then I looked at the three women at the table and cringed. "Sorry."

They smiled at me and at Trent. I looked at him then, and he looked at me in wonder, like he couldn't believe what I'd just done.

Then a scrunched up napkin hit me in the face. Brendan. He looked to the leather strand around my neck. "So, you gonna join some gay, hippy commune and hug trees and shit?" he said.

I scrunched up my napkin and threw it back at him. "Don't know, Brendan. Can you tell the difference between boy and girl trees?"

Trent chuckled quietly beside me and squeezed my hand, relieved. Brendan grinned at me. I smiled at him, and I knew we were good.

"So..." Brendan trailed off suggestively, still smiling, looked pointedly between Trent and I. "You two...are...what?"

"Together," I answered. I looked at Trent and smiled, and it felt like my chest might burst. "Trent and I are together."

There were more smiles, and I felt my father's eyes on me. Everyone at the table glanced periodically at him, then at me, as though they were waiting to see which one of us would speak to the other first.

My mom stood up, cleared the coffee cups and looked at the man beside me. "Trent dear, could you help me with these?" she asked. It was a clear, and not very subtle, excuse to give me some alone time with my dad.

Trent looked at me and squeezed my hand, regardless of who could hear, he asked, "Are you okay?"

I nodded and gave him a small smile.

"I'll just be inside," he told me. Then he whispered, "I'm so proud of you."

I looked down at our joined hands, marveling at his long fingers in mine. He stood up, pulled his hand away, picked up some uneaten food from brunch and walked inside. Kat,

Brendan and Alana walked down toward the bay, giving us some space.

Bentley started to follow them, but I called him back. "Stay here with me, buddy," I said to him, and scratched him behind his ear. I still hadn't made eye contact with my dad.

"Nathan," he said quietly. "Can you look at me, please?"

I exhaled slowly and dragged my eyes to his. He looked concerned and sad, and I really had no idea what he was about to say.

"Bentley looks like he was banged up pretty badly" he said.

"The vet was closed, and I wasn't about to let him die," I said defensively.

"Nathan—" he started again, but I cut him off.

My voice was just a whisper. "I love him, Dad. I love him." And he knew I wasn't talking about Bentley. "For the first time ever, I know what *life* feels like." It was then I realized I was crying. I scrubbed my hands at the stupid tears.

Dad was quiet for a moment. "Nathan, for years we watched you study and work, study and work," he said, looking down at the others near the water. "It was all you did. Don't get me wrong, Nathan, your mother and I are both extremely proud of what you've achieved. But it's hard to watch your child struggle with happiness. It's one of the most difficult things, knowing your son is so unhappy." He looked at me then. "And you were, Nathan. We all saw it."

I looked back down at Bentley, who was now resting his head on my thigh as I patted him. "I've never been happy," I mumbled, looking back at my dad. "Never."

Then dad smiled. "Until now."

I let out a shaky breath. "Until now."

"Nathan, a blind man would be able to see how happy Trent makes you," my dad said with a smile.

Surely he could see the scepticism in my eyes. "It doesn't bother you? That I'm gay?"

He smiled again and shook his head no. "That boy has brought you back to life. I don't care if you're gay, straight or whatever else you're into, Nathan. Just as long as you're happy."

I looked at him and fresh tears fell down my face. "Thank you," I told him, and he pulled me in for a hug, which was kind of silly and awkward, because we were both still sitting down. But he managed it.

"Just promise me you'll stay safe and healthy," the doctor in my father said.

I understood his concern. He was a doctor worried for his son. I nodded. "Of course, Dad. Always."

"Now, tell me," he said, using his loud Doctor Tierney, Senior voice. "What's this about you treating a dog in a hospital?"

Wiping my face, I chuckled softly and told him. Everything. I told him a little about Trent's history, his parent's death, how he had been alone and scared of heartbreak. I told him how Trent tried to leave me, how he barely got a hundred miles from me before he couldn't go any further. How he came back, how Bentley was hurt, how Trent begged me to fix him, I told him everything.

Brendan, Kat and Alana wandered back up to the house, but didn't interrupt us.

I told Dad why the veterinary clinic was closed until next week, about the kids in Searsport, about Dani, Adam and Steve.

"Steve's the Chief of Police," I told him. "He was the one who stood guard at the door while I treated Bentley so no one else would see."

Dad laughed and shook his head at the thought. He sighed, "You really love it here."

"I do," I answered him honestly. "My work feels more *appreciated* here," I told him. Maybe that wasn't the right word, but I didn't change it. "It's only been four weeks, I know, and maybe it'll drive me mad in twelve months, but for now, I love it."

He smiled at me, with amazement and pride in his eyes. "I'm so glad to hear it, Son."

"I know I've only known Trent for four weeks," I admitted. "But Dad... I think he's it for me. Nothing in my life has ever felt so *right*."

My father smiled and nodded, knowingly. "The moment I met your mother, it was the same for me." He shrugged. "Sometimes it's just the way it works."

I looked back inside the house, wondering why it was so quiet in there, and dad laughed. "Yes, go save him. Lord only knows what your mother's roped him into doing."

I laughed and nodded, because it was probably true. But when I walked through the kitchen and into the living room, I found the reason for their silence. They were all in there, staring at a painting.

One of Trent's paintings.

One I hadn't seen before. It was big, rectangular and now hanging on the living room wall. Kat said quietly, "Your mom saw the paintings on the floor in the corner, and wanted to see them."

Trent looked at me, he looked so scared and nervous. And I wished Mom had just minded her own business and not gotten into his personal things. He was so private with his paintings.

I was quickly by his side and put my hand on his back. "I'm sorry," I told him quietly.

But then Mom turned to face me, and she had tears in her eyes.

Alarmed, I looked at the painting, tried to see what she saw. Large, textured, feather-looking leaves of spicy browns, burnt oranges, shades of hazel and alabaster. They were falling, or flying, overlapping, swirling, different sizes, shapes, textures, and there was one red leaf in the top corner.

"It looks like the forest in fall," Alana said.

And it did. It was very beautiful.

Then Alana stepped closer and read something in the bottom corner. "Learning to Fell," she said out loud.

"Um, it's Learning to Feel," Trent said quietly. "The e kinda looks like an l."

My mom stepped in front of Trent and with tears in her eyes, she kissed his cheek. "Thank you, Trent. It's beautiful."

Trent bowed his head and smiled shyly.

Mom must have seen the confusion on my face, because she hugged me again and whispered to me, "It's you, Nathan. It's all the colors of you."

My mouth fell open. I stared at Trent, then at the painting then back at Trent. "Me? It's of me?"

He looked at the floor, but he nodded. And when he finally did look up at me, his eyes showed his vulnerability.

Still staring at the painting, Brendan cocked his head to the side. "That's not Nathan." And Kat whacked his arm, shushing him to be quiet.

Trent smiled, and his voice was barely a whisper. "It's the painting I've been working on for almost four weeks. The house painting has been done for two weeks, so I've had the time."

Me. It was of me. He had been painting me, the colors of me, almost since the day I got here. He struggled with expressing emotion, but he gave me a part of himself, he said so much in every brushstroke. I quickly wrapped my arms around his waist and pulled him against me. I didn't care that my family was right there.

"Wait. What?" I asked. "The house paintings been done for two weeks?"

He smiled at me. "Told you I couldn't leave."

I laughed. "Is that really me?" I asked, looking back at the painted canvas before us. He nodded.

I talked into his hair. "You have to teach me how to read your work."

He laughed against me, and I noticed my mother had dragged everyone out of the room. Kat stopped by the door and muttered, "Oh, I'm happy to watch." Brendan's jaw almost hit the floor, and he pulled her by the elbow into the kitchen.

I chuckled and pressed my lips against his forehead. "I can't believe you painted me." I held his face and kissed him, sweetly but soundly. "It tells me things you can't say."

His breathing hitched, but he nodded. I knew he loved me. It was there in front of me, on canvas, in browns and hazel. It wasn't in words, it was in thousands of brushstrokes. In all the colors of me, without words, he told me he loved me.

"Trent," I whispered in his ear. "I love you, too."

CHAPTER TWENTY-TWO

I SAT CURLED up on the futon-like chair with a book, a blanket and Bentley enjoying the rare sunshine streaming through the attic windows.

Trent was painting, and Bentley and I were *not* disturbing him. We didn't always join him up here, but some days, particularly on my weekends off when we stayed in Belfast, if he got the urge to paint, sometimes it could be the only way I got to see him.

When his muse lured him, encouraged him, I swear sometimes he could paint for days. And he was beautiful when he painted. He got so lost in what he was doing, he didn't even notice us up there with him. I could have watched him forever. His concentration, the way his eyebrows pinched and his lips pursed and how his hands fluttered with the brush, barely containing his creativity.

But I didn't speak to him when he painted. I just liked to be near him. So I sat up there, cozied up with Bentley on the futon, stroking the fur on his neck while he snoozed at my thigh.

And admittedly, it was one of my favourite things in the world to do.

Sometimes I read, sometimes I just enjoyed the silence and sometimes I dozed. Sometimes Trent would have his iPod playing, sometimes he wouldn't. Today, there was no music, and I found my eyelids starting to close.

I woke with a start when Trent's phone rang. So did Bentley, he jumped off the sofa and shook himself awake, while Trent spoke quietly into his phone. He walked to the dormer window and looked out across the vast forest.

"Um, when?" he said.

"Okay. Yeah, that's fine," he told whoever was on the other line. "Sure. I'll see you then."

"My pleasure," he added, before he clicked off the call. He turned to face me, all wide-eyed and a little shocked.

"Trent, are you okay?"

He nodded slowly. His voice was quiet. "Um, that was the East Gallery. They said yes."

I crossed the attic floor quickly and hugged him. "Of course they said yes, Love."

"Actually, they said they'd be honored," he mumbled into my neck.

Laughing, I pulled him back so I could see his face. "Because you're fucking talented."

He looked at the paintings scattered around us and swallowed, trying to take some deep breaths.

I held his face. "Trent, deep breaths, baby," I said, unable to stop smiling. After he'd inhaled a few times, I told him, "You deserve this. You've worked so hard."

"Do you think they'll like it?" he asked quietly.

I shook my head no. "They will love it."

"Oh, my God," he murmured. "Nathan, they said yes."

I pulled him against me, kissing wherever my lips could reach. "I'm so proud of you. I knew you could do it."

"I couldn't have done it without you," he said into my shirt.

He held me tightly, but he was almost bouncing with excitement. When he peeled himself away from me, he flipped open his phone. "There's someone we *have* to call."

I smiled at him. He grinned from ear to ear as he searched through his contacts. He looked at me, waiting for the call to connect. "I love you," he whispered to me.

But then I heard the soft click from the phone and a familiar voice answered, "Hello?"

"Julia," Trent said with a laugh. "You'll never guess who just called me."

Smiling, I remembered back to the first time he told me he loved me. He didn't even know he'd said it. It had been two months since he'd tried to leave me, since Bentley's accident, since I came out. It was a normal morning, I'd taken Bentley for a walk, I was still hesitant to stress his healing leg, and when we came back to the house, I made us our usual breakfast.

Trent, sleep rumpled and fucking gorgeous, walked into the kitchen just as I was putting strawberry jam onto Bentley's toast. He stopped and gave me one raised eyebrow. Guilty, I explained, "He likes the strawberry jam." Then I rambled, "Just after his accident, I felt bad for not taking him for a run, so I thought I'd offer him some toast with jam as a treat, and now he kind of won't eat toast without it... " my words trailed away, knowing I was probably only digging myself in further.

Trent shook his head at me as he made himself coffee. "You spoil him too much."

"He doesn't mind?" I said, my tone making it a question.

"You're fucking lucky *I* love you so much, but Brendan will kill you if Bentley ends up with diabetes." Then he shook his head again and sipped his coffee.

Now, he'd never been able to say those words out loud, but I knew he loved me. It was in everything he did. It was in his paintings, it was in the little things, like the way he'd cook dinner and leave it for when I got home from work. It was in the way he kissed me, in his eyes, in the way he made love to me.

But to hear him say it...

My heart pounded against my ribs, and I stood slowly from my seat next to Bentley. Trent looked at me, still not realizing what he'd just said. "What?" he asked.

"What did you just say?" I asked him to repeat it.

"I said, 'Brendan will kill you if the dog gets diabetes'," he said again like he was talking to a two year old.

"No, not that," I said quietly, now standing in front of him. "The part before that."

He looked at me, and I saw it in his eyes the moment he remembered his own words. His eyes went wide, and his mouth opened and closed.

I nodded and smiled and took his face in my hands. "I am fucking lucky you love me," I told him. He nodded and chuckled, his eyes filled with tears. "You're fucking lucky I love you too," I said with a laugh. Then I pulled his face to mine and kissed him. His lips trembled, but he kissed me back before he started to laugh.

So I hugged him and held him as tight as I could, until he pulled away from me to wipe his tears. Happy tears. He still hadn't said anything about his declaration, he'd only laughed and smiled, but I told him, "I love you too, Trent Jamieson."

I'd never seen him smile like that.

He'd come a long way over the last twelve months. We talked about him going into therapy for his issues, but he said he'd been-there-done-that, and would prefer to just talk to me. Admittedly, I was hesitant, wondering if he'd be telling me things I didn't want to hear. Even my father had his doubts and told us to tread carefully.

But it turned out it was the best thing for us.

He slowly opened up to me, his fears, his dreams, his past and what he wanted for his future. He told me about his parents and how his aunt and uncle, rather than dealing with a grieving teenager, had put him into therapy. It was *that* therapist who had encouraged the young, closed-off sixteen year old Trent, to use his art as his emotional vent.

It worked. He'd successfully only expressed any kind of emotion through his paintings.

Until he met me.

His painting had taken on a whole new dimension in the last twelve months. The more he opened old wounds, the more he honed his craft. The more he told me he loved me, the more he basked in being loved, the more poignant his art became.

Which was why the works of Trent Jamieson had been signed for an exhibition in the small, but prestigious East Gallery.

He clicked off the phone call to my mom and threw his arms around me. Then, taking my hand, he pulled me down the narrow attic stairs. "Come on, we've got unscheduled trips to Boston to plan."

CHAPTER TWENTY-THREE

WITH NO FOREST trails to go on, I took Bentley for a morning walk along the Boston sidewalk instead. Knowing Trent would like some, I grabbed some coffees and muffins for breakfast on our way home. I swear Trent had a nose for caffeine because he magically appeared in the kitchen one second after I walked in.

He took the coffee immediately from the coffee carrier and hummed as he tasted it. "God bless the coffee bean."

"Yeah," I laughed. "And the boyfriend who brings it to you."

He grinned. "Oh, yes. Him too."

As we ate our breakfast, we talked about our plans for the day. Trent needed to meet with the director of East Gallery. The opening was tonight, and after previous meetings last week, phone calls, emails and weeks of preparation, this was the final meeting before the big night.

I wanted to head in to see my old boss at Mass General. When I left, he asked me, unofficially, to come back and see him in twelve months, and he'd give me my job back, no questions asked.

I was going back to see him. To say thanks, but no thanks.

I signed on for another twelve months at Belfast.

Mom and Dad were so pleased with my decision. Actually, my entire family was. They loved having a weekend getaway if needed, and with my roster giving me four days off every two weeks, Trent and I usually spent every second one in Boston. We'd hit the clubs, restaurants, markets and movies.

The other days off were usually spent in Belfast. We'd made some great friends there, Dani, Adam, Lucas and Carla, the nurse who had helped me with an injured Bentley was Dani's best friend. We'd have barbeques and watch football or hockey.

Life was pretty fucking good.

And my mom basically told me if I ever planned to come back to Boston, Mass General ER and run myself into the ground and stop living again, she'd wring my neck.

Trent and Mom have grown incredibly close this last year. As thick as thieves they were. It was beautiful. It was actually my mom who had introduced the director of the gallery to pictures of Trent's work.

Trent had argued that the director felt obligated to see his paintings because Julia could be so insistent. But then the director had dismissed Trent's concerns with a click of her tongue and a simple, "Connections can only get you so far. Don't insult my eye for talent. I know talent when I see it, and you my dear boy, have a gift."

Trent didn't argue after that.

He did, however, say 'no' to showing his collection of paintings inspired by me. The one he'd painted twelve months ago, of the falling leaves in all the colors of me, and the paintings that followed, he wouldn't show. He told me later he didn't want people to tell him it was no good, he couldn't handle anyone telling him what he felt for me wasn't good enough.

He said they could show the "Two Sevens" collection he'd be working on. It was actually two groups of seven, fourteen paintings altogether.

The Seven Sins in true Trent style, color and texture, swirls and lines, some defined and some not, all a different color, infused with gold or silver. Seven representing sins, and seven opposing sins: Lust, Gluttony, Greed, Sloth, Wrath, Envy and... and... ugh fuck. Godammit, I could never remember the seventh one. I yelled out to Trent, who was getting dressed up stairs. "What's the seventh one called again?"

"Sneezy? Clumsy?" he yelled back. I rolled my eyes, even though he couldn't see. "No wait, it was Dopey!"

"Shut the fuck up," I said flatly. "Clumsy was a Smurf anyway, smartass."

He laughed, and I tried not to smile. "Pride," he answered, and as soon as he said it, it was like a lightning bolt of recognition. Yes, that was it! Pride.

Anyway, the fourteen new paintings, they loved.

So a week ago, he'd had his paintings transported to Boston. He was nervous and even wanted to drive them himself. But from my cell phone at work, I had convinced him that I was fairly certain the director of East Gallery wouldn't appreciate her next exhibit arriving in the back of a Chevy.

He walked down the stairs, dressed in jeans and a vintage tee. Casual and sexy as hell. Sweet Jesus, he still took my breath away.

I couldn't help but smile. "You will knock them dead tonight."

He exhaled nervously. "You sure?"

I smiled at him. He'd asked me this a thousand times. Kissing his lips, I told him, "They'll love your work, and they'll love you."

A car honked its horn outside, and we both knew without looking who it was. Mom. I asked him, also the thousandth time, "Are you sure you don't want me to go with you today?"

He shook his head. "No, you'll only distract me," he said. "Plus, I want you to see it for the first time tonight." And with a peck to my lips, he ran out the door to my mother's waiting car.

I fixed Bentley some dry food and checked his water, then gave him a good rub on the belly. We had a dog door installed—actually *I* had dog doors put in at this apartment and in the house at Belfast. The wake up calls for breakfast I could handle. The wake up calls for pit-stops got a bit tedious. So when I left him inside, closing the front door behind me, I knew he'd be alright.

I called in to see my old boss like I'd planned. He was happy to see me, he thought I was there to ask for my job back. After seeing the madhouse that was the ER, the understaffed, overworked medical teams that darted from patient to patient, I could only smile when I told him no.

No way in fucking hell was I coming back to this.

He laughed and told me I'd gone soft.

"Maybe," I told him.

"Or you've fallen in love," he said, raising his eyebrows.

"Or there is that," I said, grinning.

"Well, I'll be fucking damned," he snorted. With perfect timing, his pager beeped and he shook my hand, smiled and called out, "Good luck, Tierney," as he ran off down the hall.

I walked down the corridor, once so very familiar to me,

toward the exit. It used to be like my second home. It felt alien now, foreign. I used to run these corridors, I owned them. Well, I thought I did. Some faces I recognized, most I didn't. One thing that was familiar was how completely stressed and tired everyone looked.

I didn't remember thinking I ever looked that bad.

I must have looked like death warmed over.

I smiled as I left. I wondered if coming here would spark a buried desire to come back, but it only reinforced my decision to stay in Belfast. No Belfast didn't have the prestige, the money or the reputation my old job had.

But I couldn't care less. I wouldn't trade it. I had a life in Belfast. A job that I loved, people I had come to know, good friends. I had the big old house that I loved, the Bay, the running and walking trails.

But most of all, I had Trent.

The last twelve months haven't been all sunshine and roses. He had habits that drove me mad, leaving his clothes on the floor, and don't even get me started about leaving wet towels on the bed.

I have traits that annoyed him too, but we're learning. We've had our disagreements. The biggest one by far was about money. The big fights usually were, or so I was told.

He mentioned looking for work, and I told him not to worry about it, to concentrate on his painting. I thought he'd like that idea, and he thought I thought he was sponging off me. He yelled. I yelled back. He grabbed his keys, and I told him not to *dare* fucking leave. He stormed out, revved the Chevy far too loudly and took off down the drive.

He only got about a hundred yards before his brake lights came on. He stopped half way down the drive and sat in his car for a minute or two before reversing back down the drive.

He walked quietly back inside. "I'm sorry," he whispered. "I told you I'd never leave."

I hugged him fiercely. "Yes, you did," I reminded him, kissing the side of his neck. "I don't give a fuck about money, Trent. None of that matters to me. But you," I held his face and looked him in the eyes, "you matter to me."

And then we sat on the couch and talked it out like adults.

Yeah. Imagine that.

Like I said, we were learning.

After my visit to the hospital, I headed back to the apartment and took Bentley down to Mrs. Lin's to pick up some takeout for lunch. "Where's Mr. Trent?" she asked me.

"Big opening at the gallery tonight," I reminded her. Trent had come to Boston a few times in the last few weeks and had eaten here, when he wasn't fed by my mother. "I'll grab enough for two, though. He'll be home soon."

She smiled and threw in some wagashi. "Mr. Trent always like my wagashi."

I smiled and nodded. Of course he did. How very typical of Trent to have charmed his way into Mrs. Lin's good-books and she'd give him free sweets.

"You tell him good luck," she added. I paid, thanked her again and Bentley and I walked home.

When Mom dropped Trent home two hours later, he was nervous.

"How'd it go?" I asked him, standing up and walking toward him.

"All done," he said. "No going back now."

I WAS SHOWERED, dressed and ready, and Trent was

still in the bathroom. I knocked on the door. "Babe, we have to leave here in 20 minutes."

He mumbled an inaudible response.

"Can I come in, Trent?"

"Yeah," he huffed.

I opened the door, and he was wearing only a towel around his waist, fiddling with his hair. "I can't get it to sit right," he told me.

Pulling his hand from his hair, I took his hand in mine. "Trent, it's perfect."

He pulled his hand away and tried to tame a wayward curl, mumbling something about getting a buzz cut.

I took his hands in mine again and stood in front of him. "Trent, stop." He stared at me for a moment. I smiled and told him, "Let me."

I took the shaving cream and lathered it in my hand. His eyes widened. "I was only joking about shaving my head," he said with a laugh.

I rubbed the cream along his jaw. "I know, baby." When I had the cream lathered on his skin, I ran some hot water and picked up his razor.

Slowly, carefully, I shaved him. With medical precision, I placed the blades against his skin and gently drew the razor downwards. He didn't speak. He just lifted his chin for me when I needed, turned his head left, then right, and straightened out his dimple and bottom lip so the razor glided smoothly along his skin. His eyes never left mine. He watched the concentration on my face, in my eyes, as I took my time, savored the moment, and ensured his skin was flawless.

When I was done, I dabbed his skin with the towel. He looked up at me, and his eyes were clear and humbled. "Thank you," he said softly.

"Anytime." I took his hand and lead him to the bedroom, where his clothes were laid out on the bed.

He got dressed while I sorted out dinner for Bentley, and when he walked down the stairs, he literally stole my breath.

He was so fucking beautiful.

Charcoal grey pants, crisp white shirt, black vest and tie and Italian leather shoes. *My* Italian leather shoes. I looked from the shoes to his face, and he shrugged.

"'They go with the pants," he said with a smile.

I smiled. "You look... beautiful."

"Not too shabby yourself, Doctor."

I smiled at him. "Are you ready?"

He took a deep breath and exhaled through puffed out cheeks, then he nodded.

When we got to the East Gallery, we found Mom and Dad talking to a tall, striking woman who was introduced to me as the Director, Carmen. She smiled magnificently at me then whisked Trent away.

Mom and Dad were excited and nervous, more-so I think, than they were at my graduation, or Brendan's. Mom was just about beside herself.

Brendan, Kat and Alana arrived shortly after, and the gallery foyer started to fill with people. East Gallery was known to show artists who went on to become the next big thing, so the people who were here came armed with check books and high expectations.

Some of my Bostonian friends were here tonight to support Trent, the ones who were fine with my being gay. A few other friends said they were fine, but over time had faded away. And that was okay.

When Dani, Adam, Lucas and Carla arrived, Trent was so humbled. I thanked them for making the trip, and they all agreed they wouldn't have missed it for the world. I think it shocked Trent to see how many people turned out in support of him.

When Carmen called for everyone's attention, silence and anticipation filled the room. Trent stood beside her as she ran through her spiel about her gallery and the new and exciting works of one Mr. Trent Jamieson. She opened the rope barricade, and when the lights came on in the main viewing room, people wasted no time in walking through.

I'd seen these paintings before a thousand times, I'd lived with them. But to see them displayed with expert lighting and name plaques, artfully spaced and perfect, was something else entirely.

Vices and Virtues.

The seven vices, Lust, Gluttony, Greed, Sloth, Wrath, Envy and Pride.

The seven virtues, Chastity, Temperance, Charity, Diligence, Patience, Kindness and Humility.

To say people were amazed was an understatement. People nodded, smiled, gasped and stared.

The room was large, rectangular in shape. Seven Vices lined one wall, Seven Virtues the other. They faced off against their opposite. They aligned perfectly, the lighting complimented the art like it too was a part of the artist's work.

The effect was striking.

There was an open door to another room, which I could see some people going into, and I presumed it led to the rest of the gallery. As I got to the door to see what all the fuss was about, my mom grabbed me. "They're talking big things for him, Nathan. I'm so proud of him," she gushed.

"Me too," I told her. "He's come so far."

I looked toward the door where people continued to

walk through. "What's in there?" I asked. "I didn't think the rest of the Gallery would be open."

"Oh," she said distractedly. She looked around the room, grabbed Trent's eye, and he excused himself from the conversation he was in and walked over to us.

He was smiling brilliantly, and he exhaled loudly, relieved, when he got over to us. "It all seems positive," he said.

"Oh, Trent," I grinned at him. "They love it."

He nodded and looked around at the guests who were admiring his work.

I looked pointedly at the other room. "What's in there?" I asked him.

His eyes widened, just a fraction, and his smile faded. "Um, Nathan... I was going to tell you, but I wanted it to be a surprise... " he trailed off. Well, now my curiosity was more than piqued. I stepped toward the mystery room, but he grabbed my hand. "Wait. I want to show it to you."

He pulled me toward the door and told me to close my eyes. Carefully leading me inside, I could tell even with my eyes closed the lighting was darker. "Here," he said, when we'd reached some magic spot. "Now, open your eyes."

So I did.

And on the wall before me was the painting he made for me. The one of falling leaves, in all the colors of me, was there in a room all by itself. The room was dark, except for a spotlight emphasizing the canvas on the wall. It looked... it looked... fucking spectacular.

"It's here for you," he said quietly beside me.

I looked from the painting, to him. "Trent... "

He was quick to explain. "I told Carmen she could show it. But not for long, and it's not for sale. I know I said I didn't want to show any of my work that involved you. But I wanted to do this *for* you. I wanted to show you... "

"Trent," I said in a whisper, and he stopped talking. I looked at him. "You're amazing."

He smiled hugely. "You like it?"

I nodded. "I love it."

My mom and Carmen came up beside us and were all knowing smiles. I asked my mom, "You knew this would be here?"

She nodded. Then I looked at Trent, "How did I *not* know about this?"

He answered sheepishly. "I knew you were working a double shift for the two days it would be gone, and I hoped like Hell you wouldn't notice it wasn't there."

Then Carmen looked from me to the painting and then back to me when she said, "Yes, I can see the resemblance."

I felt myself blush, and I hoped the dimmed lighting hid it, but I seriously doubted it. Trent chuckled beside me and slipped his hand into mine.

"Oh, don't be shy," Carmen said flamboyantly. "If someone as talented as Trent were to paint a piece dedicated to me, I'd be shouting it from the rooftops. Especially one that shows such pure emotion, the falling leaves, the changing of seasons, the promise of new growth," she sighed dramatically. "Learning to Feel, indeed."

My heart pounded and was so full of love, it should have hurt. I swallowed and Trent squeezed my hand. But I couldn't talk, so I nodded.

Then my mom fanned her hands in front of her face, trying to dry her eyes. "You're going to make me cry," she said, and I knew exactly how she felt.

But then my dad walked up to us with two flutes of champagne and handed one to me and the other to Mom. It distracted me long enough to inhale deeply and collect myself. Carmen dragged Trent away to mingle with some VIP's. After that the night seemed to fly.

When our friends from Belfast bid us farewell, they hugged Trent then me, wasting no time in telling us how blown away they were with his work. They were proud of him, and their words meant so much to him. When they said goodbye, Trent squeezed my hand tighter. I guessed honest friendships were something he had come to value, something he'd never really known.

By the time the last of the other guests left, I'd had four or five champagnes and was cheerfully trying to convince Kat and Brendan to come out with us. "The night's not over," I told them. "You have to come out with us. There's much celebration to be had."

"Where are you going?" Brendan asked, dubiously.

"Um, a bar on Fifth Street," I explained vaguely. "I can't remember what it's called." I was lying, but I didn't think he could tell. "Kat can come with us. We're walking there, it's only two blocks away. You can drop Mom, Dad and Alana at home and meet us there."

"I'm not leaving my wife alone in some bar, Nathan," he huffed at me.

I grinned. "She'll be perfectly safe, I promise."

He looked at me for too long. "It's a gay bar, isn't it?"

I grinned and nodded, and Kat laughed. "Yay!" she cheered.

The look on my brother's face was so funny, I laughed so hard my sides hurt.

WALKING into the bar was comical. It was late on a

Saturday night, so the place was packed, full of thumping music, and moving men. We made a bee-line for the bar, and instantly got noticed. In our formal wear, we were very overdressed, and Trent did look particularly fucking hot. Some of the other men openly stared at us.

Well, I thought to myself, we did bring a *woman*.

I snorted with laughter, Trent shook his head at me and went to the bar. Kat looked around at all the men like a kid in a candy store. I laughed again, "Excellent, right?"

She smiled and nodded as Trent brought us our drinks.

Ooooooh, green drinks.

My favorite.

"How many drinks have you had?" he asked teasingly.

"Nowhere near enough," I declared. Holding out my drink, I clinked glasses with them. "To the most spectacular artist in Boston."

Kat lifted her glass high. "Here! Here!"

Trent rolled his eyes.

When Kat tasted her drink, she crinkled her nose. I laughed and told her the first couple were a bit sweet, but by the third or fourth one, they tasted just fine.

"And how do they taste after five champagnes?" Trent asked me, grinning.

I took a long sip, nearly emptying my glass. "Like water."

They laughed at me. I looked at them expectantly and said, "Come on, slow pokes. I wanna dance."

Kat thought I was funny. Trent cocked his head to the side. "You've never complained about my slow pokes before," he said, and Kat choked on her drink. I think she may have tried to swallow her straw.

When she had recovered, I picked the straw out of her glass and threw it away. "Drink it down, Miss Katrina. I won't tell Brendan you swallow."

Trent's mouth fell open, and Kat roared with laughter. "Oh my God, Nathan," she said through her giggles. "You should totally drink more often."

"No. He shouldn't," Trent said with a smile.

I pouted, and he chuckled.

I waited until they finished their drinks and led the way to the dance floor. I didn't know how many songs we danced for, but before I knew it, I noticed Brendan arrive.

He tried to look really cool and calm amidst a sea of grinding men, but he really just looked petrified.

He scouted the bar for us, and when he saw his wife dancing, with her arms up above her head, swaying and laughing, his eyes popped.

It was the funniest thing I'd seen all night.

He glared at me for laughing, and grabbing both Trent and Kat's hands, I led us over to him.

"Drink?" I asked him.

He nodded, and I made my way to the bar, leaving him with Kat and Trent. I ordered specific drinks and told the barman to watch my brother's face.

I carried the tray back to our table, chuckling to myself. "Jesus! How many people did you order for?" Brendan cried.

"Here," I said, handing him a shot glass. "This is for you, courtesy of the barman. I think he likes you."

Brendan spun around, and the barman who was looking played along, and gave him a small wave. Brendan's eyes widened, but he smiled, kind of, and he looked back to us. He held the shot glass to his lips and asked, "What type of drink did he give me?"

"A blow job," I deadpanned, and Brendan nearly swallowed the shot glass.

I burst out laughing, and so did the guy behind the bar.

Trent chuckled beside me, and Kat was doubled over laughing. Oh fuck, I amazed myself sometimes how funny I am.

"That. Was. So. Fuh. Nee," I spat out, between bursts of laughter.

Ignoring Brendan's death stare, I composed myself and handed out the other shot glasses. "My personal favorite," I declared.

"Do we even want to know?" Kat asked.

"Probably not," I admitted, but then told them anyway. "These are Cock Sucking Cowboys."

Trent laughed this time, but I was pretty sure he was laughing at Brendan's expression.

I explained to Kat, "Well, there's no such drink called a 'Sexy-as-fuck-Texan-artist' so these had to do." I held my glass up to hers, and we knocked them back together.

"Oh, good Lord," Brendan said, mortified. He asked Trent, "Is he always like this when he drinks?"

Trent grinned and nodded. "Wait until he gets all handsy and tells everyone he loves them."

I rolled my eyes at them and reminded Trent, "You've never complained about me being all handsy before."

Brendan finished his beer and put his hands up. "Whoa. No. Stop. There's certain shit a brother does not need to hear."

Trent laughed and downed his shot.

He was so Goddamn sexy in his tie and vest. He was so good tonight. As nervous as he was, he fucking put himself out there. I was so proud of him. "I'm so proud of you," I told him. "You were amazing tonight."

He smiled at me. The kind of genuine smile that made my heart thump. I kissed him, right on the lips, slid one hand down to his ass and handed him another drink with my other hand.

"Where's your drink?" he asked.

"Oh, I might have had enough for now," I told him. Actually, I'd probably had enough about three drinks ago. "I want to dance."

Trent leaned in close to my ear. "You'll have to take your hand off my ass if you want to dance."

No fucking way.

I took the drink out of his hand and keeping my other hand firmly wedged inside his back pocket, I pushed us out to the dance floor. "Mm mm," I shook my head at him. "Your ass is mine."

He groaned, and as we started to sway to the music, he ran his hand up my chest. He pulled at my tie, loosened it, allowing my shirt to open, just a bit. I think Kat and Brendan joined us on the dance floor at some point, but I was so lost in my boy, I couldn't be too certain.

Our hips were locked together, one of my legs was between his, one hand still on his ass and the other under his vest, on the small of his back. His hands were on my waist, my ribs and my back. Our cheeks were pressed together, so when I talked to him, he could hear.

"Trrrrreeeeent," I whispered, and I felt his cheek round off in a smile. "Have I told you how proud I am of you?"

He moaned his yes and nodded a little.

The display of his painting of me in the private room was the most amazing declaration. "Have I told you I love you?"

He kissed the spot near my ear and hummed.

"You're so talented," I told him. "With a paint brush, with your hands, with your mouth."

His head fell back, and I felt his chest vibrate as he groaned.

I licked along his Adam's apple up to his ear. "And what you can do with your cock——"

His hands roughly pulled my face to his, and he kissed me, fucking hard. The rest of my words died in my throat.

He kissed me until I needed air, and then he kissed me some more.

God only knows how many songs we danced and kissed to. Kat and Brendan told us goodnight, and Brendan added, "Get a fucking room. I need to have my retina's bleached with the shit I've seen you two do tonight."

Trent smiled against my lips. I mumbled, "Fuck off, Brendan."

Trent continued to kiss me as our hips pressed against each other, we swayed, grinding, dry humping, and it was getting pretty fucking serious on the dance floor. We were dancing ourselves sober.

Until his lips stilled against mine and my eyes opened and found him looking at me. It was a different look in his eyes.

"Trent? What's wrong?"

He didn't answer me for a moment. He leaned in and whispered in my ear, "Nathan, I want to go home."

It was a little odd, but I nodded. "Sure. Are you okay?"

His hands encased my face, and he stared into my eyes. "Nathan, I have a surprise for you," he said. His lips brushed against mine as he spoke. The tone of his voice, the secrecy... made me shiver.

Oh.

Fuck.

I didn't like surprises. Really, I didn't. Even though I had a feeling this one was different.

Even in the cab ride home, as much as I begged him, he wouldn't tell me. Not even a clue.

So then I tried pouting.

And even some sulking. He was so fucking stubborn.

Unlocking the door to my Boston apartment, Bentley greeted us at the door. I grumbled to Trent, "I fucking hate surprises. You know that."

"Believe me, baby, you're gonna love this one," he said with a chuckle, his eyes were bright and dancing. "I've had it for a little while, but wanted to surprise you with it tonight, after the Exhibition."

"Why couldn't you have given it to me when you first got it, in Belfast?" I was still grumbling, as he pulled me up the stairs and into our room.

"Because it'll be better to use with this headboard," he said, his eyes flickered to the solid wooden headboard.

"What? The headboard?"

Grinning, he pulled a brown paper wrapped rectangular box out of the dresser drawer and handed it to me. "Open."

I was curious, and a little bit scared, but I did as I was told. "A flashlight?"

"Not quite," he chuckled as he started undoing his shirt. "I've fantasized about this, Nathan."

I looked again at the box in my hand. It wasn't a flash light. It was a Fleshjack.

Fuck.

Literally.

I swallowed thickly and looked up at Trent. He was unbuttoning his suit pants now, grinning like the devil.

"I ordered it online," he explained, letting his pants fall to the floor. "I picked it up a couple of days ago, but thought it could wait until after the exhibition opening." He took it from me then took it out of the box. "Plus, this bed has a headboard."

I was out of my clothes before he could blink.

Trent stood before me, naked and hard, smirking. "I can't wait to show you this. I've been dreaming of what this will be like."

I'd seen Fleshjacks used in porn. This one was the ass model, the hole a cock slides into was shaped like a perfect ass. I throbbed at the mere thought of what he'd been fantasizing about. He must have read my face, because he stepped right up to me and his voice was husky, pure sex. "I'm going to fuck you, while you fuck this."

My entire body reacted, I shivered and convulsed, my cock twitched and my nipples hardened. Fuck. My boy knew what to say, what to do, how to make me putty in his hands.

Trent and I had done a lot of things over the last twelve months. A *lot* of things, countless different positions, a few sex toys, porn, you name it. We'd both learned things I never dreamed possible.

I'd even topped him a few times. It was unbelievable, the sensation of being inside him. And I did look forward to whenever we did it, but it wasn't what I craved.

Trent had always understood my need to bottom. Hell, he was the one who explained it to me. I'd told him I didn't know why, but it just seemed more natural to me. He said he wasn't surprised. "You look after people every day," he'd said, like it was the most obvious thing in the world. "You're always the caregiver, always making decisions that affect the lives of people. I'm not surprised you want someone else to do that for you."

And it made perfect sense.

He took the Fleshjack from me, jolting my mind back to the present and threw it on the pillows.

"Kneel on the bed," he instructed. "Hold onto the headboard."

I did as instructed. My body wouldn't allow me not to. I was leaking from the slit and aching as he started to rub me down, slicking his fingers and exploring, probing, right where I wanted him to.

By the time he entered me, I was quivering in sensation, anticipation. He gripped my hips and pushed himself inside me. He groaned, low in his throat. "Fuuuuuuuuuuck."

I had both hands on the headboard, my knees spread wide and he eased himself into me. It was the most perfect thing, being filled with Trent. His hands held me, his breath on the back of my neck, his dirty words in my ear and his cock so far inside me.

There was no feeling in the world to equal it.

Until he sat back on his heels, pulling me with him and told me to pick up the Fleshjack. I straddled his dick, my thighs on the outside of his and my cock bobbed heavily between my legs. Using my right hand, I pressed the tip of my cock to the waiting hole.

Slowly, so slowly, I slid the fake ass over my throbbing dick. "Oh, fuck. Oh, fuck. Oh, fuck."

Trent held my hips, and kept his cock buried inside me, while my body twitched in the dual sensation of fucking, while being fucked.

"Oh fuck, Trent," I ground out.

His voice was warmed liqueur. "Feel good, baby?"

"God yes, so good," I gasped, and I started to slide the Fleshjack up and down, fucking it, while Trent held me still.

My hips started to buck. I couldn't control it. My body moved without my permission, but I needed to fuck. My hips rose slightly, and Trent grunted every time his cock slid in and out of my ass.

But it wasn't enough. I needed to fuck.

Leaning up on my knees, Trent moved with me, still buried in my ass. And then he really moved. His hands held my hips, and he started to slam into me. I gripped onto the headboard with my left hand, my right hand kept me deep within the sex toy. My head fell back, and my hips fell forward, taking the pounding Trent gave me.

The base of the Fleshjack was on the bed, and with every thrust of Trent's cock, I fucked it.

Trent's voice was so loud and coarse. "Yeah, yeah, yeah," he grunted with each thrust of his hips. He was so far inside me, grunting and moaning. Every time he plowed into me, his hips pushed mine, thrusting my cock into the sex toy.

His knees spread mine farther apart, and the angle of his dick changed. "Oh, fuck!" I yelled. My body flexed, white heat ripped through me and my cock erupted into the fake ass. I bucked and bucked as I poured come into the Fleshjack, and Trent slammed into me one final time, before he stilled over me and inside me.

I felt his heavy cock lurching, emptying into the condom. He growled and groaned, his forehead pressed into the back of my neck and his entire body was wracked with rolling waves of pleasure.

"Oh my fucking God," was all I managed to say.

Trent chuckled, and he breathed hard. We collapsed on our sides, and he pulled out of me, convulsing as he did so. We laid like that, unable to move or speak.

When Trent did finally move, he kissed my neck and told me he'd run a bath. I heard the water turn on. And a few moments later, he came back into the room, crawled up over my naked body, kissing me as he went.

"Are you sore?" he asked quietly. "I was pretty rough."

"I have no feeling in my body but bliss right now," I mumbled, which made him chuckle.

He pulled me into the bathroom and into the hot bath. He slid in behind me, holding me, kissing my neck and shoulder. My head fell back onto his shoulder, and when he whispered into the side of my head that he loved me, my eyes closed and I smiled.

We stayed like that, with his arms around me, and I think I dozed off. "Hey babe, the water's getting cold."

I opened my eyes lazily, and he was grinning at me. We got out, dried off and climbed into bed naked. He wrapped his arms around me. "Do you feel okay?" he asked me again.

"I feel very fucking great right now," I mumbled sleepily, and I remembered the present he bought me. "I like your kind of surprises."

The last thing I remembered was the sound of his warm laughter, his arms pulling me tight and his nose in my hair.

I CLOSED my phone as Trent came down the stairs. "Mom wants us to go round to her house before we head home."

"Okay," he agreed with an easy shrug. We packed up our belongings and loaded Bentley into the car.

When we got to Mom and Dad's house, Kat and Brendan's car was also there. When we walked inside, my brother was the first to comment. "Nice to see you two aren't still fused together. I had nightmares about that shit."

Kat leaned over and whispered loudly, "I dreamed about it too."

Brendan's jaw dropped open again. Trent burst out laughing, and Brendan threw his soda cap at him.

"Oh boys, I'm glad you're here," Mom called from the kitchen. "I found this recipe online and thought Bentley might like them." She brought out a plate of bone shaped cookies. "They're a special oatmeal cookie for dogs, except for strawberry jam glaze, I added that."

I chuckled, Trent sighed beside me and Brendan barked, "Strawberry jam isn't good for dogs."

"I used the diabetic one," Mom defended herself. "I bought it just for him. Nathan told me how he likes the jam on toast."

Oh, great.

Brendan stared at me. "Nathan!"

"He likes it," I mumbled.

Mom picked up a dog cookie and offered one to Bentley. "See? He loves them."

Brendan snorted. "Next thing you know, she'll be knitting him a coat and matching hat."

Mom's eyes lit up, but Trent quickly replied. "No, please don't do that."

So Mom looked at me and asked, "Does he need a new blanket for his bed?"

Oh well, actually... I nodded, yes.

Brendan stood between us with a hand on each of our shoulders. "I'm gonna let you both in on a little secret. He's. A. Dog."

Mom and I looked at Brendan, horrified, and Dad and Trent laughed.

Ignoring them all, I patted Bentley with both hands. "Don't you listen to him, buddy."

When the cookies were re-wrapped, I picked them up

and was just about to tell everyone goodbye when Trent interrupted. "Um, just a sec."

I looked at him, unsure of what he was about to say.

"I'd just like to thank you all," he said, quietly. "For going last night, for supporting me. It means so much to me, that you support us," he motioned between himself and me. "For Nathan to have such a supportive family is a blessing. Julia, you especially."

I couldn't believe he'd just said that. My Trent, who had always struggled to voice his feelings, just said *that*. I felt my smile widening as I looked at him.

Then my Mom pushed me out of the way to hug him. "Oh, my sweet boy, Trent. We're so proud of you. You don't have to thank us. It's what families do."

She kissed his cheek, and he was thankfully saved by his cell phone buzzing in his pocket.

Pulling out of my mother's hug, he read the Caller ID. "It's Carmen," he said, and you could have heard a pin drop. He answered the call, "Trent Jamieson." His southern accent made me smile.

"Okay," he said. "Oh. Really? Are you sure?" he asked with a laugh, and we all looked on.

"Mmm," he hummed. "Oh, yes. Hell, yes. You let me know. Okay, thanks again." He disconnected the call and we all watched and waited...

"So, what's the verdict?" I asked him. "What did Carmen say?"

"Um, there are some very interested people," he told us. "They'll deal with Carmen, but I have the final say."

"About what?" Kat asked.

"About what I sell, what I could commission, what they want me to exhibit next."

Mom squealed, which made Bentley bark. Dad

declared it was cause for celebration, called for more champagne.

"Hell the fuck no," Brendan told him. "Don't let Nathan drink, or we'll all be in therapy. You have no idea what I witnessed last night."

Dad laughed, and I ignored them both. I couldn't take my eyes off Trent. This blond haired man with his Southern accent and his sexy fucking dimples. The man who owned my heart, who gave me his, this fucking talented man standing before me, was going places in the art world.

And I knew one thing.

I'd be right there beside him. Or curled up on the couch with our dog, watching him paint.

EPILOGUE

THREE YEARS LATER

"YES, MOM," I said, rolling my eyes, though the effect was lost through the phone. Jeez, I'd only left her house half an hour ago. "We will," I told her. Again. "We'll be there for lunch. Sure you don't need us to bring anything?"

"No, no," she said. "Just yourselves."

"Mom, is there anything else?" I asked. She had been acting weird all afternoon. It was as though she was trying to keep a lid on her excitement. I dropped Bentley off at her house earlier, because Trent and I had a dinner date tonight. I mean, she always loved having her 'grandchild', as she called him. 'Him' being Bentley. And she spoiled him rotten. But it was different today.

"Oh, and Mom," I reminded her, "don't give him any liver treats. Please."

I swore I heard her roll her eyes at me. "Yes, Dear. And toast for breakfast. I know this."

I smiled. "Mom, I have to go," I told her. "I have to pick Trent up in forty minutes, and I'm not even showered."

She gasped. "Yes, you go. Don't be late. Give Trent my love, and we'll see you tomorrow."

"Bye, Mom," I said to the dial tone.

See? Weird.

I was running short on time, so I raced up the stairs and grabbed a quick shower. I didn't shave, because I didn't have time and well, because Trent loved it when I didn't.

I dressed in the suit pants I knew he liked on me. He said they hugged me in all the right places. I threw on a button down shirt, grabbed my dinner jacket, and when I sat on the sofa to tie my shoes, I noticed how much this apartment had changed.

The differences between then and now were so striking. We only stayed here a few days a month, I still worked two weeks straight, and had four days off, so we still spent every alternating four day weekend here.

When I lived here, before I moved to Belfast, before Trent, there was no trace of a person living here. Despite the furniture, it was just four walls. A shell, basically, a shell of a house for a shell of a man.

Now, four years later, it was our second home. There were paintings on the walls, photos of friends and family, my neatly organized books and Trent's piles of crap. It was *our* home.

Love lived here.

I smiled as I walked out, locking the door behind me.

Tonight's plan was for me to pick Trent up from his gallery, and we'd head out to dinner. That's right, *his gallery*.

Late last year when the opportunity came up, he made the decision to do it, and he never looked back.

Successful? Yeah, you could say that.

He'd worked so hard for it. His credit and reputation was well merited. He'd worked the last few days getting an exhibition organized for Montreal, that's what he had been doing today, and I had about five minutes to get there to pick him up for the dinner reservations he made.

This weekend, we'd been together four years.

Four years.

Four amazing, hard, crazy, sometimes-fucking-trying years.

The best four years of my life.

I knew everything about him, as he did me. His faults, his strengths, his weaknesses. And he knew mine. He wasn't the angry, scared man he was when I met him. He still had the sexy, flirty sense of humour, but he no longer used it as a defence mechanism.

And sweet fucking Jesus, he got better looking every year he aged.

When we went suit shopping for Adam and Dani's wedding, good Lord, I almost died when he tried on the grey suit. And then he came out in the black one.

Fuck me.

Needless to say, we bought both suits.

I smiled as I recalled the fun we had trying those suits on again at home. And taking them off.

He got another tattoo, the solitary star on his hip, was now two stars. One for him, one for me, he said. And the two black stars looked striking against undone black suit pants and no shirt. He wore the black suit to Adam and Dani's wedding. We had fun taking it off that night too.

Traffic into the city was heavy. Stuck at a red light, I pulled out my phone and sent Trent a quick text letting him know I was on my way.

Two months ago we'd gone back to Texas. It was the fifteen year anniversary of his parent's death, and the first time he'd been back since he left all those years ago. We spent a long afternoon at the cemetery. Trent told me stories of his childhood, like things his Momma taught him and what things he did that made his Daddy shake his head. The things he did, the things he got busted doing, and the things he did and got away with.

He'd hemmed and hawed about seeing his aunt and uncle again. But he bit the bullet and contacted them, they were after all, his only living relatives.

He was nervous on the way to meeting them. Considering they rejected him when he needed them the most, I was a little unsure as to how we'd be received, too.

But holding his head high, he walked into their home, holding my hand.

The reception was lukewarm at best. When his Aunt Carolyn clucked her southern tongue and said, "I see this nancy-boy nonsense is still going on," I worried that the infamous Trent Jamieson temper would flare.

But it didn't.

He simply stood up, smiled and said, "Momma would be appalled at your manners. Gramma raised you better."

And we left.

He told me when we got home, he understood now. He really, *really* understood now, his family wasn't in Texas.

It was in Belfast and Boston.

My memories took me as far as Jackson Avenue, where I pulled up in the alley behind the gallery. I took the fire escape stairs to the upstairs office, knowing the gallery downstairs would be locked and alarmed.

I used my keys, and hurriedly let myself in, trying to get out of the rain. "Trent?" I called out, once I stepped inside. "Sorry I'm late," I explained, even though I couldn't see him. "Traffic was terrible."

He appeared from around the doorway. He smiled beautifully. Nervously.

"Hey," I said, gauging his reaction to seeing me. "You almost ready? It's already 7:30, we're late. My fault, sorry."

He shook his head. "No, it's fine," he said quietly.

"Oh. Did you phone the restaurant and tell them we'd be late?"

He shook his head and inhaled and exhaled deeply.

"Trent, what's up?"

He held out his hand. "Come with me."

Okay, well now I was confused. And anxious.

He took me past his office door and down the darkened stairs to the gallery below us. Maybe he had done something new he wanted to show me, which was odd, because the display room lighting didn't seem to be on.

The gallery itself consisted of two rooms, both about twelve feet by eighteen feet, high ceilings and wooden floors. We walked down the stairs into the first room. The blinds were drawn, the only light coming from a candle, in the middle of the room, on a table set for two.

"Oh, Trent," my words were a whisper.

"Happy anniversary, baby."

He smiled at me and let go of my hand. He nervously wiped his palms on his pants and quickly pulled out my chair. I walked over to the table, and kissed his cheek before I sat down.

The table was covered with my favourite food. "Mrs. Lin did this?" I asked.

He grinned at me, and took his seat. "I had them deliver."

"And saki?"

He chuckled and nodded. "The very best."

"Oh, Trent," I murmured. "It's perfect."

He exhaled loudly, relieved. "I wanted it to be just right."

I couldn't believe how just right it was. "You must have had this planned for a while."

He nodded and swallowed thickly. "A while."

He was still nervous, so I reassured him. "This is absolutely perfect."

His eyebrows knit together. He looked unsure, so I nodded. "I love you, Trent. This is perfect."

He grinned and turned his attention to the food on the table. Sashimi, gyoza, tempura domburi, it was all here. Trent poured two shot glasses of saki and held the first glass over the flame of the candle, warming it, before he handed it to me.

I waited for him to warm his drink and clinked my glass to his. "To us."

"Yes," he smiled. "To us."

As we ate, I told him I dropped Bentley off at Mom and Dad's, and how Mom acted a little strange.

"Oh, really?" he looked at me, startled. "What did she say?"

"Nothing really," I admitted, swallowing my mouthful. "Just excited. More excited than usual about having Bentley for the night."

Trent smiled. "And of course, lunch tomorrow."

This surprised me. "How did you know we were invited for lunch tomorrow?"

His eyes widened, just a fraction. "Oh, your Mom came by this afternoon," he said quickly. "You know she loves it here."

That was funny. I'd spoken to her twice today, and she never mentioned that she'd been here.

"Did she know you were going to surprise me with dinner?" I asked. "Is that why she was all excited and told me not to be late?"

He smiled. "Yeah, probably."

I rolled my eyes. My boyfriend and my mother, were as thick as thieves. I laughed quietly, pushing my empty plate away. "You two are as bad as each other."

"Have you had enough to eat?" he asked.

"I have, thank you," I told him. I saw he hadn't eaten a great deal, so I asked him suggestively, "Have you? Or did you have something else planned?"

He puffed his cheeks out, back to being nervous. "I do actually."

Oh.

"What is it?"

He blinked and breathed out a shaky breath. Before I could question him, he stood. He took my hand again, walked me toward the back room, and I saw it was softly lit. But he stopped as we got to the door. He didn't say a word. He just looked at me. I opened my mouth to ask him what was going on, but he stepped inside the room. He still held my hand and led me in.

All the paintings that were on the walls were now gone.

In the centre, toward the back wall was an easel holding a square painting.

I looked at Trent, and he was so nervous he even looked a little pale. I walked toward the painting. He obviously wanted me to see it.

"Is this new?" I asked. He hadn't told me he was painting something new.

He smiled. "Yes."

"Is it for me?" I asked. "Is this an anniversary gift?"

He nodded, but shrugged a little. "Do you like it?"

I looked back at the painting. It was so different from anything he had done before. It was predominately metallic and silver, glittery, but somehow like a flat base metal. The principal shapes were circular, with a spinning effect.

It was extremely well done. I'd never seen anything like it.

"Trent, it's... it's extraordinary."

His brow pinched again, like I answered wrong.

I tried again. "It's so different from your other work. It's remarkable." I looked from Trent back to the painting. "What does it mean?"

His voice was quiet. "You tell me."

Oh. Even after all this time, I still sucked at this game.

I started with the product it represented. "It's elemental. The metal, it's a raw material. From the earth?"

His lips twisted into half a smile.

See? I really sucked at this game.

He opened his mouth, but closed it again, obviously deciding on a different thing to say. "Tell me what you see."

"Silver. Metal. Wheels, turning wheels." Yes, that's it. Now in the mind of Trent, what would that mean? "Motion. Wheels in motion."

He smiled, but shook his head. "No, baby."

I looked back at the painting and started again. Two wheels, spinning. No, he said that was wrong.

Trent stood behind me and rested his forehead on my shoulder. "Come on, baby. You can do this," he whispered. "What do you see?"

Circles.

Two joined circles. Metal circles, but they were not wheels. They were almost interlinked and looked like the symbol for eternity. Yes, the symbol for eternity! That's it! It was...

Oh, fuck.

Eternity.

Two circles.

But they were not circles.

They were rings.

Oh, fuck.

I turned to face him, and he saw that I finally got it.

"Trent," my voice didn't work, my lungs had no air.

He nodded.

"Is that...?"

He nodded.

Oh, fuck.

"Two rings?"

He nodded.

"Are you... "

He nodded. "Will you?"

I nodded.

And he crushed me in his arms, he held me so tight, kissing my neck, my ear and my hair. "Oh, baby," he said into my neck. Then he pulled my face back and brought our foreheads together, his eyes were a piercing a blue. "Will you? Marry me?"

I nodded again. "Yes. Yes, yes, God yes."

He kissed me with smiling lips and tears in his eyes.

"I love you, Trent Jamieson. Of course, I'll marry you."

He laughed, relieved and ecstatic. His face was just beaming. I imagined it matched mine.

Oh, my God. I was getting married.

"I'm getting married!" I said, rather stupidly.

"So am I!" he laughed. I tried to kiss him, deeper this time, but I was smiling too much.

He held my face against his, cheek to cheek. "Nathan Tierney," he said my name, reverently. "'Thank you."

Thank you? "What are you thanking me for?"

"For everything," he said, his eyes brimming with tears.

"For saying yes. For loving me. For teaching me how to feel, how to love, how to live."

Oh, Trent.

"For making me believe in myself, for giving me a family, your family."

"They're your family too," I corrected him.

He smiled, and his tears fell. "For helping me be the man you deserve."

I kissed him then, our lips and noses crushed together, my tears mixed with his. There was so much I wanted to say, so much I could have told him; what he meant to me, how much I adored him, how much he completed me, how he'd made me whole.

But I didn't. Instead I told him, "It would be an honor to marry you."

His hands held my face to his and he nodded. "Thank you, thank you, thank you," he mumbled again and again.

He folded his arms around me, his hand at the back of my neck, holding me so close. So fucking close. I might have been holding onto him just as tight.

We stood like that for the longest time. Yet nowhere near long enough. He pulled away from me and looked down between us. "So," then he smiled coyly. "We'll be in Montreal in four weeks."

Like usual, Trent had lined up the opening of the exhibition with my four days off. I nodded, "We will be."

"Do you think your family could make it?" he asked with a suggestive smile.

Oh, fuck. "You want to get *married* in four weeks?"

He shrugged and laughed. And I laughed and nodded. "Yes. Holy fuck. Yes," I said with a laugh. "Ohmygod. I'm getting married."

Trent laughed. "So am I."

He smiled and kissed me then. It started out innocently enough, but soon heated-up into something serious. His mouth opened wider, his tongue pressed harder, his hands held me tighter. I was soon moaning into his mouth, but then he pulled away from me.

"Take me home," he whispered against my lips. Then he added, "Fiancé."

I chuckled. "It will be my pleasure, Fiancé."

"Yes, it will be your pleasure." He grinned and pecked my lips. Then he closed his eyes and whispered, "It's been a while since you've topped me."

Oh, fuck.

Suddenly very keen to leave, I looked back at the table with empty food containers. "Leave it, Nathan. Bridgette said she'll take care of it."

Ah, Bridgette. The assistant sent from heaven, who took his messes in stride. "She knew you were planning this?" I asked.

"She helped me this afternoon," he answered with a smirk.

"Did anyone else know?"

He answered quietly. "Your mom."

My eyes widened in shock. He quickly explained, "She called in when we were taking the paintings down from the back room," he explained. "She saw the painting... of the rings. It took her a minute, and she didn't say anything, but I could tell she knew."

"So that's why she was acting so weird," I said with a nod.

Trent smiled sweetly. "More than likely. When she left she was grinning like a mad woman."

This made me laugh. "Can I ask how long you've been planning this?"

He smiled shyly. "At Adam and Dani's wedding, Lucas joked that you and I would be next, and that got me thinking. But when we went back to Texas... I knew then... I just knew... I couldn't live without you."

"I couldn't live without you either," I told him, smiling. "I tried. For twenty-seven years. It was horrible."

He ginned, and pulled me in for a quick, hard kiss. "Take me home," he said again, "and have your way with me."

Oh, fuck.

"Your wish, my command, Fiancé."

He smiled and laughed quietly, took my hand and led me toward the exit. "Oh, wait!" I cried out, and quickly ran in to grab the painting from the easel. I passed the table on my way and grabbed the bottle of saki as well.

"HELLO?" I yelled out.

"We're out back," Dad's voice called back.

The familiar sound of canine claws clicking on the floorboards greeted us, along with a slobbery tongue and wagging tail. "Hey little buddy."

Trent chuckled as Bentley bounded back through the house, showing us where the other humans were currently located. Taking Trent's hand, we walked out to where my family was.

Alana and Chris, her boyfriend of two years were there with Dad and Kat, while Brendan sat with his gorgeous daughter, one-year old Lily, on his lap.

Mom came out from the kitchen, grinning ridiculously. "Happy anniversary, boys," she said, kissing our cheeks.

Then she asked, like she was privy to some great secret, "How was dinner?"

I looked at Trent, unable to stop from smiling. "Dinner was great."

Mom looked at Trent, her eyes conveyed some unspoken question. Trent's lips twitched in a telltale smirk, and Mom's eyes popped.

Yep. She knew.

I had to do something before she had an aneurysm, I looked around at my family, and shrugged, and tried to play it cool. "Oh, I'm um, I'm getting married."

Eyes widened simultaneously, and Trent laughed loudly. He pretended to look surprised, "What a coincidence! I'm getting married too!"

There was a whole three seconds of utter silence, and then my mother screamed. She collected me in a hug-like tackle that would make a footballer proud, jumping up and down and squealing.

Then she left me, somewhat violated, only to inflict her assault on Trent. We were hugged and kissed, congratulated and hugged again.

"I thought that was what the painting meant," Mom said through her tears. "I saw the rings, and I hoped... oh, I hoped that was what it meant." Then she turned to Trent and asked, "Did he take long to get it?"

"I'm not completely clueless," I defended myself.

Trent laughed. "He thought they were wheels."

Mom looked at me like there was something wrong with me.

Oh, come on.

"Wait!" Kat exclaimed, her eyes wide. "You proposed? With a painting?" Trent nodded and smiled. Kat's mouth fell opened. "How romantic!" she swooned.

Kat collected little Lily from Brendan and hugged her. "Don't you listen to your Dadda for advice on men, baby girl," she said with a kiss to her daughter's temple. "You listen to your two uncles."

"Listen to your Uncle Trent, Lily," I corrected her. "He's the romantic one."

I told them we had not made any plans, or set any dates yet. "It will be small, personal, just family and a few friends," I told them. "In a church, in a park, I don't care."

Trent smiled, and his eyes danced. I kissed him, lightly on the lips. "As long as you're there."

We sat at the table for lunch, and talked, and planned, when Dad stood and made a toast. "Trent," he started, "when we first met you, sorry to tell you this, but it wasn't you that we noticed. It was the difference in Nathan. It was like night from day. You've made him so happy."

My father smiled fondly, proudly. "Trent, I'd like to thank you for saving my son." He raised his glass higher. "They say love is blind," he said with a shrug, "but I think it had perfect vision."

~ THE END

ABOUT THE AUTHOR

N.R. Walker is an Australian author, who loves her genre of gay romance. She loves writing and spends far too much time doing it, but wouldn't have it any other way.

She is many things; a mother, a wife, a sister, a writer. She has pretty, pretty boys who live in her head, who don't let her sleep at night unless she gives them life with words.

She likes it when they do dirty, dirty things...but likes it even more when they fall in love.

She used to think having people in her head talking to her was weird, until one day she happened across other writers who told her it was normal.

She's been writing ever since...

Blind Faith

Through These Eyes (Blind Faith #2)

Blindside: Mark's Story (Blind Faith #3)

Ten in the Bin

Point of No Return – Turning Point #1

Breaking Point – Turning Point #2

Starting Point – Turning Point #3

Element of Retrofit – Thomas Elkin Series #1

Clarity of Lines – Thomas Elkin Series #2

Sense of Place – Thomas Elkin Series #3

Taxes and TARDIS

Three's Company

Red Dirt Heart

Red Dirt Heart 2

Red Dirt Heart 3

Red Dirt Heart 4

Red Dirt Christmas

Cronin's Key

Cronin's Key II

Cronin's Key III

Exchange of Hearts

The Spencer Cohen Series, Book One

The Spencer Cohen Series, Book Two

The Spencer Cohen Series, Book Three

The Spencer Cohen Series, Yanni's Story

Blood & Milk

The Weight Of It All

A Very Henry Christmas (The Weight of It All 1.5)

Perfect Catch

Switched

Imago

Imagines

Red Dirt Heart Imago

On Davis Row

Finders Keepers

Evolved

Galaxies and Oceans

Private Charter

Titles in Audio:

Cronin's Key

Cronin's Key II

Cronin's Key III

Red Dirt Heart

Red Dirt Heart 2

Red Dirt Heart 3

Red Dirt Heart 4

The Weight Of It All

Switched

Point of No Return

Breaking Point

Starting Point

Spencer Cohen Book One

Spencer Cohen Book Two

Spencer Cohen Book Three

Yanni's Story

On Davis Row

Free Reads:

Sixty Five Hours

Learning to Feel

His Grandfather's Watch (And The Story of Billy and Hale)

The Twelfth of Never (Blind Faith 3.5)

Twelve Days of Christmas (Sixty Five Hours Christmas)

Best of Both Worlds

Translated Titles:

Fiducia Cieca (Italian translation of Blind Faith)

Attraverso Questi Occhi (Italian translation of Through These Eyes)

Preso alla Sprovvista (Italian translation of Blindside)

Il giorno del Mai (Italian translation of Blind Faith 3.5)

Cuore di Terra Rossa (Italian translation of Red Dirt Heart)

Cuore di Terra Rossa 2 (Italian translation of Red Dirt Heart 2)

Cuore di Terra Rossa 3 (Italian translation of Red Dirt Heart 3)

Cuore di Terra Rossa 4 (Italian translation of Red Dirt Heart 4)

Intervento di Retrofit (Italian translation of Elements of Retrofit)

Confiance Aveugle (French translation of Blind Faith)

A travers ces yeux: Confiance Aveugle 2 (French translation of Through These Eyes)

Aveugle: Confiance Aveugle 3 (French translation of Blindside)

À Jamais (French translation of Blind Faith 3.5)

Cronin's Key (French translation)

Cronin's Key II (French translation)

Au Coeur de Sutton Station (French translation of Red Dirt Heart)

Partir ou rester (French translation of Red Dirt Heart 2)

Faire Face (French translation of Red Dirt Heart 3)

Trouver sa Place (French translation of Red Dirt Heart 4)

Rote Erde (German translation of Red Dirt Heart)

Rote Erde 2 (German translation of Red Dirt Heart 2)